CATCH AND RELEASE

A MILWAUKEE GROWLERS NOVEL

TRACY SOLHEIM

Sun Home Productions

CHAPTER ONE

THE TENSION PERMEATING the air felt a lot like being pressed into the turf by a three-hundred-pound lineman. *Heavy.* It was a sensation Milwaukee Growlers' quarterback Trey Van Horn didn't care for on--*or off*--the gridiron.

To avoid the combative stares of the other two occupants of the room, he shifted his gaze down to his hands. His money-makers, so to speak. The body part most fans considered Trey's greatest asset.

Sure, there were a slew of women out there who might be inclined to make a case that another part of his anatomy was equally talented. Just not the woman currently trashing him in *Vanity Fair.* The asshole trolls on social media who were piling on didn't help matters. Hence this little trip to the principal's office.

"Do you realize your pithy comments have potentially alienated half the fans of this team?" the Growlers' owner remarked.

Trey tried not to cringe at her disappointed tone. Mrs. Ciaciura inherited the team from her late father, Norm Clarkson, a decade ago. Since then, she'd risen to become one of the most respected owners in the league. She was gracious and fair-minded when it mattered, and a bulldog when the situation warranted one. Trey considered her to be not only his boss, but a friend.

For the past eight years, he'd used his brain, his feet, and his money-makers to lead the team to the playoffs every season. She, in turn, treated him like the son she and her husband never had. Up until now, apparently.

"Now, hold on just a second," Collin Slater, Trey's agent, chimed in.

Make that "acting" agent.

Trey's long-time business representative, Marty Slater, recently suffered a mild heart attack. One that had his wife forcing him to take a sabbatical or face a divorce. Likely calculating how much the single life would cost him, Marty succumbed to her demands, leaving his clients in the hands of his overly ambitious son, Collin.

Trey and Collin were once teammates on their prep school football team. Collin believed that made them each other's emergency contact. It didn't. But since Trey's contract with the Growlers was set for the next three years, he didn't see any harm in letting Marty's son handle what little needed to be managed while his agent recovered.

Although, he could have navigated this unexpected performance review just fine without a wingman.

"That's not fair of you to accuse my client," Collin whined. "Trey didn't—"

Mrs. C raised her voice to drown him out. Trey would have laughed, but he could feel her angry gaze boring into him, and she didn't seem to be in a joking mood.

"Women make up nearly fifty percent of the league's fan base. I don't care how high your passing rating is. When you say something stupid like 'marriage is a trap,' you risk offending them. Most women—most *people*, for that matter—don't consider marriage to be 'an exercise in torture,' Trey."

"No one can prove he actually said that," Collin argued. "It's her word against his."

The weight of the older woman's gaze had Trey reluctantly looking up to meet her troubled grey eyes. They both knew he had said exactly what was printed in the magazine. The problem was, she still thought he didn't mean it.

"Have you ever been in love, Trey?"

Collin just about lost his shit at her question.

"What the hell? If a man asked a woman that, he'd be publicly eviscerated." Collin shot to his feet. All five-foot-eight of him. "This is getting out of hand. What we have here is a simple case of a jilted lover spouting off some nonsense so she can remain in the social media spotlight. That's all." He rocked forward on his heels, seemingly trying to appear more forceful. "As we speak, we are putting together a slander case against her. The Growlers don't have to get their hands dirty. Let us do our job, and this ridiculous story will be in the rearview mirror by week's end." He moved toward the door of the owner's suite. "I'm sure you've got more important things to do today. We'll leave you to it."

Mrs. C arched an eyebrow at Trey.

He sighed heavily. "I'll meet you outside, Collin."

His pseudo-agent didn't like that one bit. "Unless it involves football, I think we should consider the matter settled."

Out of the corner of his eye, Trey could see the team owner digging her painted fingernails into the arms of her chair. "Please wait for me outside, Collin," he repeated.

If Collin didn't appreciate being dismissed before, he was downright livid about it now, judging from the flush that was crawling up his neck. But Trey held all the cards in their relationship. And Collin knew it. With an abrupt nod to Mrs. Ciaciura, he yanked open the door.

"I'll be right outside if you need me."

It was on the tip of Trey's tongue to say he wouldn't need him. Except he still wasn't out of the frying pan with his boss. Hopefully, things wouldn't get so testy that he'd actually have to call Collin in for backup.

When the door closed a bit more firmly than was necessary, Mrs. C made a sound that was half laugh, half sigh.

"Well, that was fun." She rose from her chair and went to refill her coffee cup.

Trey groaned as he shifted in his seat. "Is that what you'd call it?"

She laughed. "He's an entitled brat with short man's issues. He needs to be taken down a peg. As I'm sure you're aware, Marty also represents Alek Bergeron, the goalie for the Mayhem. They're locked in some intense contract arbitration right now. I was just toying with Collin. I want him to go into tomorrow's negotiations all riled up. My little brother has it much too easy, only having to deal with the contracts of twenty or so hockey players."

He should have known. Norm Clarkson's assets, including a brewery and three professional sports teams, had been divided between his four children. Naturally, the brewery went to the oldest son. The baby of the family, a love child half his sister's age, was gifted the town's hockey franchise at the tender age of twenty-four. Norm's other daughter was the proud owner of the Timbers, Milwaukee's baseball team. The good-natured rivalry among the siblings was legendary in the sports world.

Mrs. C gestured at the coffee pot before realizing her mistake. "That's right. According to your 'jilted lover,' you no longer put caffeine in your body. Or anything else worth eating." Making a face at the kale smoothie in Trey's hand, she returned to the table and gingerly sat down beside him. "Please tell me there is at least honey or something more decadent than leaves in that sludge."

He took a long pull from the straw before answering. "My diet isn't as ridiculous as she made it out to be. I've always done my best to eat healthy. But if I want to play ten more seasons, I need to tighten things up a little, that's all."

"Mmm. I wish I had your ability to simply flip a switch in my brain and completely change up my eating habits."

He sighed in frustration. His former girlfriend hadn't minced words when she described Trey's commitment to football as "obsessive" and "robot-like." Of course the social media trolls had wasted no time creating memes and posts depicting him as a machine with no social graces or feelings whatsoever.

So what if Trey played the game with single-minded intensity? How was it anyone's business if he became a hermit during the season so he could focus all his energy on football? That was how games were won. Wasn't that what he was getting paid to do? Wasn't that what fans wanted?

"What I put in my body directly correlates to my performance."

She mumbled something that sounded a lot like "Too bad not everyone gives your performance high marks" while blowing on her coffee.

Trey snapped to attention. "I've put my ass on the line for this team for eight seasons now. This is the first I've heard any complaints."

"Relax," she said with a sly grin. "No one's complaining about your performance *on* the field, Trey."

She sobered up then.

"Look. Your private life is just that. Private. But, having grown up in the limelight, you of all people, should know how fickle the world we live in can be. How they want to cheer you on and tear you down at the same time. I'm speaking as a friend here, not the woman who signs your paycheck, when I say you can't approach every aspect of your life as if you're a machine. It's not healthy. You're a living, breathing organism. I need to know that you realize there's more to life than football. In the end, it's just a game."

Trey snorted. "You pay me millions to play 'just a game.' To win every one of those 'games' so you can make the millions you need to pay me and a crap ton more. I'm not going to half-ass it because I'm too busy looking for a soulmate to—" he made air quotes "—complete me."

She studied him over the rim of her coffee cup. "You never answered my question."

"Which one was that?" He knew damn well which question he hadn't answered. The same one he wasn't ever going to answer.

"Have you ever been in love?"

He exercised that machine-like control he was now famous for, keeping his face and body from reacting, to hide the truth from her. Because, in what felt like a past life, he thought he had been in love once. She'd been innocent, yet whip smart, challenging him at every turn. Generous and creative, she was everything his twenty-year-old heart had been yearning for his entire life.

Until she wasn't.

Instead, she'd been a mirage. Another woman after him solely for his legacy. Like mother, like daughter. He was lucky to get out when he did.

Ever since, Trey kept his heart locked up tight. The more he micro-managed every aspect of his life, the better he felt. The better he performed on the field. No longer was he at the mercy of his parents using him as a pawn in their game of one-upmanship for the tabloids. He controlled his agenda. And he damn well liked it that way.

Not that he was averse to women and what they offered. He gave as good as he got in the bedroom—with the exception of his heart. The Van Horn men didn't do commitment. Up until now, the women he'd been with understood that. He'd just have to be more careful in the future.

Of course, he couldn't tell any of this to the woman sitting before him. She was happily married to her husband of over forty years, with three daughters blissfully married themselves. Mrs.

Ciaciura believed in the bullshit premise that was happy ever after.

Trey knew it for the lie it was.

His teammates may fall under its spell, but he never would. Not when it meant giving up the rigorous control he'd carefully cultivated. Not when it opened him up to having his heart sliced in half. *Been there. Done that.* Wisely, he kept his thoughts to himself.

The charged silence stretched until she huffed an irritated sounding sigh. "Suit yourself." She held up her hand. "Your love life is your business. But that doesn't mean I can't chastise you about your public image. Hopefully the little whelp is right about something for once, and this will die down long before we get to training camp next month."

"I'm not going to dignify the story with a statement, if that's what you want."

"No. Of course not. I may be nosy, but I'd never ask that of you. Besides, actions speak louder than words."

A trickle of unease scraped down his spine. "Don't tell me you want me to marry one of your granddaughters," he joked.

She laughed. "Don't toy with the emotions of the seven-year-old. She still sleeps in your jersey every night. The thirteen-year-old?" Mrs. C shook her head. "Who the heck knows what she'd do. She's giving her mother fits with her mood swings. I wouldn't wish her on my worst enemy right now." She settled back in her chair. "No, Trey, I have something much less dramatic in mind."

The tension building at his temples eased, but only slightly. "Hit me."

"The gala."

Seriously?

Was that all she wanted from him? He was a regular contributor of auction items and funds to the annual event benefitting Milwaukee's Children's Hospital. It was the one night during the season when he allowed himself to socialize with anyone other than his teammates. There was no question he would be a part of it again this year.

"Let me know what you need donated and it's yours."

"You're always more than generous with your donations every year," she said. "If only you weren't so closed-mouthed and anonymous about it. Fans here in Milwaukee should see the real you. The guy your teammates follow into battle every week. Not the cold machine the media is making you out to be. I want people to see that there really is a heart beating beneath your shoulder pads."

Her tone was a bit cagey. Trey suddenly had the feeling she'd been toying with him all along. That the confrontation about his so called "pithy remarks" was simply a smokescreen to get him to agree to whatever the hell she wanted from him. He was instantly on alert.

"I'm not sure where you're headed with this." *And I don't like it,* he nearly added.

She jumped to her feet and scurried behind her desk.

Not a good sign.

"Let me cut to the chase then. You're chairing the gala on behalf of the Growlers this year."

"Excuse me? What?" He practically catapulted from his seat, following her across the room. "You've got to be kidding me? I don't have time for that. In case you forgot, I'm going to be busy preparing for, *and winning,* football games. You know. That thing you *hired* me to do."

"And you are the best quarterback in the league. Lucky for you, the role as chairman is mostly proforma. The team has a committee that works exclusively on the preparations. They've been working on it since January." She shuffled some papers on her desk. "In addition, we hire a wonderful outside PR guru from the Westwood Agency to do the rest. We've been partnering with her for the past six years and she is brilliant." She waved her hand as if to brush his concerns away. "They'll need you for a few publicity events in the fall, but nothing you can't handle on your off days."

What the actual fuck?

"Don't you usually task one of the retired players with the . . . honor?"

She narrowed her eyes at him, knowing full well he didn't consider it an honor at all. Instead, he saw her request—*make that order*—as an unnecessary interruption to the season. Trey had a strict rule about endorsement work of any kind after the first day of training camp. As in, he didn't do any. Period. That way he could keep his mind laser-focused on the game. Those off days she was so cavalierly giving away were for breaking down film. Nothing else. That's the strategy that made him a winner.

"I'm changing it up this year," she announced. "My siblings have decided to trot out their superstars, so I will, too. My brother and sister will certainly not be showing me up."

Trey had spent all of his life wishing for a sibling or two. Suddenly he was rethinking that wish.

"Am I allowed to point out that the gala takes place in the middle of the football season, whereas baseball is over, and hockey will have barely started? It makes more sense for them to trot out their so-called superstars. The guests won't care who's listed as the chairs."

"Actually, this year the event is scheduled for mid-October. You'll still have two-thirds of your season to be a football hermit. But this event will go on with this city's biggest sports star at the helm. Even if it's in name only."

He opened his mouth to say something—anything—but she was right. Football was king in Milwaukee. In the entire state of Wisconsin. The Growlers were one of the original teams in the league. And Trey was the two-time league MVP who captained them. There wasn't an athlete in the city with as much shine on his or her star.

At any other moment he would be proud of that fact. Right

now, however, the label felt like a yoke. The smile she gave him forestalled any additional discussion on the matter.

Check and mate. The bulldog has spoken.

One of the receptionists poked her head in the door. "Excuse me, Mrs. Ciacuira. Your ten-thirty is here."

"Perfect timing. I need to introduce her to Trey as they'll both be working on the gala together. Show her in."

Collin squeezed in behind the receptionist.

"Dude," he murmured. "You need to let me handle this."

"It's handled. At least at this end. But there aren't going to be any lawsuits for slander, you hear me? That's not how I want to play this. I'd rather—"

A melodic laugh rang out across the room. Its sound was lighthearted and genuine. And one Trey never expected to hear again in his lifetime.

"Trey?" Collin was trying to get his attention.

Too late. Some unknown force was already pulling Trey toward the door to see who was standing in front of Mrs. C. He was surprised he could move at all, given how heavy his limbs suddenly felt. Not only that, but his rapid heartbeat was almost deafening to his ears.

It couldn't be her. She was in California, chasing after her dream of becoming a filmmaker. Her eye for photography had been keen for an untrained eighteen-year-old.

Besides, Mrs. C said she'd been working with this woman for the past six years. There's no way they had both been in the same city together for that long. Trey would have known she was close by. He once had a sixth sense about her.

"Ah, here she is," Mrs. C was saying as she moved to the side to allow the other woman to enter.

The room tilted slightly when his gaze collided with an equally distressed pair of blue eyes. Eyes that he'd fallen into ten years earlier. One iris was still darker than the other. He wondered if anyone else besides him had ever noticed. Her lopsided mouth was pulled tight in a grim line and her nostrils flared ever so slightly when her gaze landed on him.

Gone was the carefree gangly girl with the dreamer's smile. She'd been replaced by an adult version, wearing uptight clothes and a fierce glare. Even her wild and wavy strawberry-blonde locks had been tamed into submission.

Yet, parts of his body were already barking at him to take her in his arms and pick up where they'd left off all those years ago.

The very idea pissed him off.

Mrs. C was still chattering. "Trey Van Horn, allow me to introduce you to the Westwood agency's secret weapon—"

"London Headley," he finished for her.

London's chin inched up.

"You two know each other?" The older woman shifted her gaze from Trey to London and slowly back again. "That's fortunate."

Her tone didn't match the words.

The silence grew awkward, and Mrs. C's smile dimmed. She sidled up closer to Trey.

"Please tell me you don't *know her*, know her," she practically hissed at him.

London bristled.

For crying out loud.

"No," he reassured his boss. Fortunately, he'd discovered the truth of her identity before he'd made that colossal mistake. "Not a chance."

That had London pursing her lips and narrowing her eyes to near slits. *Too bad.* He crossed his arms in front of his chest, tucking his fingers into his armpits before dropping his bombshell.

"London is my little sister."

"Holy shit," Collin murmured from somewhere behind him.

"Pardon me?" Not much flustered Mrs. C, but she was well on her way to being chuffed.

Next to her, London let out a delicate snort and rolled her eyes.

"*Was*. Past tense. And only for a hot minute, a long time ago," she explained. "My mother quickly saw the error of her ways." She directed that last shot at Trey.

Bullshit. But he wasn't keen on airing his father's dirty laundry in front of his boss, not to mention Collin—a guy who made a living trading in secrets.

"How is . . ." *Shit.* What was the woman's name? In his defense, his father didn't make it easy for him, marrying four women after leaving Trey's mom. Trey made it a habit not to get too invested in any of them. They didn't stick around long. London's mother held the title for quickest trip through the revolving door of step-mothers, lasting barely five months.

Not that Trey's mother was much better. She'd racked up three husbands since her highly publicized divorce. Needless to say, his views on marriage were shaped by real life experience.

"How is your mom?" he asked. They had an audience after all. Best to appear polite.

London arched an eyebrow at him smugly. It was obvious to her he couldn't remember her mom's name. It irked him that he felt a smidge of guilt.

"Landed on her feet, I assume?" he shot at her.

Her mouth curled up in a wicked grin. "She did. In fact, she traded up. She married a prince."

A guffaw escaped his lips before he could stop it.

Sensing the blood in the water, Mrs. C stepped between them. "Well, then. I guess we can do away with the get-to-know-you chitchat." She pierced Trey with a glare. "That saves us a lot of time since QB One here needs to be downstairs for OTAs with his teammates. I'll have the community relations department forward you the information regarding the first committee meeting when it's finalized, Trey."

"Looking forward to it," he lied.

Mrs. C was shooing him and Collin out the door. There was no room for London to move and his arm accidentally brushed against her bare shoulder. He felt it all the way in his groin. She sucked in a strangled breath. A gentleman would have apologized. But if she was expecting an apology from him, she'd be waiting until hell froze over.

CHAPTER TWO

London's hand shook as she poured herself a generous cup of coffee the following morning. She mumbled a curse when some of the hot liquid scalded her fingers. Yet another thing to blame on freaking Trey Van Horn.

It was bad enough the asshole had caused her to endure a sleepless night. And on the eve of one of the biggest meetings in her career, too. Instead of tossing and turning while over-analyzing the Gunther Cheese account, she'd been pounding her pillow in frustration as the memories of her greatest heartbreak played in a nauseating loop behind her closed eyes.

Yesterday wasn't the first time she'd seen Trey since he'd left her holding her heart in her hand ten summers before. One couldn't live in the city of Milwaukee and not see the Growler quarterback's likeness plastered on the side of a bus or a billboard. Or flickering on the television screen during his post-game press conferences.

They'd even been to the same event on multiple occasions. Not that Trey would have noticed her. He'd been too busy strolling across the red carpet of the Milwaukee Art Museum, a different fabulous woman adorning his arm every time, oblivious to London standing in the background busily directing the media.

Standing inches from him was different, though. Those amber leonine eyes of his instantly homed in on her, making her breath still and her panties damp—just as they had the first time their gazes locked across a dock. And, dammit, he still smelled *ahhmazing*.

She hadn't meant to inhale the rarified air surrounding him, knowing the perils of such a mistake too well. But her body didn't bother listening to her brain's distress signals. As a result, that familiar intoxicating scent haunted her for much of last night.

Up close, she could see the changes in him the filtered photos and camera lenses missed. The hardness of his square jaw, the tightness bracketing his mouth. Gone was the boyish wonder of a young man eager to find his path in life. It was replaced by a level of arrogance only a guy with unlimited wealth, skill, and good looks could command.

The jackass.

All these years, London had waited for—*hoped for*—an explanation. An apology of some sort. But it was obvious that none would be forthcoming. She should have known. She'd just been a blip on the surface of his enchanted life. Nothing special to him. Not like he'd been to her. And he didn't care that he'd hurt her. Heck, the jerk couldn't even remember her mother's name, for crying out loud.

"Kim! It's a common name with only three letters in it," she mumbled. "How hard is that to remember, you . . ." She slammed her mug down on the conference room table in frustration.

"Relax, kiddo. You've got this." Bennie Westbrook, founder of the Westbrook PR firm, strolled into the room juggling a mug of coffee and his daily cheese blintz from one of their long-time clients, Swanson's Bakery. "Butterflies are normal before a big presentation. We both know you've got the details to this campaign outlined to perfection, though. It's what they call a slam dunk. Seth Gunther is about to become a national name and a very rich man." He groaned slightly as he lowered his sixty-eight-year-old portly frame into the chair at the head of the table. "Which means he'll be a real pain in the patookis at poker night."

London smiled in spite of herself. Somehow, Bennie always made things, if not better, more tolerable. The big softie was more than just her boss and mentor. He was like the father she never knew she needed.

Thirty-five years ago, he'd left a job at a major ad agency in Chicago to help promote the little guys in his hometown of Milwaukee. He'd never looked back. Seth Gunther may become wealthy when he took his cheese brand national, but Bennie would be the one smiling the widest, basking in his friend's good fortune.

"Does that mean you won't be letting him win anymore?" She took the chair beside him and sipped her coffee.

Bennie laughed. "You betcha. It's about time that old fart paid me back."

"I'm going to miss this," she said softly, careful not to be over-heard by the other members of the agency who were milling about outside the conference room. "Are you sure this is what you want?"

Her boss's brown eyes softened. He reached over to pat her hand. "You've delayed your dream long enough, young lady. It's time for you to step into the big time." His gaze focused on something beyond the glass door. "Besides, this place isn't the same without Robyn."

Bennie's wife of thirty-three years, a talented graphic artist, passed away eighteen months before, leaving an empty office within the agency and an even bigger hole in Bennie's heart. Unable to have children, the agency, its staff, and their clients became the couple's extended family. It was that feeling of community that had London never considering working anywhere else after a summer internship at Westbrook her sophomore year in college.

Public relations and advertising were never on her radar. Neither was the University of Wisconsin. She was all set to go to film school at UCLA. Until her mother's midlife crisis sent London on a different path.

All her life, it had been just the two of them. Kim and London sharing a small apartment above Kim's parents' garage on Lake Geneva. London's father was never in the picture, and it had not mattered one bit. Kim was a flight attendant with a major airline out of Chicago. Grandma and Gramps filled in while London's mom traveled. All in all, it was a very simple, yet comfortable life growing up in a small town where she was loved. London had no complaints.

Until the summer she graduated from high school.

No longer needed to watch after London while their daughter was away, Kim's parents relocated to the Arizona desert. London was soon to follow them out west, headed to Los Angeles that September. At thirty-nine, Kim was suddenly staring at an empty nest.

Needless to say, she freaked out. Nothing as dramatic as Thelma and Louise, fortunately. Instead, she fell in love with a passenger she'd met on an eighteen-hour flight from Fiji.

Jay Van Horn was the playboy son of multi-millionaire Lars Van Horn and a competitive yachtsman. He had the golden looks and hefty bank account to sweep Kim off her feet. And he did. After a whirlwind weekend of romance in Beverly Hills, the two tied the knot in Vegas.

It was a very un-Kim-like thing to do. Although, London couldn't blame her mom. Not when she'd fallen under the spell of a very similar charming smile that summer.

Like father, like son.

It wasn't long until both Kim and Jay recognized their mistake. The two newlyweds laughed it off and parted as friends.

Six months later, Kim found her happy-ever-after with an insurance agent and life returned to normal. Except for the part about London going to college in Madison, Wisconsin, instead of L.A.

Her mom and grandparents tried to convince her to transfer. To follow her dream. But she wouldn't budge. Her excuse was that she wanted to remain close in case her mother succumbed to another wild whim. Her family didn't understand. Probably because she'd never told them anything about her and Trey.

He was lighting up the football field at Stanford. Sure, California was a big state. Just not big enough for London to be so near the man who had shattered her heart. She didn't have the guts to risk it. Karma was definitely a bitch, however, because Trey was drafted in the first round by the Milwaukee Growlers, putting them in the same town once again.

"It's not like I'll be far away," Bennie said, interrupting London's runaway thoughts. "You're only going to Chicago."

Thank goodness. Suddenly Milwaukee wasn't big enough for her and the football superstar.

"Let's not get ahead of ourselves," she reminded him. "Even if everyone at Gunther's buys into my campaign, I'll still be auditioning for Nolan and Hemphill while I manage the account."

For twenty-seven years, Bennie and the team at Westbrook had served Gunther Cheeses in lieu of their own in-house advertising. But taking a brand national required a larger skill set. Hence the partnership with the Chicago ad agency.

Nolan and Hemphill. One of the largest advertising firms in the world. London still had to pinch herself. She'd finally transition from organizing galas and grand openings to producing national commercials for television and social media. It was a dream come true.

If she pulled it off.

"They could not like my work." Just uttering the words had her stomach in knots.

Bennie's booming laugh echoed off the glass walls of the conference room. "Not a chance. You are a genius with your social media videos." He gestured to his blintz. "Gretchen said your shots of their baked goods have customers running through the door with their mouths watering. And your idea to have Orlando post a joke of the day over at the tire shop has people driving from Kenosha to get new tires. Brilliant!" His eyes grew wide. "They had one guy comment all the way from Ireland. He said if he could get his car to the U.S., Orlando was the only guy he was buying his new treads from. Can you imagine? That is all you, kiddo. And that's why Nolan and Hemphill agreed to partner with us."

Except it wasn't really a partnership. Or an "us." At the end of the year, the Chicago agency would absorb the clients and staff from Westbrook. And Bennie would ride off into retirement. She and Bennie had deliberately kept the news from staff and clients. Until it was a done deal, there was no sense getting everyone invested.

Brenda, the agency's receptionist, waltzed into the room carrying a dozen red roses in a vase. "Someone has an admirer," she sing-songed before setting the flowers down in front of London.

"Who is it this week?" Bennie joked.

The only person ever to send her flowers—at home or at work—was her mom. But never a bouquet as gorgeous as this one. The knot in London's stomach grew tighter. Surely it wasn't—

"Well? Don't keep us all hanging," Brenda demanded.

London reached for the card. Her breath hung in her throat when she read the words.

You are a goddess of public relations! Your social media posts really paid off. New contract is

being inked today. I owe you big time. Dinner is on me. Let me know when you have a free night.
Alek Bergeron

Dammit. She hated that her heart couldn't decide if it was relieved or disappointed that they weren't the long-awaited apology from Trey.

She forced her lips up into a grin. "It seems the Mayhem have come to terms with their goalie, thanks to us."

Bennie applauded. "Thanks to *you,* you mean."

"Way to go." Brenda sighed. "I'd miss those gorgeous eyes if they went to another city. On behalf of all the women in Milwaukee, thank you, London."

"Well done, kiddo." Bennie got to his feet. "The team from Nolan and Hemphill just texted. They are five minutes out from the meeting. Now let's go knock this next one out of the park."

London stood as well, taking a moment to steady her breathing. She needed to focus her mind on what was ahead of her. There was a lot riding on today's presentation. There was no time to dwell on Trey Van Horn. She'd managed to avoid him for the past ten years. Once she had the Gunther account moving along, she could delegate her duties involving the gala to another staff member. If she was lucky, she'd never have to come face-to-face with the Growlers' quarterback ever again.

CHAPTER THREE

THREE TABLES HAD BEEN SHOVED TOGETHER in the back room of the Oak Creek Diner, a popular breakfast spot in Milwaukee. Crowded around them were a few of Trey's Growler teammates, along with a group of geriatric men who acted as though they were involved in this meeting somehow. One of the geezers clapped his hands to get everyone's attention.

Trey pinched the bridge of his nose.

"What kind of fresh hell have I gotten myself into?" he mumbled.

Dex Fletcher chuckled softly beside him. "Knowing your ugly views on marriage, I woulda thought you woulda found an excuse to avoid this fracas." The Growlers' Scottish placekicker gently shifted the baby sleeping on his lap.

"It's marriage he objects to," Luke Kessler chimed in from Trey's other side. "The bachelor party is an entirely different animal. Although, the jig is up about your views on marriage, old man. No one believes the BS that woman said."

"Yeah," Fletcher added. "Imagine our surprise when both our lasses fessed up. They told us it was you who talked them into giving each of us a second chance."

Trey glared at Fletcher. "That's because I was tired of the two of you playing football like love-sick fools. I needed you both to have your heads in the game."

"Uh, huh," Kessler said.

His favorite wide receiver's smirk was starting to royally piss him off.

"This doesn't look like a planning meeting for a bachelor party." Trey gestured forcefully to the trio of septuagenarians seated in the corner before waving at the baby. "It feels like we're planning a trip to the circus. It's a wonder you didn't bring that big goofy mutt with you."

Kessler grinned. Besides football, the guy's passion in life was rescuing dogs and finding them forever homes. "Hey, that's not a bad idea," he said. "Maybe we can find a place that allows dogs."

"I thought we were having this stag party in Vegas," one of the white-haired men at the other end of the table grumbled. "We can't take a dog to Vegas."

"I rest my case," Trey murmured to his teammates. "No one from this century calls it a 'stag' party."

"Relax," Kessler admonished him. "They're harmless. I want Summer's grandfather and his friends at the weekend. They're a big reason why the two of us are together in the first place."

The baby suddenly jerked awake. Her blue eyes grew wide before she let out an excited gurgle, complete with a few spit bubbles, when she locked onto her father's nauseatingly adoring gaze. Dex lifted her to his chest. As if on cue, the old men chorused a pitch perfect "aww."

"And this little lass will be staying home with her mother. The first time she even mentions bachelors, I'll be sending her to the convent."

Kessler's younger brother Brady and Growlers' receiver Antonio McGraff chose that moment to hustle into the diner and over to the table.

Brady turned a chair around, straddling it before helping

himself to a slice of bacon from his brother's plate. "What'd we miss?"

"The senior citizens want to go to Vegas," Trey announced. "Your brother wants to bring his fart-machine dog. And Fletcher needs to find a convent for his daughter. We still haven't decided who's going to order the bouncy house."

"Cool," Brady said before shoving another piece of bacon into his mouth.

Trey reached over and moved the plate out of the teenager's reach. "Just because you're redshirting this season doesn't mean you can let your body go to shit."

"Ack. Leave the lad alone. He doesn't need your Faustian diet. He's still growing." Fletcher tossed a bagel in Brady's direction. The kid caught it with two fingers.

"Vegas works for me," Brady said around a mouthful of bagel.

His statement prompted a trio of enthusiastic nods from the geriatric set and a thumbs up from Antonio and the other receivers at the table.

"We're not going to Vegas." Trey and the men on either side of him spoke in unison.

"Man," Antonio moaned.

"Yeah," one of the seniors added. "What a bunch of namby-pambies."

The waitress came around to refill the coffee cups. Brady ordered a breakfast of pancakes, eggs, bacon and some sort of home fry situation.

"Too many paparazzi in Vegas," Fletcher explained. "We want a place where we can let loose without having to read about it online."

"Fletcher's worried one of us will get hitched at one of those wedding chapels just like he did," one of the Growlers said.

That got a laugh from the rest of the group.

The kicker grinned at his daughter. "I've no complaints with how that particular business deal turned out."

"Some place close is better because it cuts down on the travel. We only have one night over Labor Day weekend," Kessler added. He pitched his voice in a poor impersonation of Trey. "Once the season starts, we can't afford any distractions."

His teammates guffawed. Trey rolled his eyes.

"Our only other weekend off is taken up with the gala," Antonio announced. "Speaking of which, Van Horn, now that you're chairing the thing, maybe you'll class it up a bit with some fine musical accompaniment, like from yours truly."

"Wait. What?" Kessler jerked his head toward Trey so fast it was a wonder his eyeballs stayed in their sockets.

"You're chairing the gala?" Fletcher practically gasped out the question.

"How did you find that out?" Trey demanded of the wide receiver.

"Astrid told me," Antonio replied with a shrug, as if that explained everything.

Kessler let out a little wolf whistle of appreciation.

"Who the hell is Astrid?" Trey wanted to know.

All the Growlers looked at him like he'd just asked what a football was.

"She's one of the receptionists for Mrs. C," one of them enlightened him.

"Tony-O here wants to shag her," Fletcher added.

"They'd make beautiful music together," Kessler said. "Summer says Astrid is a very promising violinist."

Trey glanced between his two teammates. "How do you know all this about a receptionist in the team's office building?" He didn't think he could pick any of the support staff out of a lineup.

Fletcher shook his head. "Jaysus. You really are a robot. There's more to this team than just the guys in the locker room. You're too singularly focused on the game to know it."

"The only reason this team exists is to win championships.

Period. Excuse me if I'm the one person at this table who gets that," Trey argued.

Kessler snorted. "Testy much? Maybe you should rethink your no sugar rule. Not that I think it would make you any sweeter."

Sighing in frustration, Trey dropped his head into his hands. Why did it seem he was the only one on the team who cared so much about the game's outcome?

Fletcher nudged him with his shoulder. "Is that why you look like shite this morning, Van Horn? You don't like the idea of chairing the gala because it breaks your silly 'no PR during the season rule?'"

Hell no, he didn't like it. Not one bit. But that's not what had him looking and feeling like "shite."

He was still reeling from his close encounter with a woman he thought he'd shaken from his system years ago. And the overwhelming way his body continued to react to her. Memories he believed long buried suddenly were replaying in vivid detail every time he'd tried to shut his eyes. Images of a quicksilver smile, her sassy mouth and those luscious lips kept his body on tenterhooks most of the night. Twice he'd gotten up to brush his teeth because he could have sworn that he could taste her. As a result, he'd barely slept a wink.

Pissing him off even more was how unaffected she'd been seeing him for the first time. Except it wasn't the first time she'd seen him. Apparently, she'd been at the same galas Trey had been attending all these years.

And he'd never realized it.

Probably because she hadn't made a scene and called him out on the way he'd left things between them. Trey had endured more than one embarrassing incident like that. Case in point, the ugly *Vanity Fair* article.

Something shifted within his chest cavity.

Those other women claimed to have been in love with him. London obviously hadn't felt the same way. He'd been right all these years to think her interest in him was a ruse. A mother-daughter plot to get their hands on the Van Horn money. Lucky for him, only one of the two women was successful.

The back of his neck was unexpectedly tight and hot. Trey was angry that he'd avoided returning to his grandfather's house for over a decade because he'd been carrying around a sliver of guilt at walking away from London that summer night. The old man was still vital and in good health, but he traveled less and less, preferring to spend three seasons at his Lake Geneva home. Trey always found an excuse for why they had to meet somewhere else.

Suddenly he realized how ridiculous he'd been. He could go back there and enjoy all the area had to offer with a clear conscience. In fact, the men gathered around the table could, as well.

"I've got the place," he announced loudly. "My grandfather has a house on the lake. It sleeps twenty. We'll have a chef, access to golf and all the privacy we need. There are even a few boats we can use out on the lake."

"Hey, speaking of boats, maybe your dad can join us? He's always up for a good time." Kessler looked at him expectantly.

One of the downsides to having a dad who'd become a father before he was old enough to drink legally was that the guy thought they were more like brothers instead of parent and son. Lars Van Horn Junior, or Jay as he was dubbed by the paparazzi years ago, was very much like Peter Pan: He refused to grow up.

Whenever he visited for a game, he was the life of the party. Carousing with the guys, picking up the tab and chasing every skirt he could. Unfortunately, he had a habit of marrying some of the skirts he caught.

Trey loved his dad. But he also loathed the man's laissez-faire approach to life. It was downright embarrassing. His dad definitely hadn't inherited his carefree lifestyle from Trey's grandfather. Just the wealth that allowed him to live that way.

The senior Van Horn was a self-made millionaire who worked doggedly to build a small electronics firm into a giant within the semi-conductor industry. After his wife died giving birth to their son, Lars Senior devoted himself to acquiring more wealth. The man's self-discipline made him a role model for his only grandchild.

That and his attitude about committed relationships.

The elder Van Horn's grief after losing his wife nearly destroyed him. Once he recovered, he vowed never to give his heart to another. He insisted that doing so made a man weak.

Words to live by.

"Jay will be on his way to Australia by then," Trey lied. He had no idea of his father's schedule. He doubted his father did either.

"You two have the coolest relationship," one of his teammates remarked.

Jay insisted his son call him by his first name. Most people thought that meant Trey and his dad had a close relationship. They were wrong.

"What about a stripper?" one of the old-timers asked. "Will we be able to get one to come to the lake?"

"No!" Trey, Kessler, and Fletcher practically shouted.

"What about a theme drink?" Brady asked.

Kessler smacked his brother on the head. "You're eighteen, dumbass."

"We need a hashtag," Antonio insisted.

While the rest of their group began debating options, Trey relaxed in his chair, surprised that he was looking forward to the outing. Not only would he get the bachelor party behind them before the season started, but he could finally exorcise the remaining ghosts of London from his life.

"I need the loo. Hold her a minute."

Before Trey could even voice a protest, Fletcher placed his young daughter in his arms.

"Don't drop her," the kicker growled before disappearing down the hall.

What the hell?

Trey had never handled a baby before. He'd never even been around one. How was he supposed to hold her?

The baby let out a little squeak. Trey realized he was gripping her too hard. When he relaxed his fingers, her rosy lips moved from a pout to a little "o" of surprise. Any second now, she was going to let her displeasure with him be known to the entire diner.

Dammit. How long would it take the Highlander to take a leak?

Holding her wasn't quite the same as holding a football. For one, the little imp was squirmy. She gave Trey a drunken smile while thrusting her arms and legs out like a little starfish. His shoulders relaxed ever so slightly when she gurgled a happy sound.

A startled gasp had him jerking his gaze away from the baby currently bewitching him. Only to collide with the first pair of female eyes to ever wrap him up in a spell. For the second time in as many days, London Headley was close enough to touch.

CHAPTER FOUR

*T*HIS CAN *NOT* *BE HAPPENING.*

London's feet seemed to be frozen to the floor. A few yards away from where she was supposed to launch her new career, Trey Van Horn was holding, of all things, a baby. The kaleidoscope of butterflies fluttering in her stomach ahead of her pitch-meeting abruptly stilled.

Probably because she was no longer breathing.

Trey Van Horn was holding A BABY, for crying out loud!

And he was looking at the infant as if she hung the moon. His face was relaxed into the easy grin she'd so quickly fallen for. It still had the power to melt a piece of her heart. The lucky baby gazed back at him with worship in her eyes.

I feel you, sister.

The scene was so unexpected, it was impossible for London to stop a gasp from escaping. Trey's head snapped up, his eyes filling with frosty annoyance. He was giving off a vibe that clearly conveyed she had no right to breathe the same air as him.

She didn't have time for this. Evan Millar and the team from Nolan and Hemphill were waiting with Seth Gunther. Bennie was already shaking hands with everyone at the table. London forced her feet to move in their direction.

The scouting reports on Trey Van Horn's quickness were not exaggerated, however. He blocked her path before she could take two steps. He'd only moved a few feet, but he was breathing as though he'd just run the length of a football field.

"What are you doing here?" he demanded.

Excuse me? "Last time I checked this place was owned by one of my clients. Clearly, he isn't discriminating about who he lets through the front door." *Take that, you egotistical ass.*

The baby chose that moment to reach out and grab hold of the long silver chain London had paired with her navy sleeveless sheath dress. Her mom called it her power dress. She was abruptly proud of the way it made her look professional, yet feminine. Especially given the way Trey's gaze lingered on her chest.

London had no choice but to move a step closer to him when the baby tugged the necklace into her mouth and began gumming it.

"I meant why are you in Milwaukee?"

The baby flinched at Trey's hard tone.

He lowered his voice. "Why aren't you in L.A. filming movies? Or was that just a lie, too?"

A lie, too?

What was he talking about? Before she could demand an explanation, a large hand reached between them. London didn't dare move as long fingers gently extracted the chain from the baby's mouth.

"Pardon me, lass. I'll just take what's mine, Van Horn," he took the baby from Trey's hands. The baby issued a warning wail before her father cooed to her. "Hush, sweet Lily. Daddy will buy you a chain of your own."

London blew out a calming breath, then forced her lips into a bright smile. "It was nice to see you again, Trey," she lied. The sooner she could get away from him, the better it would be for her equilibrium. "If you'll excuse me, I have people waiting for me."

She went to take a step, but his palm against her bare arm stopped her forward progress.

And nearly her heart.

The skin tingled beneath his fingers. She swallowed roughly at the unfairness of the sensation. "What do you want from me?"

"Answers."

Well, so did she. But this wasn't the time or place. Besides being years too late. She'd waited for him that night. *All night.* He was the one who had to answer for his behavior. She didn't owe Trey Van Horn anything.

"People are watching us," she said quietly. "I've got an important client waiting. I'd really appreciate it if you'd just walk away. We both know how good you are at that."

His hand dropped from her arm as if she'd scalded him. Bennie swiftly materialized by her side. Her boss's brows were hiked to the top of his forehead.

"Everything okay here, kiddo?"

He looked between her and Trey before cupping her elbow and edging her away. She could feel Trey's eyes boring into her back as she made her way to the round table where Evan and his team waited along with Seth Gunther, their rapt gazes all focused on her. Feeling like a fool, she took her seat and gulped down a few ounces of water.

"I apologize," she said. "I just wanted to say hello to an old friend."

Seth shot a fist pump into the air. "Well, what do you know? She's got famous friends. Today is my lucky day."

The man's exuberance helped to calm her nerves. She knew they had put together a solid campaign. Bennie was correct. Given Seth's enthusiasm, this was a "slam dunk." From the corner of her eye, she saw Trey and his friends exit the diner.

Exhaling a last steadying breath, she launched into her presentation.

"We're proposing that we target two separate shoppers with your campaign," she explained. "First, we'll go after moms during the upcoming back-to-school season. They're always looking for something interesting to put in their kids' lunchboxes. Based on our market studies, Gunther's string cheese outperforms the national brands in the regions where it is available. All we have to do is get moms to put it in their children's hands, and we think that when you take the string cheese national, it will grab the same market share within eighteen months. If we are lucky, perhaps even sooner."

Bennie pulled a cow puppet from beneath his chair.

"Mooz-R-Ella will be the face of Gunther's string cheese for that purpose," she continued. "We've developed print ads and video for both television and social media targeting moms and kids. There will even be replicas of the puppet that kids can win with a certain number of UPC codes found on the inside of the string cheese wrapper."

Bennie handed Seth the cow puppet. "Your grandkids are going to love this."

"Yeah, sure," Seth replied as he absently took the puppet and put it on his hand. "But there is more, right?"

"Yes," London said, trying not to be too disappointed by Seth's lack of enthusiasm. "Of course." She opened her tablet and slid it across the table. "The rest of your cheese products will be targeted to our biggest demographic: the foodie. Millennials and Gen Xers are cooking at home more now thanks to the pandemic and the *Food Network*. It's our plan to appeal to them using these fun social media reels and recipes emphasizing the quality of your products. Research indicates they aren't afraid to spend more on something that tastes better."

She sat back while Seth quickly flipped through the videos she'd painstakingly researched and recorded. The recipes, the actors, the sets, and even the lighting, were all carefully curated to appeal to their target audience. She was proud of the work she'd put in. Everyone at the table seemed to be holding their breath as Seth swiped at the tablet.

"I don't understand," Seth was saying. "He's not in any of these videos."

Evan moved forward in his chair. London exchanged a confused look with Bennie.

"Those are for the foodies," Bennie explained to his friend. "The cow will be in the videos for the string cheese."

"I realize that." Seth slammed the cow puppet onto the table. "I don't care about the damn cow. I want to see the videos with Trey Van Horn promoting my cheese."

London nearly swallowed her tongue. "Tr-Trey Van Horn," she croaked.

Evan cleared his throat. "Mr. Gunther, your budget doesn't allow for a paid spokesman." He gestured to the discarded puppet with his chin. "Other than Mooz-R-Ella, that is."

Seth glared at the account executive before turning to Bennie. "Who's this guy to tell me that I have to use a puppet for a spokesman? I don't want a damn puppet. I want someone people look up to telling them to buy my cheese."

Bennie tried to pacify his friend. "We talked about this, Seth. The money isn't there right now. But that doesn't mean it won't be in a year or two. You heard London's stats. When we get that market share, then you can think of hiring a major spokesman."

Seth pointed at London. "But she just said they're friends."

London's stomach dropped. That's what she got for lying. *Damn Trey.* Wasn't ruining her life once enough?

"Didn't that article say he doesn't eat cheese?" One of Evan's team mumbled the question.

"I think he's lactose intolerant," another added.

"Nah, just a food weenie," one of the others chimed in.

London was pinching the bridge of her nose so hard she

wouldn't be surprised if it suddenly snapped off. That would certainly put an end to this inane conversation. She looked over to find Evan eyeing her speculatively.

"If we can get more money in the budget . . ." he began.

Oh hell no. Not him too.

"As was just mentioned, Trey Van Horn practices a crazy diet that doesn't include cheese or he would be perfect," she ad-libbed, shrugging her shoulders for effect. "But if it's a spokesman you want, I can do my best to get you Alek Bergeron."

Beneath the table, London crossed the fingers on both hands. But the goalie did say he owed her.

"Who's that?" Evan was apparently not a hockey fan.

"The goalie for the Mayhem." Bennie blessedly followed her lead. "He'd be perfect and he's very popular here."

"Yeah, *here*," Seth emphasized. "But I'm taking my brand national. I need someone everyone will recognize. Who better than football's reigning MVP? Kids will care more about what comes out of his mouth than some damn stuffed cow." He stood abruptly. "It's my money we're spending. I should get to choose my own spokesman. Make it happen."

Seth tossed down his napkin and stormed out. Everyone at the table sat in stunned silence for a long moment.

"Well, I certainly didn't have that on my bingo card." Evan's Gucci loafers squeaked on the tile floor when he shifted in his seat.

Bennie shot up from his chair. "This is a big step and he's under a lot of stress. It happens." He gave London a pacifying pat on the arm. "The campaign is perfect. I'll talk to him. Worse comes to worse, we can send Van Horn's agent an offer. It will be ridiculously lowball, but that's all Seth can afford. Van Horn will turn it down and we can proceed as planned." With a reassuring nod to Evan, he hurried after his friend.

The rest of the advertising team avoided making eye contact with London.

Evan leaned back in his chair, exhaling heavily. "We've already invested a lot of upfront money in the development of this campaign, London. I don't have to explain to you the many reasons why we need to make this work. And quickly. We are slated to kick off in seven weeks."

The ominous comment hung in the air as Evan and his coworkers solemnly filed out.

CHAPTER FIVE

"How did I not know about this," Lucy Tham demanded as she struggled with the cork on the Prosecco bottle. "I mean, this is big, London. I can't believe you never told me." She curled her lips in a pout.

Lucy's husband, Mike, took the bottle from his wife. The pop of the cork and the fizz rising from the bottle were music to London's ears. Mike poured a generous amount into a flute and passed it across the tasting bar. London gave him a chagrined smile before taking a healthy sip.

"I'm sorry," London told her friend. "I guess I just thought it wasn't a big deal."

"*Not a big deal?*" Lucy's voice rang out through the vacant liquor store. "Are you kidding me?"

This was exactly the reason London never told her best friend.

The two met during London's internship at Westbrook when she'd stopped in at Lucy's mother's nail salon next door. It was only London's second cold call soliciting business for the agency. Mrs. An was a lot harder sell than her daughter, but by the end of the summer, the nail salon had a PR strategy and London had a new best friend.

When Lucy married Mike, whose dad owned the dry cleaner in the same shopping center, London was their maid of honor. Two years later, when the couple opened a liquor store between the two shops, it was London who came up with the idea for the tasting bar and events. It was Lucy who kept London from hiding out in her apartment on weekends.

Lucy was generous, steadfast, fun-loving, and a social butterfly. She was also the drama queen to London's pragmatic introvert. Mike shot London a look of commiseration while his wife grumbled on.

"Honey," Mike said. "Just because you are friends, it doesn't mean London has to tell you everything."

Lucy stopped her rant and looked at her husband as if he'd told her there was no such thing as Ben and Jerry's ice cream.

"Of course she does," Lucy snapped. "I tell *her* everything."

Mike stiffened behind the bar. "Not . . . *everything?*"

His wife arched both eyebrows at him and jerked her chin up and down once.

London avoided his flustered gaze. Lucy *was* guilty of oversharing. There were many times when she wished her friend would keep the particulars to herself.

The tips of Mike's ears grew red. He threw down the dishtowel he was using to wipe the counter. "I'm going next door to check the alarm at the drycleaners."

As soon as he was out of earshot, Lucy sat back down next to London. "He's gone. Now you can spill the tea. And don't leave anything out."

London sighed before taking another sip of her Prosecco for courage.

"You've heard the story before. Girl crushes on guy. Guy makes girl fall in love with him. And then guy . . .vanishes."

"The dirtball," Lucy hissed. "Mike has one of his jerseys in the closet. I'm going to burn it as soon as we get home tonight."

London laughed at her friend's bloodthirsty tone. "You're the best, you know that? I wish I'd known you back then. You would have found a way to help me find the humor in the situation. My mom was preoccupied with her new marriage when it all went down."

"You never told anyone?" Lucy reached over and gently tucked a strand of hair behind London's ear. "That's not healthy, girlfriend. It might make you feel better if you let it all out," she urged. "I promise to listen silently. And I'd never judge."

She refilled London's glass and waited patiently, wearing London down.

"I met Trey the summer before college," she began. "I was working as a mail jumper on Lake Geneva. Every day we would sort the mail in the morning, then climb aboard a boat filled with sixty or so tourists who watched while we jumped onto the docks and left the mail in the mailboxes of the seventy-five estates lining the lake. When we finished, we had to jump back onto the moving boat and chat up the passengers with info on the famous houses."

"Wow."

"I know. It's the coolest summer job ever." She grinned wistfully remembering. "I first spotted him in the boathouse of his grandfather's estate. I didn't know Lars was his grandfather, though. And Trey never mentioned that little tidbit."

A sound of disgust escaped Lucy's lips before she mimed zipping them up and throwing away the key.

"There he was. This golden god, lifting weights wearing nothing but a skimpy pair of shorts. He had the graceful, fluid movements of someone in tune with every fiber of his body. He was so intently focused on making every move precise that he was unaware of anything around him. I was so captivated by him I ended up messing up my timing and instead of landing on the stern, I landed in the lake. I'm embarrassed to admit it was the first and only time I ever missed a jump that summer."

A melancholy feeling settled over her as the memories of that day flooded back.

THE WATER WAS STILL chilly in June, but London barely noticed. Her body was warm with embarrassment. She surfaced to the cheers of the passengers. And a sexy guy with brown locks blowing in the summer breeze crouched on the dock. His arm was stretched out toward her.

"Here," he said. "I've got you."

She wasn't in any danger of drowning. Years of swim team guaranteed that. Not to mention the life vest she wore. It was a good thing she had it on, too, because when he grinned at her, she lost all feeling in her body. The captain was circling the Walworth *around to pick her up. London had no choice but to take his hand and climb onto the dock.*

Before she knew it, he was draping a beach towel around her neck. The gesture was both natural and intimate at the same time. London shivered beneath his hands resting on her shoulders.

"Do you do that every day?" There was a touch of awe in his voice.

"Fall into the lake?"

His smile grew wider, revealing two perfect dimples that instantly stole her breath.

"No, silly. Do you jump to and from that boat delivering the mail?"

She nodded.

"Cool."

"Uh, huh." His smile had stolen her brain cells, too, apparently, because she couldn't think of anything more impressive to say than that.

The captain honked the horn to indicate the Walworth *was making its final turn to the dock. London tried to shrug out of the towel, but his hand stopped her.*

"You're still shivering. You can return it tomorrow with the mail." He winked. "I'll be here waiting."

London's stomach did a loop-di-loo. She sank her teeth into her bottom lip to keep her mouth from gaping open. Several wolf whistles coming from the passenger section of the boat startled her into action. With flaming cheeks, she leaped back on board, grateful she didn't splat against one of the windows like a bug. When she looked back, he was still standing on the dock, hands on his hips, staring at the departing boat.

And her.

LUCY'S SIGH brought London back to the present.

"I can't believe he's the same guy," Lucy said. "He sounds so much less uptight and machine-like than how he comes off now."

"Yeah. He was." London took another sip of her Prosecco.

Except she'd seen behind that robot mask he wore earlier today. When he was making goo-goo eyes at a baby. That guy she'd met on the dock was still in there. Her heart ached wondering why he chose to hide him.

"So, was he there the next day?"

London smiled coyly. "And the day after that."

THE THIRD DAY, he was waiting for her at the marina following the cruise. They'd spend the afternoons wandering around the lake talking about everything and about nothing. On the evenings she worked at Sandy's ice cream parlor, he'd camp out at one of the tables in the back spearing her with smoldering looks in between watching sports on his tablet or reading.

He was smart. Going into his junior year at Stanford, of all places. But he never made himself out to be too sophisticated for her, a townie with limited world experience.

He claimed to be Trey Micheals. His excuse for being at the Van Horn estate was something involving setting up a new computer system for the mansion. He said he was dragging the job out for the month until he had to return to California for a mini-semester. London was too smitten not to believe a word out of his gorgeous mouth.

Especially when he said he was falling for her.

The physical part of their relationship progressed slowly. From holding hands to delicate kisses on the cheek at the end of the evening, to more heated make-out sessions by the shores of the lake late at night. Having never had a boyfriend before, she appreciated that Trey didn't pressure her, despite the desire shining in his eyes.

Her aunt was chaperoning her while her mother was flying internationally for the month. Bringing Trey home to her place was out of the question. The boathouse at the Van Horn estate became their rendezvous spot.

Nearly three weeks into their relationship, she was officially head-over-heels in love. Stanford and UCLA weren't that far apart that their relationship had to end, she reasoned with herself. She could use her mom's buddy miles to fly back and forth. This didn't have to be a summer romance. There wasn't any reason they couldn't take their relationship to the next level, she decided at the end of their third week together.

Earlier that morning, Trey had hitched a ride with the estate's caretaker for an appointment in Chicago. She hated how much she missed his presence when he wasn't around. Especially when she got a troubling prank phone call from a supposed reporter asking her about her mother's recent marriage. She tried to shake it off. Her mother wasn't married. But when she reached out to her mom, Kim had been all giggles telling London she had a surprise when she returned home the next day. Something was definitely up.

Even more unsettling, Trey wasn't responding to her texts. She worried something had happened to him, too. Needing reassurance, and to feel his arms around her and his lips on hers, she huddled in the dark, counting down the minutes until he was supposed to meet her at the boathouse.

She ended up waiting all night.

. . .

"OH, HONEY." Lucy draped an arm over London's shoulder before reaching out to wipe a tear off her friend's cheek. "I'm such a beast for making you relive that. That jerk broke your heart."

London leaned into her friend's embrace. "Nah. My heart survived." It was mostly true. But there was still a part of it she suspected was lost forever. She was convinced it was that missing piece that doomed every relationship ever since. "He was just one in a long line of guys who decided they wanted something better."

Starting with my dad.

"Shame on them all. They're jackasses who didn't know a good thing when they had it." Lucy slammed her palm down onto the counter. "You were too good for that boring insurance guy you dated, anyway. We put up with him for a year because we love you. But he always acted like he couldn't wait to get out of here. And when you told me he slept with his socks on—" Her friend shivered. "Oh, and the frat boy you wasted three years on in college? The one who couldn't keep his hands off every woman's ass? I'll bet he's already got a pot belly."

London snorted a laugh. Leave it to Lucy to put a positive spin on her train wreck of a love life.

"Don't you dare give up on finding 'the one' just because of a few rotten eggs," Lucy told her.

"I'm not giving up. I'm just taking a break from relationships for a while. I have a career I love and family and friends who keep my heart full."

"Ohhh." Lucy swiped at her own tears. "Now you're making me cry. Still, I want to take Trey Van Horn out at the knees for deserting you like that."

"He's not worth the energy," London announced. "Besides, the next day I found my mom had lost her mind and did actually marry someone: Trey's dad. How awkward would that have been?"

"I read a book about that once. It was called *Stepsiblings in Love*. Very kinky."

London rolled her eyes at her friend and finished off her drink.

"Too soon?" Lucy joked.

"Is it safe to return?" Mike asked from the doorway.

"Please do," London said. "Your wife is being a freak."

"Did you solve the problem of getting a spokesman for Gunther's?" he asked.

"I still think the puppet is a winner. It's adorable." Lucy folded her fingers while making mooing noises. "Mooz-R-Ella says 'buy my string cheese.'"

London sighed. "Bennie said Seth was being a bit petulant. He thinks there's more to the story. Seth's wife left him a few months ago. It's almost as if she took Seth's personality with her because he's not been himself."

"Bennie's a very smart and intuitive man," Mike said. "He'll fix this."

"I hope so. My only other option is Alek Bergeron. But at least he and I get along."

"Oooo," Lucy cooed. "He's way into you. And *he* has a personality. Not to mention very sexy eyes. You should totally do him."

Mike groaned and refilled London's glass while pouring some for himself. He raised his flute up. "It'll all work out, London. You're going to kill this one."

London laughed. "As long as it doesn't kill me."

As she took a sip from the glass, she noticed Lucy wasn't drinking. "Hey, what's going on with you? I've never known you to pass up a glass of sparkling wine."

Her friend smiled demurely before exchanging a telling glance with her husband.

"Oh my gosh!! Are you—?

"Preggers!" Lucy finished for her.

London threw her arms around her friend. "This is so awesome."

Lucy and Mike had been trying to conceive for a while. Both came from large families, and they wanted the same. Their first two pregnancies resulted in early miscarriages, however.

"It's good this time?" London whispered.

"Very. This one is going to stick. We just told our families. But as our child's godmother, we wanted you to know right away." Lucy squeezed tight. "Our baby will be so lucky growing up with you in his or her life."

The words made London's breath hitch. If this deal went through, she'd no longer be popping in for a glass of wine most nights. She'd be nearly two hours away. Or perhaps even farther if she was working on a film. She'd been trying to work up the courage to tell her friends for the past several weeks. Given the way things went today, though, she might not have to break the news to Lucy at all.

CHAPTER SIX

THE SOUND of the water lapping against the boathouse dock helped to ease some of the tension in Trey's shoulders. Unfortunately, not all of it. He'd decided to rip the bandage off quickly and cleanly by beginning his visit to his grandfather's estate with the place that held the most memories of those few weeks spent with London. He didn't figure on the sting being so painful, however.

Images of her hair flying in the wind as she jumped onto the dock had his throat tightening. Remembering the way that same riotous hair looked spread out beneath him on the cushions of the chaise lounge had him hard. He swore violently as he stormed out into the sunshine.

This was a stupid idea. He should have stuck to the house. There wouldn't be any lingering flashbacks there because he'd never brought her inside. He'd have to come up with some excuse to avoid this part of the estate when the bachelor weekend rolled around.

Or find himself another woman to help him cure this insane lust that had resurfaced after seeing London again. Except his ex-lover's tell-all wasn't doing him any favors in that department. The older he got—and the larger his bank account grew—more and more women began to look at him through a marriage lens rather than just as a casual fling with a famous sports star. It wasn't likely he'd find relief easily.

"Who are you?" A young voice interrupted his disquieting thoughts.

Shoving his sunglasses up on top of his head, Trey turned to find a boy of about seven or eight standing on the dock, a hockey stick in his hand. He'd been so absorbed with trying to vanquish thoughts of London, he hadn't heard the kid approach.

"Whoa." The boy grinned. "Never mind. I know who you are. Pops said you were coming for lunch."

Pops? Since when were strangers using the nickname Trey had given his grandfather?

The boy dropped a red rubber ball onto the dock and began to dribble it with his hockey stick as if he'd done so in this spot many times before. Not only that, but he was freakishly good.

"My dad says I'll never be big enough for football. But that's okay because I love hockey. It takes a lot more skill to play a game on ice skates, you know?" He grinned sheepishly. "No offense."

There was something so achingly familiar about that grin it had Trey leaning a shoulder against one of the posts to steady himself.

"None taken," he said. "But it seems you have me at a disadvantage. Who are you?"

And what the hell are you doing here calling my grandfather Pops?

"I'm Kyle," the kid said matter-of-factly. He stopped his dribbling abruptly. "Hey, do you know Alek Bergeron?"

"We've met." Milwaukee was a small city. The hockey goalie and Trey ran in the same dating circles in addition to sharing the same agent.

"I'm going to his sleep-away camp next week. In Canada! I've met him once. He likes my sister. He sent her flowers to her office the other day."

"Kyle! That's my private life!"

Trey wasn't sure which stunned him more: The sight of London standing at the edge of the dock wearing short shorts and a T-shirt, her long hair whipping in the breeze as though she'd just jumped off the mail boat. Or the fact that fucking womanizer Alek Bergeron was sending her flowers.

"Look who's here," Kyle was saying.

London stayed where she was, her hands on her hips defensively. "I see that. Mom and Dad are waiting for you. We're going to lunch."

"We're not having lunch here?" Kyle glanced over at Trey then back to his sister.

His sister. That explained the familiar smile.

Kyle wasn't going without an argument. "Pops is always talking about Trey, and I've never met him before."

London shook her head. "Not today. It's a family lunch."

"But we're family," Kyle insisted.

What the ever-loving fuck?

"There you are, Trey." Pops' voice boomed in the distance. "We've been waiting for you up at the house."

Trey's grandfather ambled down the wooden stairs leading from the terrace surrounding the mansion to the dock. Two women and another man trailed behind him. Kyle raced over to them. Smiling broadly, Pops palmed the top of the boy's head.

"Can we stay for lunch?" Kyle asked.

Pops tousled Kyle's hair. "You're always invited for lunch, young man. But today you've got to get ready for your big trip. Besides," he said with a stage whisper. "We're serving only healthy stuff this time. We'll plan a gentlemen's lunch at the club where we can eat junk food. Just you and me. When you get back from your grand adventure. I want to hear all about it."

Kyle's shoulders slumped briefly. "I guess."

Pops chuckled. "Of course, I'll just be a boring old man after two weeks with The Alek Bergeron."

"Never." Kyle threw his arms around Pops' waist and hugged him.

Everything about this scene was making the back of Trey's neck squeeze. "Who the hell are all these people, Pops?" he demanded tersely.

A stunned hush fell over the dock. Kyle's bottom lip began to quiver. London leveled an angry glare in Trey's direction as she pulled her young brother's back against her chest. Not exactly Trey's finest moment.

His grandfather's eyes narrowed. "Trey Van Horn. That's no way for you to speak to my guests."

"We should get going," the younger of the other two women said.

"No one is going anywhere until my grandson apologizes for his rude behavior." Pops gestured to the woman who just spoke. "You've met your father's ex, Kim."

Ah, ha. That was the woman's name. If she aged in the previous ten years, she hid it well. She had the same build as her daughter, long, trim limbs with just enough curves. Where London's hair was strawberry blonde, her mother's was dark. Kim's gray eyes were an exact match to her young son's.

Of course he'd met his father's former wife once before. In Chicago. The day she and his dad returned from Las Vegas, both of them wearing wedding bands and love-struck smirks. It was then that she told him about her daughter. It was then that Trey's life changed in an instant. The woman he believed he'd fallen in love with was now his stepsister.

His stomach lurched recalling the episode.

THE CARETAKER for his grandfather's estate snickered as she watched the scene unfold. "Won't that be awkward," she murmured to Trey. Obvi-

ously, he and London had not been as discreet as they thought. "I wonder if the girl will be disappointed that she didn't get you to the altar first."

"She has no idea who I am," Trey growled.

"Don't be a fool. That girl's no dummy. You're college football's golden boy. She's delivered half a dozen sports magazines to the house with you on the cover. She knows exactly who you are," the caretaker said. "Both mother and daughter have lived in Lake Geneva all their lives. Kim has been scheming to land a big fish forever. I've no doubt she pushed her daughter in your direction."

Heart in his throat, Trey skipped out on the celebratory dinner and took the first plane back to California.

FAST FORWARD TEN years and the woman he'd rudely snubbed was standing in front of him with her hand out and a serene expression on her face.

"Nice to see you again, Trey," she said. It even sounded like she meant it.

Surprised at the embarrassment he felt, he hesitated briefly. The low rumble emanating from his grandfather's throat propelled Trey into action, shaking her hand. "Same here."

The man standing behind her reached his hand around and stuck it in Trey's direction.

"Chuck Prince," he said. "Kim's husband. And dad to this little imp."

Prince. Trey glanced over at London as he shook Chuck's hand. She met his look head on with a superior smile and a sassy shrug.

"I don't think you had the opportunity to meet Kim's daughter." Pops gestured to London.

Oh, no way was he playing that game. "We've met," he bit out.

Pops looked between them wearing a perplexed expression before the lines on his forehead smoothed out.

"Ah," he said. "Of course. London works with all sorts of famous people in Milwaukee. She doesn't share her client list with us, though. Except we know about Alek, certainly."

For fuck's sake. Not Bergeron again.

"I'm a little perplexed to see you all here today." Trey directed his comment at Kim. "You and my dad were only married briefly."

"True," Kim replied. "But we parted on good terms and we're still friends."

Her words surprised the hell out of him. But he figured the number of zeros in her alimony checks likely kept her on "good terms" with his dad.

"It's been nice having some family around when I'm here," Pops added. "Especially since you never visit."

Trey felt a lot like he'd been blindsided. And damn if it didn't hurt just as much as when it happened on the football field. These people were no longer a part of the Van Horn family tree. Why was his grandfather still hanging around with them?

The woman he hadn't met yet edged up next to Pops. "Don't I deserve an introduction?"

Pops' eyes crinkled at the corners. "Of course, my dear. Trey, this is Olivia."

"Kim's mother, I presume," Trey said as he took her hand.

Everyone laughed.

"Oh, my, no." Olivia tittered. "Although I've known her all her life, so I could be. And, were I allowed to pick out the perfect granddaughter, it would be our sweet London."

"Hey!" Kyle interjected. "What about me?"

Olivia reached over and stroked his cheek. "I was getting to you, dear boy."

Pops draped his arm around Olivia's neck. "If you had come straight up to the house, you could have enjoyed the champagne toast with the rest of us while your father was on the satellite phone." He and Olivia shared a bemused smile. "After much cajoling, Olivia has done me the honor of agreeing to be my wife." He pointed to the woman's hand. "We did the deed at the courthouse yesterday."

***

LATER THAT EVENING, Trey sat out by the pool of his sprawling Tudor situated on the shores of Lake Michigan. He'd bought the place on a whim five years earlier because it reminded him of Pops' estate. He'd hoped living in a similar type of home would bring him some peace about his decision to avoid Lake Geneva. He realized today it hadn't.

He kicked a pebble across the flagstone patio and took a pull from his vitamin water, wishing like hell it was bourbon and Coke instead. To say the past few days had not gone as expected was an understatement. Starting with the publication of the tell-all. Then discovering London lived in the freaking same town as him, followed by the bombshell today at his grandfather's.

Make that bombshells.

In spite of everything, London and her mom had somehow wormed their way into his family. To what end, he couldn't figure out. He just knew he didn't like it.

Then there was the shocking announcement of his grandfather's marriage. *Pops.* Who never missed an opportunity when Trey was growing up to reinforce the idea that love wasn't worth the pain.

His grandfather had certainly done an abrupt about-face given the adoring looks he showered on his new wife throughout the awkward lunch. Trey had been so shell-shocked by Pops' declaration, he didn't notice London and her family slip away. Part of him wished they'd stayed. Kyle would have been a welcome distraction from the stilted get-to-know-you conversation Trey had to endure.

Not that he learned anything about the woman who'd just

become his grandmother. The two had eloped, for crying out loud. Pops made some comment about life being too short and not wanting to waste another day. Still, it stung that his grandfather had up and married a stranger without so much as a word. Both Olivia and Pops had been very evasive about her background, saying only that they'd met at the club. She'd obviously been a longtime resident of the area given her affection for Kim and her family.

Trey sat up straighter in the chair. Could that be it? Was Olivia a third player in their little con to marry into the Van Horn family?

He swore savagely.

This was ridiculous. Surely his grandfather could see through such a scheme. Yet, every time Trey attempted a private conversation with the man this afternoon, Pops rebuffed him. Except of course for the little lecture about Trey needing to "have a care" how he was portrayed in the media. According to Pops, Trey's exploits shouldn't reflect badly on the Van Horn image. Not to mention any future political hopes Pops had for Trey. That one had smarted. Especially since Trey took great pains to keep his image intact.

Too bad Pops hadn't given Trey's father the same lecture. Jay Van Horn's life had been played out in the tabloids ever since he got a young Palm Beach socialite pregnant at her cotillion. He'd been nineteen at the time. Trey's mother, Reese, barely eighteen.

The pair believed themselves in love. Their lavish wedding filled an entire issue of both *Bride's* magazine and *Town and Country*. Two years and one young son later, their wedded bliss met a fiery conclusion. There were rumors of infidelity on Jay's part, but the paparazzi were never able to substantiate them. Knowing his father like he did, Trey had no doubts.

Jay was racing somewhere off the African coast, well out of cell range. Trey wanted to speak with his dad not only about

Pops' news, but he was curious about the continuing relationship with Kim. Why would his father let it continue, especially when he married again? Nothing seemed to make sense anymore.

He called his mom instead.

"Sweetheart," his mother drawled after picking up on the second ring. "You've been a naughty boy."

Trey massaged the back of his neck with his free hand. "Don't believe everything you read, Mom."

She laughed. "Where the Van Horn males are concerned, nothing said about marriage surprises me. But believe it or not, I would like grandchildren one day, you know. Please don't make it so no woman will have you."

Despite their frequent trips to the altar, neither of his parents ever had more children. That didn't surprise Trey. His mother was proud she could still strut through South Beach in a bikini with the coeds. Jay's reasons were a little harder to figure out. Perhaps it was just luck.

"Speaking of marriage," Trey began.

"Oh, for heaven's sake. Who has your father proposed to now?"

For the first time in his memory, neither of his parents was presently hitched. Jay's three-year marriage to an Australian actress ended a few years earlier. His mom's seven-year stint as wife of a young Argentinian polo player fizzled out last year. But that didn't mean she wouldn't be out seeking a new Mister Right if Jay was planning to wed again. It felt to Trey like they always had to be one-upping the other on the matrimony front.

"Not Dad. Pops. He freaking eloped."

His mom was quiet on the other end of the line for a long minute before she responded. "Well, isn't that wonderful. Lars is getting up there in years. He deserves another great love in his life."

What was it about women and "great love?"

"Just as long as her real intent isn't to take him to the cleaners."

"Really, Trey? How is it that you are so cynical about marriage?"

Seriously? She of all people was asking that question?

"Gee, Mom. I have no idea."

His quip was met with a heavy sigh. "How is your father, by the way?"

It was the same every time he spoke with either parent. No matter what the conversation was about, they'd always steer it around to asking him about the other one. His father seemed to be on speaking terms with at least one of his exes. Why not his mom?

"Dad's doing great. His yacht is leading in the standings for the Cup. Ironically, I met one of his ex-wives today. She and dad still speak all the time, apparently."

He regretted the dig as soon as the words left his mouth. Especially when the line went silent.

"She lives in Lake Geneva with her husband and young son," he said, attempting to soften the blow. "I think she checks in on Pops for dad. I assume that's probably why they're still in touch."

His backpedaling did the trick.

"Which one is she?"

"Kim," he replied, grateful he remembered her name this time. "The flight attendant."

"Ah. Well, that's nice of her. I guess she wasn't with your dad long enough to be too disgusted with him."

An awkward silence followed, and Trey felt the guilt ripple through his belly. He tried to alleviate it by reminding himself of all the holidays where both parents had used him as the go-between in their incessant squabbling. It didn't work, though. He loved both his parents despite their ridiculous relationship.

"You promised you'd come to see me this summer," she said, adding to his guilt.

"I'm still planning on it. How does the day after tomorrow sound? You can make reservations at some swanky restaurant where you can show me off to your friends."

That made his mother laugh. "You're getting too old for me to parade you around. I can't have everyone knowing I have a son so mature."

The teasing tone in her voice took away the bite of her words.

"You just said you want grandchildren."

"I do. But I want you to be happy more."

"I am happy."

He'd spouted that lie so many times to his mother he almost believed it.

His phone buzzed with a text from Collin.

Are you free?

If it meant getting out of this line of questioning from his mom, hell yes, he was free.

"Mom, my agent is on the other line. I'll call you tomorrow with my flight info. See you in a few days."

She blew a few kisses before hanging up. Trey texted Collin back.

Sure.

"Hey, man," Collin said when Trey answered. "I've been trying to call you all day."

"I was out at my grandfather's lake house. The reception out there is pretty poor." It wasn't. Trey just didn't need his agent's annoying son adding to the shit-show of this day. "What's so important?"

"Nothing. I just thought we could grab a bite before I left town. Bergeron's contract is all firmed up and my work here is done."

Bergeron. There was a name he didn't want to hear again today.

Or ever.

"But I'm already at the airport so it will have to be another time," Collin said.

Trey tried to sound disappointed. "Yeah, sure. Next time."

"By the way. An offer came in late last night. Some cheese company here in Wisconsin wants you to be their spokesman."

"I'm not taking on any new sponsorships until after the season. And anything having to do with cheese wouldn't be on my radar anyway."

Collin laughed. "Yeah. You and that nutty diet you've adopted. That's what I thought, though. Besides they're offering chump change. I would normally send them a proforma 'no thanks' but one of the contact names on the email is London Headley. I thought it was a funny coincidence since your long-lost little sister has the same name."

Trey shot up in his chair, his pulse racing.

"What's the name of the agency?"

"Uh, West-something. Why?"

"Email me the info, Collin."

"What the hell? Does that mean you're actually considering it?"

Was he?

No. But it would give him an opportunity to find out what London knew about Pops' new wife.

At least that was the excuse he was giving himself.

"Just send it to me before you get on the plane. I'll turn them down in person."

"It is the same woman, then. What's with you two anyway? I was picking up some very serious vibes the other day in the dragon lady's office."

"Nothing." It was the first truthful thing he'd said to Collin the entire call.

"Good, because I'm pretty sure Bergeron has a picture of him and her on his phone."

Well, fuck.

CHAPTER SEVEN

"WELL?" Lucy demanded from the other end of the phone. "How was dinner with Alek last night? Please tell me you at least let him kiss you goodnight. Or even better, kiss you good morning?"

London slumped back against her desk chair with an exasperated sigh. "There was no good morning kiss."

Lucy groaned. "Don't tell me you missed a chance to test drive that gorgeous mouth of his."

"I didn't say that."

There had been a very nice goodnight kiss when Alek dropped her off at her place last night. Better than nice, actually. Not that London had a catalog of men to compare it to. Her scorecard was less than a dozen. But the goalie definitely knew how to use his lips and tongue with the same finesse with which he played hockey.

"That's what I want to hear," Lucy squeaked. "Tell me all about it."

"Dinner was fun. We went to Oliveti's and sat at one of the more secluded tables.'"

"I knew it!" Lucy practically purred. "He wanted to focus all his attention on you and not on being seen. So romantic."

London chuckled. "I think it's more like the guy would prefer to eat his meal in peace rather than have fans constantly interrupt him. I told you, last night's dinner was a thank you for my help with the social media campaigns I developed for him."

"Social media campaigns that he *paid* Westbrook PR for," Lucy pointed out. "Stop selling yourself short. He took you out to dinner because he wanted a date. He wouldn't have kissed you otherwise. Now tell me what his kisses are like."

"You're more nosy than usual this morning."

"I know. I'm just trying to live vicariously through you. No one tells you pregnancy makes you horny."

"You do realize you have a very fine husband who is willing and able to satisfy all your needs?"

Lucy sighed. "He's afraid to touch me. He's worried about another miscarriage. Luckily, I have you around to help keep me sane. So don't leave me hanging. The kiss. Give me the deets."

London took pity on her friend. "It was very satisfying."

And it had been. But like every other man she kissed, it didn't leave her breathless with want like Trey's once did. She tried to chalk it up to the fact that she'd been young back then. Still discovering things about herself and her sexuality. About her desires. Very likely, if she kissed Trey Van Horn today, she wouldn't experience the same feelings.

At least that's what she kept telling herself.

For some reason, she didn't share with her friend about her third run-in with Trey this weekend. Given Lucy's thirst for gossip, it was probably a wise decision. Mostly because London was at odds with the feelings the man stirred up in her.

Seeing him standing on the dock chatting with Kyle had done something to her equilibrium and she still hadn't quite recovered. He'd looked almost . . . vulnerable. He'd clearly been stunned to discover her mom and his dad were still in contact, not to mention that London and her family had a relationship with Lars. But there was palpable pain in his eyes when his grandfather introduced Olivia as his new wife. She couldn't help but wonder why.

Why do I care? she asked herself for the millionth time. *He's not my problem.*

"That's it?" Lucy thankfully interrupted her wandering mind. "Alek Bergeron's kiss 'was very *satisfying?*'"

London could practically hear Lucy's eyeroll.

She decided to placate her friend. "It was a nine out of ten, okay. He probably would have knocked my panties off if he didn't have to catch an early flight to Canada this morning. Hockey camp starts this afternoon."

"That makes sense." Lucy snickered. "And just think of all the extra attention Kyle will get because Alek wants to 'knock' those panties off his big sister."

"I hope not." The coffee London drank earlier sloshed around in her stomach. "I want Kyle to be noticed because he works hard at the game. Not because of any interest Alek might have in me. Besides, Kyle's really good."

"Not to mention absolutely adorable," Lucy added. "Alek won't be able to resist either one of you."

"You're forgetting that I've sworn off relationships right now."

"Who's saying anything about a serious relationship? You don't need one for a booty call. You've been in the middle of this dry spell forever. And trust me when I say a real man beats a vibrator every time. And who better to get back on that horse with than Alek. Have you seen the naked photos of him from the body issue of that sports magazine? Yum."

London rubbed her fingers along her aching forehead. "Luce, please call your OB and get a note for Mike because you're starting to freak me out."

The sound of Bennie wishing everyone good Monday morning gave London an out to this uncomfortable conversation. Her boss's tone wasn't as jovial as usual which likely meant he hadn't made any headway with Seth.

"Gotta go, Luce," she said. "I've still got the mess with the Gunther account to resolve."

"You'll figure it out. Don't forget spa night tonight."

London wasn't likely to forget. It was her favorite night of the month. Lucy's mom opened up her salon to family and friends for manicures/pedicures, wine and lots of laughter. She'd miss those evenings when she moved to Chicago. Even if her move was still a big "if" right now, no way was she missing out on spa night.

"Ow."

The stitch in her side squeezed when she stood. The stress of the past week was really doing a number on her body. Between seeing Trey three times in as many days and the mess of the Gunther account, sleep was hard to come by. Added to that was the quick trip up to the lake to say goodbye to her family before they went "off grid" for two weeks. Then her dinner with Alek. There had been no time for her barre class in days and her body was letting her know it.

"My joints should not be this cranky at twenty-eight," she announced when she joined Bennie in the conference room.

Her boss managed a wan smile. "You ain't seen nothin' yet, kiddo."

The dark circles under his eyes told her that he, too, had been stressing about the account all weekend.

"Seth?" she asked.

He shook his head. "I tell ya, the guy has got his heels dug in and he won't budge. He's not the same guy since his divorce. I suspect the new chippie he's involved with might be egging him on. She's got serious dollar signs in her eyes, that's for sure."

There was no mistaking the disgust in Bennie's tone.

She slumped her shoulders. "I sent the proposal off to Trey's agent. I'm sure we'll hear something back within a few days. Then maybe when the 'no' is coming from them, Seth will see the light." She tried to infuse enough optimism into her voice that maybe it would come true.

"Let's hope so." Bennie lowered his voice. "In the meantime, I have a call into Nolan and Hemphill. I'm going to ask Evan to take you on no matter what comes from this account."

"What? No!"

Bennie held up his palm. "Listen to me, kiddo. I'm closing the doors to this place at the end of the year, no matter what. Everyone else here will either retire or land with one of our clients." He pointed a finger at her. "You, though, are far too talented for this market. And you're young, despite your damn complaints about aches and pains. I want to see you take those gifts of yours to the next level. Evan has made no secret that he thinks very highly of your work. Hell, the guy will be happy to get you and not have to deal with the excess baggage of the staff." He sighed heavily. "I won't let damn Seth torpedo your career."

London's stomach had gone from gentle rolls to a tidal wave. Was Bennie even being serious right now? Or was there a bigger piece to the puzzle she was missing?

"Bennie, is there something you're not telling me?" She blinked a few times to ward off the tears stinging the back of her eyes. The idea of not seeing him every day made her sad, but he'd still always be a phone call away. Wouldn't he? "Are you—is everything okay?"

Please don't let there be something wrong with Bennie.

He waved her off. "I'm fine. But life is short. Losing the love of my life showed me that. There are things we talked about doing and seeing. I wanna honor her by actually accomplishing them." He reached across the table and squeezed her hand. "Robyn was so proud of you. She'd want this for you, too."

As guilt trips went, Bennie had just laid a pretty good one on London's shoulders.

She didn't know what to think. It was her dream to move on to bigger, national projects. To work with a company like Nolan and Hemphill would be the ultimate. But it was all happening so fast. It was a lot easier to swallow when her "future" was months away.

"I think we should stay the course for a few days longer," she insisted. "I floated the idea of a big national ad campaign by Alek Bergeron last night. He said he'd be thrilled to work with any client of ours."

He'd really said he'd be delighted to "couple" with London and her team, but Bennie was a lot like Lucy about reading into things. She didn't want him to get the wrong idea about her and Alek. Even though he *had* winked at her when he mentioned "couple."

She was relieved to see Bennie's face break out into a wide smile. It was all the foolishness about the account that had him talking nonsense about sending her off to Chicago early, that's all. If she could get Alek to save the day, they could progress at the planned pace.

Then she noticed Bennie wasn't exactly smiling at her. His grin was directed somewhere over her shoulder. A throat cleared behind her. Bennie got to his feet.

"I hope I'm not interrupting. The woman up front said to come right in."

The sound of Trey Van Horn's voice had London launching from her chair, the twitch in her side be damned. She turned to find the object of her anxiety standing in the doorway, looking like he was there to pose for a cover shot for a men's magazine. He was wearing charcoal slacks that hugged his thighs smartly and an ecru golf shirt, perfect for showing off his buff chest and perpetual tan. Unlike the other players on the Growlers, there wasn't a hint of gold on him except for within his eyes. Eyes that were presently trained on London.

"What are you doing here?" she demanded, sounding just as rude as he did on the dock the past weekend.

"London," Bennie chastised her.

The room seemed to spin.

Damn this man.

She pressed her fingertips to her forehead. "My apologies. I just didn't expect to see you at my place of work." *Or anywhere.*

He grinned suavely making the room tilt even further. Through the conference room's glass windows, she could see Brenda fanning herself as she looked on. It was all London could do not to gag.

Trey moved deeper into the room. "You know what they say, bad things come in threes."

Was he making a *joke?*

"We're up to four now." The words were out of her mouth before she could stop them.

His smile grew more predatory. "You're keeping score, then?"

The expletive she was holding back threatened to escape. Fortunately, Bennie was quicker.

"Mr. Van Horn. How nice of you to stop by." Bennie ushered Trey into the conference room. "To what do we owe the pleasure?"

Trey held up several folded white sheets of paper. "You sent me an offer. I thought since I'm in town we could discuss it in person."

London rocked back on her heels, resisting the urge to pinch herself because surely this was some sort of stress-induced nightmare. Beside her, Bennie was nearly busting out of his buttons with renewed energy.

"Of course." He pulled out a chair. "Have a seat. Can I get you a coffee? Cheese Danish?"

"Nothing for me," Trey said as he settled into the chair across from her.

"That's because he doesn't consume either one." London plopped back down into her chair. "Which makes me wonder why you'd want to promote cheese products."

"How about I get our guest a bottled water." There was no

mistaking the "be nice" Bennie mouthed to her behind Trey's back before hurrying from the room.

Great. Now her head was pounding as much as her side.

Trey eyed her speculatively. "If you didn't think I'd do the campaign, why did you send it?"

She'd forgotten the man had a brain beneath his helmet. Of course he would wonder that. But he wasn't supposed to find out about the offer. His agent should have already vetted it and sent it to the slush pile.

"Because the client, Seth Gunther, wants you. He saw us at the diner the other day and misinterpreted our relationship."

He flinched ever so slightly. "You're saying he's not serious?"

"Oh, *he's* serious."

"Just not you."

Now she was the one squirming beneath his golden gaze. "He can't afford you."

"You don't know that."

She slapped a palm on the table. "What kind of game are you playing here, Trey?"

He was quiet for a long moment. London tried not to fidget beneath his gaze.

"I'd like to hear a little more about this campaign. How about we grab dinner tonight and discuss it."

It was all she could do to keep her jaw from dropping to her chest. No way was she having dinner with this man to discuss anything. Tonight or any night. It was spa night, dammit.

Too bad Bennie had other ideas.

"That sounds like a wonderful plan," her boss chirped when he reentered the room.

"But—"

Bennie held up a hand. "It can be just between us and Trey, here. We don't need to alert Seth or anyone else." He clapped Trey on the shoulder. "I appreciate you giving this some thought. Even if it doesn't work out, this is a classy way to handle things."

Trey shot her another man-eating grin before standing and shaking hands with Bennie. "Thank you, sir. London, Pops' assistant gave me your address. I'll pick you up at seven."

He was out of the door before London could react.

"Well." Bennie rubbed his hands together. "Maybe this isn't over after all."

London leaned her forehead into her palm. "He's not going to do it. He's just jerking our chain."

Bennie's enthusiasm waned. "Now I'm the one who wants to know if I'm missing anything. He's got the reputation in the business for being a straight shooter. I don't always agree with his opinions, but he's a winner." He sat down next to London. "But I get the feeling there's more to this story. Is there something going on between you two?"

She groaned softly as she tried to adjust her body to a more comfortable position. "My mom was briefly married to his dad. Just unfinished sibling rivalry, that's all."

Evidently that's what she was calling it these days.

Her boss whistled. "Holy smokes. Look, if dinner is too much, I can go in your place. Try and appeal to his Everyman side."

She laughed. "I don't think he has one of those." Once, she believed he did, but not anymore. "No, it's me he wants to hash things out with. I'll go."

But she wasn't going unprepared. If she had to break bread with Trey Van Horn, she was going to show him what he walked away from. And to do that, she needed an afternoon of primping.

LONDON'S PLACE was located in the Third Ward in an early 1900's Art Deco office building that had been converted to condos some years ago. It had all the character and charm he'd expect of the artistic woman he used to know. It also had an annoying intercom system that didn't seem to be working.

Either that or London was blowing him off.

Trey was acting like a colossal asshole. Multiple times throughout the day, he'd tried to force himself to call and cancel this nonsense dinner. He knew better than to use London to get information about his grandfather's new wife. And he wasn't that much of a dick that he'd string some company along only to turn down a deal. Not only was that bad for his image, it was bad manners, period.

Yet, something was still tugging him toward London. Something he couldn't seem to shrug off. And when he entered that conference room this morning and heard her mention Alek *fucking* Bergeron, the pull became more intense. Not to mention his pride being a bit stung when she admitted she never thought he'd consider taking on the campaign. She was right, of course. But that didn't mean he had to like that she knew him so well.

Now he was standing outside her building, buzzing her unit like a lunatic. He was going to cancel on *her*. No way was he letting her ghost *him*.

A guy dressed in gym clothes emerged from the lobby. Trey thrust his shoulder in to keep the door from closing. The other man shot him a look before recognition dawned.

"Oh, hey," the guy said.

"Hey, man. I think my date must still be in the shower," he improvised. "She's not answering."

The dude gave him a conspiring smile. "You'll need the elevator code then."

He led Trey to the elevator bank and punched in a series of numbers.

"Thanks."

The guy held up his phone in the universal "can-I-get-a-picture-with-you" gesture.

Trey nodded sanguinely. Selfies had replaced autographs as the main way for fans to document meeting him. As weird as it was to know his mug was on the camera rolls of perfect strangers, likely somewhere between pictures of their dog and their dinner, he always put up with the intrusion.

Photo complete, Trey stepped into the thankfully empty elevator and traveled up to the seventh floor. London's condo was at the end of the hallway. With a corner unit, he imagined she'd have some great views of the lake. The image suited her. She always loved to look out over the water at Lake Geneva.

He knocked on the door brusquely. If she was hiding in there, he wasn't going to let her get away with it. Something that sounded like a moan greeted him from the other side of the door.

Trey was instantly on alert. "London?"

"Oh, God, of course it has to be you," he thought he heard her say.

Trey tried the door handle, but it was locked. Another groan, this one a lot more urgent sounding, came from inside. An unfamiliar lick of panic ran up his spine.

"London, dammit, open up."

"What do you think I'm trying to do," she cried.

The door handle clicked. Trey was leaning on the door so hard he nearly fell into the entry hall. His heart skipped several beats when he saw London crumpled against the wall.

"Are you okay?" he demanded stupidly as he crouched down beside her.

"Does it look like I'm okay?" she huffed.

She was dressed in a little black dress that was currently riding nearly all the way up her sleek thighs. He swallowed roughly, trying to ignore the glorious skin his fingers itched to reacquaint themselves with.

"Enjoying the show?" she asked through labored breaths.

He jerked his eyes up to hers. Even laid out by whatever this was, she looked sexy as hell. Her hair hung past her shoulders in silky strands. He brushed a piece of it back off her face, only to discover that her skin was hot to the touch.

"Tell me what's wrong." He spoke softly, gently tracing his finger along her cheek.

"I have to cancel our dinner." She swallowed roughly. "I'm afraid I'm under the weather."

Trey nearly laughed. He'd forgotten how fierce she could be. "You don't say?"

She winced again, grabbing at her side with a cry. Trey scooped her up and lifted her to his chest. He peeked into the living room, looking for what he wasn't sure. He took in the gorgeous, framed photos on the walls, knowing instantly they were hers.

"How long has this been going on?"

"All day," she said, dropping her head down on his shoulder. "But I'll be okay. We can talk about the Gunther account another time. I just need a good night's sleep and I'll be better in the morning."

"Uh, huh."

He spied her purse and grabbed it with his free hand, fishing inside it for her keys.

"Hey, get out of there." Her complaint was half-hearted given her lack of strength.

"We're going to need this where we are going." He looped the strap of her purse over his shoulder.

"No! I don't want to go anywhere with you," she whispered.

The truth in her tone had his chest constricting painfully. Still, he wasn't leaving her alone. Fortunately, she didn't have the energy in her to put up much of a fight.

CHAPTER EIGHT

THE EMERGENCY ROOM was crowded for a Monday evening. Luckily, Trey's recognizable face and the nearly unconscious woman in his arms allowed him to bypass triage. He wasn't normally "that" guy who used his celebrity to jump the line. But at the moment, he'd do anything to ensure London was taken care of. When one of the staff suggested he wait in the lobby, Trey pinned her with the murderous glare reserved for receivers who dropped his passes. As a result, he was loitering in the hallway, trying not to get in the way.

On the other side of the curtain, he could hear the staff murmuring to London as they undressed her before beginning their exam. Every time she hissed or moaned in pain, it felt like moments were being shaved off his life. A portable X-ray machine was wheeled in. Trey sucked in a breath when London cried out. It was all he could do not to storm in there and wrap his hands around the throat of whoever was manhandling her.

There seemed to be a choreographed dance to the chaos of the ER. One Trey didn't know the steps to because every time he started to pace, he nearly collided with someone. If they recognized him, no one made a big deal. Twenty agonizing minutes went by before he heard someone behind the curtain ask if London had any family with her.

Trey stormed in. "She does."

Three heads turned to look at him inquisitively. For her part, London scrunched her face up in disgust.

"And you are?" one of the men wearing a surgical cap asked.

"Trey Van Horn." No way was this guy going to keep him from making sure London got the care she needed. "I'm her brother."

The looks directed his way were a bit more incredulous now. The woman manning the IV bag in the corner arched an eyebrow as if to say "for real?"

"Oh please," London moaned. "Not this again."

Trey ignored her protest. "Will someone please tell me what you are doing to make her feel better and *when the hell that is going to start happening?!*"

The guy in the surgical cap analyzed Trey for a long moment before turning to London. "Miss Headley, do you give me permission to share your medical information with—" He glanced back over his shoulder. "*—your brother.*"

She nodded her head with a huff. "He's just going to bully you for it anyway. He's an ass like that."

Scrub cap guy nodded to the woman in the corner who began administering something through the IV tube stuck in London's arm. Then he stood and extended his hand to Trey.

"I'm Doctor Chang. Miss Headley here has a bad case of appendicitis. As soon as I get an open OR, I'm going to remove the offending organ and she'll be feeling better by morning. Is that amenable to you?"

Trey didn't appreciate the guy's snark. But given that he was here under false pretenses, and they likely knew it, he ignored it. He also bit back the questions swirling through his brain about the guy's credentials. Instead, he nodded brusquely.

"Excellent," Dr. Chang replied. "I'll see you both in pre-op."

The doctor and one of his companions pushed through the curtain. The woman remaining readied the gurney to be moved.

"Pre-op?" London wheezed. "I can't have surgery without my mom knowing." She gestured frantically at Trey while the nurse pushed the gurney out into the hallway. "Give me my purse. I need to call her."

Trey dug through the evening bag still draped over his shoulder and pulled out her cellphone. The nurse steered them into an elevator.

"You won't be able to get any real reception downstairs," she announced.

London sucked in a shaky breath. "Just great. I'm not even sure I'll be able to reach her anyway," she groaned. "My mom is in Banff, out on some mountain with no cell reception." A tear leaked down her cheek. "She won't know if something happens to me."

Trey reached up to loosen the laces on his shoulder pads compressing his chest, only to realize he wasn't wearing any. "Nothing is going to happen to you."

The elevator doors opened into another beehive of activity. A large man in scrubs appeared at the end of the gurney wearing a welcoming grin as if he was the greeter at Walmart.

"Hey there, gorgeous," he said. "I hear you've got a little gremlin inside of you that needs to be evicted." He took over steering, guiding London into another curtained-off area.

The ER nurse followed, handing off the IV.

"My name is Victor. I'm your attending nurse slash bartender this evening. I'm going to get you ready for the main event, starting with this lovely cocktail." He injected something into the IV line.

"Actually, it really doesn't hurt anymore," London said. "Maybe we can postpone this until another time."

"That's just the pain meds talking," the ER nurse told her. She handed Trey a plastic bag, presumably filled with London's clothing. "Good luck, you two."

"He's not staying," London protested, her voice beginning to rise. "Whoa. What the heck was in that cocktail?"

Victor chuckled. "Right? Can't beat it on a Monday night."

He began sticking pads and wires to London's chest. Trey danced out of the way when the nurse came over to the other side of the bed.

"Looks like you guys were on the way to a nice evening out," Victor said. "The little buggers always seem to pop up when you've got something fun to do."

Trey looked down at the sparkly handbag he still carried against his sports jacket.

"Oh, definitely not fun." London let out a little giggle. "It was supposed to be work. I had to miss spa night for it. Now *that* is fun." She attempted to make air quotes with her fingers, but the bulky pulse monitor on her finger suddenly distracted her.

"Ah." Victor slipped some heavy socks on her feet.

London continued to fiddle with the monitor. "My client wants Mr. *I-Only-Eat-Clean* to be the national pitchman for his cheese. I had an awesome campaign laid out but *nooooo!*" She barked out a frustrated laugh. "Seff wants *him*, a football player who eats cardboard and has the personality of a robot, to be the face of his cheddar."

Ouch.

Whatever was in that IV line had turned her into the drunk date of every guy's nightmares.

"Not gonna lie, he does have a pretty face," she continued. "But Mooz-R-Ella has more personality. And who doesn't love a cow puppet? Am I right? But does Seff see that? Nope! Now Seff is going to take his money and run." She seemed to deflate. "And there goes my best shot at moving into big-time advertising."

Wait, what?

London smacked Trey in the chest. "All because this guy

couldn't resist getting in my face at the diner. I had to tell everyone I knew him. Even though I rather I didn't."

Victor moved to the head of the bed where he hooked up the cables and avoided looking in Trey's direction.

"Trey thinks he can boss me around because his dad once bamboozled my mom into marrying him."

For fuck's sake. What were they pumping into her arm?

"London, maybe we should table this discussion until later," Trey said.

She ignored him. "Thankfully they didn't last long. Turns out this guy's dad likes the *idea* of being married more than the actual marriage." She shook her head. "Of course, my mom shoulda known better. She'd been buhboo—baaboo--*bamboozled* before. And look what that got her." She gestured a little wildly at her head. "Me."

Her voice trailed off. The beeping of the monitors became jarring in the awkward silence that followed.

That long ago summer, Trey had wondered about her father. She'd told him she'd been raised by a single mom, but he hadn't pursued the subject. It felt a little hypocritical to pry when he was concealing his own identity. But now he wondered where the bastard was. Why would he abandon his child? Trey's own parents were selfish at times, but they'd never walk out of his life.

"Are you married, Victor?" London asked out of nowhere.

The other man looked up from where he was entering something on the computer. He winked at London. "Eight wonderful years."

"Mmm." London sighed contentedly before reaching up and taking Trey's chin between her fingers.

Her grip was still surprisingly strong.

And warm.

And arousing.

"This guy doesn't believe in marriage, ya know. Just breaking hearts."

Trey was beginning to get annoyed at her rambling. Especially since most of it was directed at him. He wrestled her hand away from his chin.

"I do not break hearts," he ground out. "Some women just want to change the game plan midway through the relationship."

That got a belly laugh out of her. "No chance of that anymore. Not after that article. Everybody knows your game plan verbatim." She dropped her voice several octaves. "Marriage is a trap. An exercise in torture."

Trey glanced over at Victor in desperation. "How much longer until they take her in to surgery?"

Victor moved toward the curtain, presumably to check. London grabbed the man's wrist before he could escape, however.

"Ohmigosh! You should have seen his face when his grandfather told him he'd eloped. He looked like he swallowed a bug." She broke out into another round of giggles, pointing to Trey's face. "Yep, jus' like that."

"What do you expect?" he snapped before he could stop himself. "My grandfather is suddenly married to a woman I've never met. Maybe I'm concerned she'll take him for everything he's got."

"Ooooh, that's so sweet of you to be worried about Lars." She slapped a palm against his chest. "But dumb." Her head lolled back over toward Victor. "His pops married Olivia Parsons. Of the timber Parsons. Her toilet paper touches more butts than my ex-boyfriend." She was overcome by another fit of giggles.

Well, shit.

He was beginning to feel like the dirt bag depicted in the *Vanity Fair* article.

"Oh, don't look so sad." London reached up and delicately traced her fingertip along his bottom lip.

Her touch mesmerized him.

"You have the most amazing mouth," she whispered as her

eyes followed the movement of her finger. "Did I mention he's a great kisser, Victor?"

Victor cleared his throat. "I'll just go check—"

London sighed. "Even better than Alek Bergeron."

Fuuuuck.

Trey followed Victor to the end of the bed.

"Hold up," he whispered frantically. "That damn drug you filled her with is making her spill her guts. She's a private person and she'd be mortified if anything she said made it out there." He gestured toward the hallway with his thumb. "Even if what she's saying is a bunch of nonsense. Spread whatever the hell gossip you want about me, but her life stays private. Got it?"

The corners of Victor's lips slowly turned up into a smile. "Dude, not to worry. What happens in pre-op stays in pre-op. *She* won't even remember what she said afterwards. But it's not nonsense. That stuff is actually used as a truth serum in some instances." He looked over at London who was mumbling more nonsense about kissing. "She's lucky to have you." The nurse winked at him. "I mean, for a brother."

Trey dragged his fingers through his hair. Could it be true that everything London was going on about was a fact? If so, how had he gotten everything so wrong?

"You were my first kiss, you know."

London's softly uttered words slammed into Trey's chest with the force of a defensive lineman.

For the first time all evening, Victor looked flummoxed. "Uh, I'm just gonna go check the status of the OR," he mumbled before hurrying out.

"It was so magical," London continued. She was tracing her own lips now. "I thought I was special. That it meant something."

He returned to her bedside. His throat was so tight, words weren't possible. Good thing, because Trey had no words. His head was reeling with the idea that everything he had believed about her these past ten years might have been a lie.

She slapped him on the chest again. Hard.

"I waited for you," she hissed. "I waited *all night*. My mom had just done something insane, and I was so scared. I needed someone to talk to." She slapped him again. "I *needed* you."

Trey was having trouble reining in his pinballing thoughts. He'd messed up. Instead of trusting his gut—his heart—he'd listened to the words of Pops' caretaker. A woman he didn't know from Adam. A woman he'd like to strangle right about now.

Victor entered the room. "We're ready to rock and roll."

"Wait." London's voice rose in panic. "If something happens to me, you have to make sure my mom knows I love her. And Kyle. Tell him to be a good boy." She hiccupped a sob. "And Chuck. Thank him for loving my mom. Omigosh the baby! And Lucy. And Bennie."

"Shh." He brushed a kiss onto her forehead. "I got this, London. You're going to be just fine. I'll be waiting right here for you."

Her blue eyes were awash with unshed tears. "You promised me that once before. And I believed you. I trusted you with my heart. I *waited*." She shook her head. "I won't ever make that mistake again. I'm doing just fine on my own."

Victor rolled her through the curtain, leaving Trey standing alone among the now silent monitors, gutted.

CHAPTER NINE

LONDON FELT *like she was floating on air. The summer breeze had goose bumps forming on her exposed skin. The boat beneath her bobbed gently on the peaceful lake.*

She risked a glance over at Trey, reclining beside her on the forward deck. Wearing only a pair of board shorts, he was a mouth-watering display of sculpted sun-kissed skin that she wanted to reach out and touch. Everywhere. Only she couldn't bring herself to lift a finger. Her fear of doing something naïve kept her body frozen in place.

They'd only known each other for a little over a week and she still had to pinch herself that a guy like him wanted to hang around her. There were certainly plenty of young women more sophisticated than London vacationing on the lake. She'd seen them casting speculative glances in their direction when she and Trey were walking through town.

For his part, Trey didn't seem to notice. He only had eyes for her. Wherever they went, he was quick to lace his fingers through hers, almost as if he couldn't bear not touching her. It was a heady feeling for a girl who only ever went to her prom with a group of friends rather than a date.

She could get used to the tender way he stroked a finger down her cheek before he kissed her. Or the way his hand felt, possessive and fail-safe, resting on the small of her back. Not to mention how electrifying his hard body felt pressed up behind her, his arms wrapped around her middle, as they watched the sun set over the lake in the evening. Fortunately for London, the cautionary tale of her mother's twentieth summer on Lake Geneva kept her from completely losing her head over Trey's attention. And considering she could barely get up the courage to initiate a touch, it wasn't likely to ever become an issue.

In less than two weeks, when he was gone, all she'd have left of him were the photos she'd collected when he wasn't looking. While pretending to be capturing images for her college portfolio, she'd surreptitiously snapped enough images of Trey to make a five-minute film that she watched in her room each night. Except photos wouldn't be enough to sustain her, she was beginning to realize. She itched to know if the light dusting of hair on his chest was soft or coarse. If the muscles on his abdomen were as hard as they looked. Would his legs feel nice wrapped around her hips?

His eyes remained closed as she unabashedly let hers roam over him. When she landed on his lips, the corners of his mouth slowly turned up in a smug smile, as if he could feel her checking him out.

"See something you like?" His husky voice was wreaking havoc on her nerve endings.

London surprised herself by rolling over on her belly so that her arm and leg were brushing against him. She was rewarded for her bravery by the sound of his sharp intake of breath. She shifted her eyes to the horizon, propped her chin on top her hands, and asked the question that had been nagging at her since they'd met.

"Do you have a girlfriend at school?"

"If I did, I wouldn't be here with you."

His quick response bolstered her confidence. "Why are you here with me?"

The boat shifted when he slowly rolled over onto his side to face her. London immediately missed the sizzle of his body.

"You have to ask that?"

Her skin heated beneath the weight of his intense stare. He hesitated only briefly before reaching down and skimming his finger along the back of her thigh and up again before stopping abruptly at the vee of her bikini bottom. The movement made her insides tremble.

"You're fun to spend time with," he murmured softly. "You don't take things too seriously. You're easy to talk to. You call me out on my shit. And your smile lights up my world every time you gift me with one."

She sucked in a breath when he leaned down to sweep his tongue along her shoulder.

"And you have to know how hot you are," he whispered against her skin. "I can't help but want to touch you. Hell, I can't think half the time, I'm so busy imagining all the things I want to do with you."

"I don't have any experience with that kind of thing." There. She'd said it.

His lips stilled against her skin and London suddenly wanted to throw herself in the lake. As if reading her mind, his hand settled lightly on her lower back, anchoring her to the boat.

"Look at me," he commanded.

It took everything she had to do as he asked. She nearly wept at the tender expression in his golden eyes.

"We don't have to do anything you don't want to," he said.

An exasperated sigh escaped the back of her throat. While she appreciated his gallantry, she wanted to do things. Lots of things.

Trey chuckled wickedly. "But if there's anything you do want to do, I'm all yours."

London sank her teeth into her lower lip before tentatively placing her palm against his chest. His eyes grew dark, and his breath seemed to still beneath her touch. She ran her fingers through the coarse hair on his chest before following the trail lower along his abdomen. He hissed sharply when she let a finger skim his belly button.

The sound had her jerking her eyes back to his face just as his eyelids fluttered closed. Now it was him chewing on his lip. Emboldened, she leaned forward and traced her tongue along the swollen flesh of his mouth. Trey growled, then ruthlessly took over the kiss. He rolled onto his back. London followed, practically crawling on top of him. He sank his fingers into her hips, adjusting her so she was straddling the hardest part of him. A sudden jolt of pleasure coursed through her body at the feel of his arousal between her legs. The thin barrier of both their bathing suits did nothing to diminish the hot, hard feel of him. He groaned when she slid her core along his erection.

Breaking their kiss, she stretched up on her elbows and gazed down at him. He was breathing just as hard as she was. He dragged his eyelids open. The passion she saw reflected there made her stomach flip.

"You're a fast learner," he told her. "Anytime you're ready for another lesson, let me know."

He'd barely finished his sentence when she was kissing him again. This time, he let her control their tempo, her tongue tangling with his. His fingers sank into her butt cheeks, kneading and squeezing until she was perfectly placed along his hot length once again. Her body moved on its own, grinding against him as a sense of urgency grew deep within her belly. Dragging her mouth from his, she sank her teeth into his shoulder, to keep from wailing.

The sound of a boat horn startled them both apart.

"Ohmigosh!" she shrieked as she frantically skimmed the boat deck for some sort of covering.

"Shh," he said. "No one can see us. I rigged the sunscreen to shield us from view."

His reassurance did nothing to calm her racing heart. Or the throbbing that lingered between her legs. Still gasping, she was embarrassed at her inability to stop squirming.

"Let me help you, London," Trey whispered.

"I—"

"I've got you."

Reverently, he traced the pebbled nipple beneath her bikini top. She nearly jumped out of her skin at the contact.

"Mmm," he said right before he lowered his head and took the bud into his mouth.

London's hips bucked. She'd never known such pain and such plea-

sure. A sound of male satisfaction filled her ears right before he slipped a finger beneath her bikini bottom and dragged it through her tight seam.

She threw her head back with a moan. Trey moved to her other nipple. The ache inside her built to a feverish pitch. She buried her fingers into his hair, pressing his head more firmly against her.

When Trey slid a finger inside her, London lost all conscious thought. She could hear him whispering words of encouragement, urging her to let go. To take what she wanted. Her head was thrashing from side to side when suddenly, a cataclysmic wave of sensation over-took her. Her stomach dropped as though she'd leaped off the high dive while a thousand pinpricks of light danced behind her eyelids.

"LONDON." A far-off voice called to her. "Wake up, honey. We're finished."

CHAPTER TEN

"Any news?" Pops demanded.

Trey pressed the cellphone to his ear trying to drown out the sound of *SpongeBob* on the television. The only other people in the surgical waiting area were a mom and her two young sons. The mom was frantically texting while Patrick and Mr. Krabs babysat her kids.

He'd called his grandfather as soon as London had been taken back to surgery. Mainly because Pops was the only person he knew who could help track down Kim.

"Not yet." Trey rubbed the back of his neck. "It hasn't been an hour yet. They said it could take as long as ninety minutes. Or more if there are complications." His mouth went dry at the thought.

"Kim and Chuck are on their way. There are storms brewing up in Canada, but hopefully they can get out tonight. Olivia sent her plane to get her."

Olivia.

Trey had been a total dick about the woman. Hell, he'd been a dick about a lot of things, apparently. His grandfather's impromptu marriage being the least of them.

Two of his best friends had found their soulmates recently and the team still made it to the playoffs. Trey had been more gracious to teammates about marriage than he had to his own grandfather. He still didn't understand why Pops needed to tie himself to someone so late in life, but now that he knew the woman wasn't a gold digger, the least he could do was eat crow and wish his grandfather well.

"Yeah, you know, if I didn't say it the other day, congratulations, Pops. Your new wife seems like a nice lady. I'm looking forward to getting to know her better." Or course, he wouldn't get too attached to the woman. Given the Van Horn track record for successful marriages, he had no idea how long Olivia would be in the picture.

His grandfather harrumphed. "I wouldn't have married her if she wasn't nice."

"The real question is why did she agree to be leg-shackled to a grumpy old fart like you?"

"No," Pops replied. "The real question is how were you and London in the same place when she collapsed?"

"I told you. I'm chairing the gala for the Growlers. London handles the PR." That part wasn't a lie. "We were at a meeting. She looked like crap. I brought her here. And you know the rest."

"Hmm," was all Pops said.

His grandfather was like a bloodhound on the trail when he sensed there was more to a story. He'd have a difficult time getting more out of Trey, though. Mostly because Trey wasn't sure if he knew the real story. He *thought* he knew the story once. London's medically induced revelations blew everything he believed for the past decade to smithereens. For someone so smart, he'd been unbelievably dumb.

He rubbed at his chest hoping to alleviate the hurt he felt there.

"Hey, Pops," he asked. "Whatever happened to the woman

who was caretaker of the Lake Geneva property when I was in college?"

Pops made some grumbling noises. "The only female caretaker we had here was Kellianne. If I recall, your father let her go some years back."

"Jay did? Why?"

"I don't remember exactly. Kim would know. She and your father were still married then, I believe. I know both women butted heads from the get-go. Why are you asking about her?"

Because she royally fucked up my life.

"Nothing in particular," he fibbed. "Being back at the lake brought back memories, that's all."

Victor poked his head into the waiting room and motioned for Trey.

"Hey, Pops, I think she's out of surgery. I'll text you shortly."

Trey sprinted out into the hallway where Dr. Chang was waiting.

"Everything went as expected. The appendix was still intact, and I was able to remove it cleanly. Her fever is still higher than I would like, however."

A wave of dread rolled through Trey's gut.

"I'm confident the antibiotics will take care of that in a few hours," the doctor continued. "She's a little restless coming out of anesthesia so we'll keep her in a post-op room tonight where we can monitor her more closely. Not to worry though. She'll be good to go home in the morning."

Was this guy for real?

Of course Trey was worried. Hadn't the doctor just said her fever was high? And what if the antibiotics didn't work? What then, he wanted to ask, but the doctor was already on the elevator.

"Relax." Victor clapped Trey on the shoulder. "All of that's normal. She's going to be fine. Come on, you can peek in on her and see for yourself."

The scene that greeted Trey did not reassure him.

Not one bit.

"She's been coming in and out of anesthesia for the past twenty minutes," the nurse at London's bedside explained. "Maybe you can help?"

She waved Trey into the room. The monitors were beeping relentlessly again. The nurse untangled the IV tube from the wires connected to the heart monitor. Trey stared down at London, pale and listless, her hair forming a corona around her head.

He had never felt more helpless in his life.

"What can I do?" he whispered.

"Talk to her." The nurse pushed a chair up to the bed. "Let her know you're here for her."

Given how they left things before she was wheeled into the OR, he wasn't sure she'd be glad he had stuck around. He sank down onto the chair. "London, Pops got hold of your mom. She's on her way."

London groaned.

"See that? It's already working," the nurse said. "Keep talking. I'll be right back."

He blew out a ragged breath. "Hey, Lon, you need to wake up. Otherwise, your mom is going to freak out when she gets here."

Just like I am.

He reached for her hand, alarmed at how clammy and feverish it felt. Without giving it a thought, he brought her fingers to his mouth and brushed his lips over each one.

"Come on, London," he pleaded. "You're scaring me. Wake up so you can chew me out about what an ass I am. Lord knows I deserve it."

The nurse came back. Trey felt like an epic failure. Not only had London not woken up, she appeared even more lifeless than before.

"I'm no help," he murmured in disgust. "I'm going to go back upstairs and text her family."

He laid her hand back on the bed. As soon as he released her fingers, however, alarm bells rang out within the room.

"Don't. Move." The nurse gestured to London's hand while she did something with the monitors.

Trey wrapped his fingers around London's again and the alarms quieted.

"Not helping, huh?" The nurse arched an eyebrow at him. "She knows you're here. Stay right there. It won't be long before she wakes up."

She disappeared out into the hall again, leaving Trey alone with his racing heart and a sleeping beauty. With his free hand, he brushed a lock of her hair from her damp forehead.

"You weren't my first kiss," he whispered. "But you were the last kiss that took my breath away. The only one that did that, for what it's worth. Being with you made me want things. Things I never expected. Things I haven't felt or wanted with anyone since."

Sighing heavily, he wrapped both hands around hers.

"You're right to call me a robot. I had to become one. It's the only way I know how to live my life. Growing up with loads of money sounds awesome, but it doesn't mean life is perfect. Not when your life is played out in the tabloids. It always felt like my parents cared more about hurting the other one than about loving me. I was constantly caught in the middle." His chuckle lacked humor. "Still am to this day."

He glanced toward the open door wishing he could get up and close them both in the little room. But he didn't dare let go of her hand.

"When I was eleven, I was sent to a boarding school in Connecticut. I was so relieved to be out of range from the paparazzi and around kids my age. I guess I thought it would be fun." His throat grew tight at the painful memories. "I'd spent the first ten years of my life eating junk food to cope with my loneliness. I arrived at school a chubby kid with the unfortunate name of Lars. I'm sure you can imagine what they did with that. I swear even some of the staff called me Lard.

"I endured it for two years before Pops rode to the rescue. He enrolled me in a Chicago prep school as Trey Van Horn since I am Lars the third. Luckily the summer before school started, I had a huge growth spurt. I picked up a football about the same time. All I wanted to do was show those assholes from boarding school that they were wrong to mess with me."

He kissed the palm of her hand.

"But then something happened. I got really good at the game. So good, my dad and mom noticed. They bragged about me to their friends. They were actually proud of me. I decided then and there to be the best there ever was at the game. That meant keeping close control over my body and the other elements of my life."

London moaned softly as she drew in a breath.

"Hey. Please wake up. I need to know you're okay."

He made an aggravated sound when she didn't respond.

"They always say be careful what you ask for, right?" he continued. "Well, that summer we met, I was hiding out at Pops' place. I'd gotten my wish. Everyone noticed me. And everyone seemed to want a piece of me. The pressure of being the best college quarterback was crushing. But then there you were. This gorgeous diversion. You didn't seem to know who I was. Or care. I was the real me when I was with you and I don't think I'd ever been that guy before."

Or since.

"I couldn't get enough of you. Whenever we were together, the weight of my future felt lighter. It wasn't lost on me that I created that future. But suddenly it wasn't enough to be the best. I didn't care if my parents noticed me. The only person I wanted to see me was *you*. And you did. You saw everything with that camera of yours. And you still smiled at me anyway. I hate that you never knew that you made me feel whole for the first time in my life." He swallowed around the lump on his throat. "I hate that I messed it all up. All because I can't trust myself to believe in the fairy tale."

Trey took a bite of warm chocolate chip cookie. It had been years since he'd allowed himself to indulge in anything sugary, but he'd sooner slice off his arms than hurt London's feelings.

"I don't think anyone's ever baked me cookies before," he said, helping himself to another one because, damn, they were delicious.

London paused with a cookie midway to her mouth. "Your mom never made you cookies?"

He swallowed a hollow laugh at her shocked expression. Trey doubted his mother knew how to turn on an oven much less bake anything from scratch. "My mom is not very domestic."

"Oh my gosh, that didn't come out the way I meant it." She looked out over the lake as dusk began to fall. The reflections from the lights in the boathouse illuminated the water, casting her face in shadows. "I mean, there's nothing wrong with that. There are many ways for a mom to show her love besides baking cookies."

Her abundance of compassion was one of the many things that made her so adorable. And so rare. London accepted people for who they were, without judgment. That she would defend Trey's mom, who she'd never met, made his chest ache.

"Any kid would be lucky to have you as their mom." He hadn't realized he'd said the words out loud until she ducked her head to hide her blush. But now that they were out there, he wondered about her dreams beyond film school. "Or maybe you don't want to be saddled down with kids." He was surprised how much he didn't want that to be true. "You won't be able to be a globetrotting documentary filmmaker with kids in tow."

"Who says I can't?" She challenged, wearing a grin that radiated confidence.

Trey tucked an arm behind his head and rested back on the chaise. "Ah, ha. You want the fairy tale."

London carefully lifted her camera from around her neck and placed it in its case. "Not every woman dreams of a prince coming along to sweep her off her feet. To make her life complete and uncomplicated. My mom certainly didn't have that. But her life is pretty fulfilling anyway." She pulled her knees to her chest and rested her chin on them. "My 'fairy tale' as you call it, is pretty simple really. To be with someone who supports my dreams. Who picks me up when I fall. Who loves me as I am. All the same things I'd do in return. That's all I need."

His throat was suddenly painfully tight. Trey's mother was constantly chasing her "great love story." The man who would put her first over everything else in life. Given his father's tales of woe about his ex-wives, Trey was pretty certain all women were selfish like that. Yet, here was an uncomplicated woman who wanted to partner with someone simply to love and be loved. Almost as if she was a unicorn among females.

"And you?" she surprised him by asking. "What's your fairy tale?"

Trey didn't dare tell her he didn't believe in them. Not even the simple one she dreamed of. In twenty years of life, he'd borne witness to the complications of love and fairy tales gone horribly wrong. Enough to know both were for dreamers and out of reach.

Still, the weight of her gaze had him wishing he were programmed differently. Wishing he could give her everything she hoped for. Wishing he could be that guy.

He skimmed a finger along the bare skin beneath her shorts before taking hold of her wrist and tugging her down next to him.

"I'd rather live in the moment," he murmured against her neck, hoping to distract her.

She tasted like fresh air and vanilla. Trey groaned when she pressed her body up against him. Her lips found his in the darkness, almost as if she'd traveled the landscape of his body her entire life. Her fingers tangled in his hair as she angled her mouth over his. Thoughts of fairy tales and what could be evaporated with the heat of their passion. Along with Trey's surprising unease about not being able to be the man she deserved.

"You're here."

London's craggy voice startled Trey from sleep. His neck and his back immediately began complaining about a night spent in the stiff chair. It took him several tries before his gritty eyes could withstand the glaring fluorescent lights. But the most painful sensation of all was London's hand no longer wrapped in his.

"Oh, honey," Kim cried as she rushed to her daughter. "I've never been happier to see your face."

Mother and daughter hugged while Chuck patted London's leg. He glanced over at Trey and mouthed "thank you."

Trey nodded at the man, suddenly feeling out of place. Stifling a groan, he slowly got to his feet. "I'll leave you all to it," he murmured.

If either woman heard, they didn't acknowledge him. With every step, Trey felt the gulf between him and London widening again. He could swear his breath rattled in his hollow chest.

"Trey!"

He'd just reached the hallway when Kim came bounding out after him. She immediately threw her arms around his neck.

"Thank you," she said into his shoulder. "Thank you for looking out for her."

Her expression of gratitude caught him off guard. "Uh, no problem. All in the name of family, right," he replied, trying to keep from sounding curt.

Kim stepped back and eyed him warily. "The nurse said she

can go home later today. I'm sure she'd like to thank you once she's a little more like herself."

Little do you know, lady.

He glanced back into the room. Chuck was regaling London with some story from their trip. She managed a smile for her stepfather. Trey's chest rattled once more. He'd never be gifted with one of those lopsided grins again.

You don't deserve one.

"I've got a flight to Miami in a couple of hours," he heard himself saying. "My mother is expecting me."

"Oh, of course." Kim took a step back.

"London will be fine now."

"Will she?"

Trey's gaze snapped from London to her mother. "What is that supposed to mean?"

How was it that he just noticed mother and daughter shared the same stubborn chin?

"It means that the last time you left her, it was years before she was 'fine.'"

"I don't know what she told you, but—"

Kim held up her palm. "She didn't tell me anything. She still hasn't. But having been through something similar, the signs were easily recognizable. Not to mention the fact we live in a small town where people know everyone else's business."

He squared his shoulders, refusing to comment.

"Look," she continued. "I'm not selfish enough not to realize that my crazy wrong turn with your dad knocked London off her axis. But I don't believe my rash decision was the only reason she gave up on her dream."

A cold dread settled over him. He knew what was coming next and he didn't want to hear it. No way, no how. Try as he might, though, he couldn't get his feet to move.

"You ghosted her. Not only did she walk away from the life she dreamed of, but it nearly broke her." She waved a hand at him. "Go. Enjoy Palm Beach. I'm incredibly grateful for everything you did for her last night. But please don't toy with my daughter again."

Kim headed back into London's room, closing the door firmly behind her. Trey swore violently, not caring who heard him. There was no way of turning back the clock a decade. Even if by some miracle he could, he wasn't sure that guy who'd fallen in love with London that summer still existed.

One thing he knew for sure? He couldn't give London the fairy tale. He couldn't love her the way she deserved to be loved. It wasn't in the Van Horn DNA.

But he could support her dream. He could pick her up and give her back what she lost when he left her waiting in his grandfather's boathouse. Luckily, he had a good idea where to start.

CHAPTER ELEVEN

Lucy handed London a glass of water before sitting down on the ottoman. London was propped up against some pillows, resting on the sofa in her living room. Thankfully, her mother was no longer fussing over her. She'd taken Chuck to the airport so he could return to Canada. Neither parent felt comfortable being far away from eight-year-old Kyle. London had hoped for some quiet downtime while her mother was gone so she could process everything that had happened in the past twenty-four hours.

Instead, Lucy showed up to take over babysitting duties.

"I'm so glad you are okay." Lucy smacked London on the thigh. "But I'm pissed at you for not calling me."

"Hey!" London rubbed her leg even though it didn't hurt. "I didn't call you because it all happened so fast. It felt like a stitch in my side for most of the day. Then suddenly it wasn't. Honestly, I thought it was anxiety. I wasn't looking forward to dinner with Trey."

"And that's another thing." Lucy lifted her hand again, only to slap her own thigh when she encountered London's scowl. "How could you not tell me you were going on a date with Trey Van Horn? I can't believe you're still holding out on me about him."

"Because it wasn't a date," London insisted. "It was a dinner to discuss the Gunther account."

"Yeah, right. Since when do you get your hair done for a business dinner?" Lucy reached across and tugged on a strand of London's hair. "Rosalind did an awesome job, by the way. Even with what you've been through, you still look *ahh-mazing*."

London sighed. "I think I just wanted to look my best so I'd feel like I had on some protective armor, you know?"

"Ooo, let him see what he walked away from. I love that plan."

"Yeah, well, he was punking me with his interest in the Gunther account. He has no intention of signing the contract. I just wanted him to know two could play at that game." She sighed again. "Fat lot of good it got me. I threw up on the hood of his car. Real glamorous."

"Yet he still carried you in his arms into the ER." Lucy donned a goofy smile. "*And* he spent the night with you."

"Ohmigosh, you are beyond ridiculous."

Lucy smiled smugly. "Alek Bergeron is going to be so jealous when he finds out."

"Alek isn't going to find out. Nor will he care. I'm focusing on me, remember? Alek is remaining in the friendzone."

"*Ooo!* Friends with benefits. That works, too."

Thankfully, the sound of the intercom put an end to their ridiculous conversation.

"That'll be Bennie. He insisted on coming by to check on me in person. Can you buzz him in?"

A few minutes later, Bennie ambled into London's condo, his arms laden with flower arrangements and shopping bags.

"Seriously, Bens, this isn't a wake. She's still with us," Lucy teased as she took one of the bouquets from him.

His booming laugh echoed off the high ceilings. "I come bearing sustenance to nurture her back to health." He pulled a Swansons Bakery box from one of the bags. "Gretchen sends her love in the form of champagne cupcakes."

London moaned. She didn't have much of an appetite, but she'd have to be dead to resist one of Gretchen's cupcakes.

"I'll get the forks." Lucy headed for the kitchen.

"How ya feelin', kiddo?" Bennie settled into the leather recliner Chuck had insisted she buy for when the family visited.

"A lot better than twenty-four hours ago."

His face softened. "You should have said something."

"That's what I've been telling her," Lucy called out from the other room.

"Although, suffering through a major illness to win over a spokesman is pretty rad," Bennie teased.

Lucy carried in a plate of cupcakes and some forks. "No one says 'rad' anymore, Bens."

"They don't?" He swiped a cupcake and began peeling back the wrapper. "Here I thought I was being hip."

"Yeah, they don't say that either." Lucy shook her head at London as if to say, "this guy."

"Well, I don't recommend the appendicitis tactic," London said. "It doesn't work. I'm so sorry, Bennie." The pain from her incision was nothing compared to the guilt she felt for letting her boss down. She knew how much he wanted to make the merger with Nolan and Hemphill come about.

Bennie mumbled something before pulling a sheet of paper from one of his bags. He handed it to London.

"What's this?" She unfolded the paper.

"You might want to walk back that part about it not working," he said.

London skimmed the page. It was the spokesperson agreement she'd sent to Trey's agent last week. And it was signed. The room grew fuzzy as she traced a finger over Trey's name, boldly sprawled on the bottom line.

"Is this really his signature?"

"Uh, huh," Bennie replied. "His agent called me first thing. Said Trey was all in."

"Holy snot." Lucy moved so she could read over London's shoulder. "He didn't tell you last night?"

"No. He was gone when I woke up."

Not really. The first time she'd woken up, Trey was conked out in the chair, his head resting on the bed. In his sleep, he looked so easy-going and approachable. Much like the Trey she'd fallen in love with. It was hard for her to reconcile the man gently comforting her by holding her hand in his with the cold, hard machine he'd become. She'd ached to reach over and brush the hair from his forehead. But she didn't dare risk waking him and having him let go. She hadn't realized how much she missed the sensation of his skin against hers after all these years.

"Seth is promising to name a cheese after you," Bennie was saying. "And Evan wants you to direct the new commercials. He liked what you did with the other ones you shot so much he's giving you carte blanche on the campaign, kiddo."

Her boss beamed at her proudly.

"Huh." London was still having trouble wrapping her head around this sudden change in events. She continued to stare at Trey's signature on the white page as though it would disappear if she looked away.

"There is one caveat," Bennie added, sheepishly.

London crumpled the paper. "I knew it."

"Oh, course there is," Lucy said. "Let's hear it."

"It's minor." Bennie gently pried the contract from London's fingers. "Because we'll be filming during training camp, he'd prefer to do it here rather than Chicago."

"Well, of course you'd film here," Lucy said. "Why the heck would you do it in Chicago?"

London was careful to avoid Bennie's eyes. "Oh." She nodded. "That makes sense."

"I told you it would work out." Lucy leaned down and hugged London. "Now all you have to do is figure out how to make a man who professes to avoid all snack foods look like he loves Gunther's cheese."

That wasn't the part London was most concerned about. She was worried how she was going to spend more time around Trey and still keep her sanity—and her heart—in one piece.

"Have you lost your fucking mind?!"

Trey lowered the volume on his cellphone so everyone in the gym wasn't subjected to Marty's colorful tirade. Fortunately, the place was nearly empty. The summer heat and humidity typically turned Palm Beach into a ghost town during July.

That didn't mean one of the college kids surreptitiously stalking him around the leg machines wouldn't overhear. Hell, they could fund the rest of their summer on this type of gossip. The last thing Trey needed was another shoutout on *TMZ* this week.

"I swear," his agent roared on. "You and Collin are going to give me a second heart attack before I get over the first one."

Trey didn't doubt that given the way the man was carrying on.

"Collin had nothing to do with my decision. In fact, he advised me against it."

As much as Collin annoyed Trey, he wasn't going to throw him under the bus. Too bad his defense of the turd didn't calm his agent one iota.

"He never should have shown it to you in the first place!" Marty bellowed. "You always give me a song and dance about how you can't take on any endorsements during the season because it will screw up your vibe or something. Then, *pow,* you sign a deal the minute my back is turned. Explain that to me, will ya?"

Trey sighed as he picked up his towel and headed toward the

locker room. He had no intention of admitting to his agent that his decision had been a kneejerk reaction. A way to make things right with a beautiful woman he'd wronged. The man would blow a gasket.

"Marty, it's done already. You really need to dial it down a notch. You're getting all worked up over nothing."

"Nothing? *Nothing!* Of course, I'm getting worked up about nothing. That's because those weasels at Gunther got away with one and are paying *you* nothing to hawk their damn cheese! You, who doesn't even eat damn dairy!"

Trey loaded up his gym bag, opting to shower back at his mom's place. With seven bathrooms, there was a lot more privacy and less chance of someone eavesdropping. "Actually, I allow myself some dairy now and then during the offseason. This whole thing about my diet has been blown out of proportion because of that article."

"That's another thing! That damn article!" Marty made a gasping sound.

"Marty! Are you okay? Is someone there with you?" Trey debated texting Collin before his agent came back on the line.

"Of course there is someone here with me," Marty snapped. "My wife won't let me take a crap without a nursemaid hovering over me. Look, Trey, this Gunther guy lowballed you. It's okay if you want to do something for charity, but Mr. Cheese just torpedoed every other endorsement deal in your future. No one is going to pay you what you're worth now."

"You're blowing this way out of proportion, Marty. Gunther's is a privately held company. Therefore, the terms of the deal are private."

"Except when the arrogant jackass is blabbing to everyone and anyone who will listen that he got you for a song!"

Well, fuck.

Trey plopped down onto one of the benches. He should have seen that coming. From what he could decipher from London's ramblings in the ER, Seth Gunther had thrown a temper tantrum to get Trey to endorse his cheese. The ink on the contract was barely dry when the man started hounding Trey, texting him multiple times a day like they were golf buddies. Just this morning, Gunther sent a text regarding the annual bike ride to open training camp.

The bike parade was a tradition dating back to the team's formation nearly seventy-five years earlier. Local kids decorate their bikes and wait outside the Growlers' stadium, hoping one of the players will pick theirs to ride the near mile around the parking lot to the practice facility. Players navigate the two-sizes-too-small bikes along the route crowded with cheering fans. The kids get the honor of carrying the player's helmet while they walk, run, or skip beside them.

It was the best tradition in professional sports and Trey loved everything about it.

Right up until he had to bow out when he earned his first MVP four years ago.

After receiving the honor, the pressure from outsiders for Trey to choose their kid rose exponentially. Not only that, but kids began showing up from all over the country hoping for some facetime with Trey. No matter what he did, some kid was going to be hurt and an advertiser or well-connected fan pissed off. Knowing what it felt like to be ten years old, and the last kid chosen in gym class, Trey began skipping the bike parade. It pissed him off that he had to miss one of the most unique experiences a pro-athlete could have. At the same time, he recognized it was the price he paid for being the best.

Seth "suggested" in his text that Trey select one of his two grandsons for the first day of practice bike ride, and the other one later on in the week. *As if.* It was all he could do not to call the man and tell him in no uncertain terms why that wouldn't be happening. Except he didn't dare do anything to jeopardize London's career. So, he foisted the problem off to Collin to take care of instead. It was about time the guy did something to earn the large percentage he and his father took from Trey's paychecks.

The one positive to come out of the situation, however, was the follow-up phone call he had received from Bennie Westbrook. London's boss was quick to reassure him that Seth wouldn't be making any further demands of Trey's time other than what was stipulated in the contract. More importantly, the call had given him an in to ask about London without looking too obvious.

It had taken everything he had to leave her in that hospital room, much less to hop on a plane and fly fourteen hundred miles away from her. Which was ridiculous because she was in good hands with her guard dog mother watching over her. The only thing he added to the situation was a truckload of guilt.

Trey had hoped taking the Gunther Cheese deal would alleviate the weight of that guilt. Only it hadn't. When he should have been getting his mind and body ready for the upcoming season, he'd been too busy obsessing over London.

The idea that she would never trust him again ate at him day and night. The image of her helpless in that hospital bed kept him from a decent night's sleep. The breathless way she'd described his kiss had him in a constant state of semi-arousal. Which was ridiculous because she'd made it very clear she wanted nothing to do with him. And she was right to want that.

The night he'd left her alone in the boathouse, he'd given up any right to have her by his side. He'd been a fool, listening to poison gossip and not his heart. Losing London was the painful price he had to pay for his idiocy.

For his part, Bennie felt guilty about what went down the night Trey and London were supposed to have dinner. It was obvious the guy adored London as if she were his own daughter. Bennie was sick about encouraging her to go out with Trey when she was ill. He heaped on the praise, thanking Trey for rescuing her when he did. Thankfully, he'd told Trey, she was recovering remarkably and would be ready for the first commercial shoot on schedule.

The news should have quieted Trey's endless thoughts of her. It didn't. He needed to find a way to stop wanting something—or someone—he could never have.

"Are you listening to me?" Marty's aggravated voice cut into Trey's wandering thoughts. "Christ, you're getting to be as bad as your airhead father."

"Hey," Trey admonished his agent. He grabbed his gym bag and headed to the hot parking lot to retrieve his mother's Bentley. "I've heard every word you've said."

"Yeah, well, as soon as I'm allowed out of my home jail, we're going to come up with a course-correction for your endorsements," Marty announced. "And if the cutie whose life you saved the other night can make America believe you eat fucking cheese, I'm hiring her, pronto."

"I didn't save her life. I just happened to be in the right place at the right time. And she already has a pretty good gig lined up after this campaign."

"Semantics, Trey, semantics. Any way you slice it, it was the perfect rebuttal to that bullshit article claiming you lack feelings for anyone or anything except football. If Gunther were paying you what you're worth, it would be a win-win." Marty sighed dramatically. "I guess it's in the genes. Your father was always a sucker for a pretty girl. If I had to guess, I'd put money there's a woman behind him dropping out of the Cup race."

Trey's fingers froze on the key fob. "What are you talking about?"

"He hasn't reached out to you, either?" Marty mumbled something. "They were in contention near Cape Horn three days ago when Jay abruptly notified officials he was pulling out. Your grandfather is in the dark about what's going on, too. I've got four sponsors riding my ass wanting to know what the hell is going on with your old man. The yacht is docked in Cape Town but there's no sign of Jay."

Trey turned the AC up to full blast in an attempt to dry off the sweat forming on the back of his neck. His father often made decisions with the wrong body part, but Jay was as competitive as Trey. He'd never leave his yacht and crew in the middle of a race. Not even for a woman.

At least Trey hoped so.

"You've tried reaching him by email? Or on the satellite phone?"

"I've tried everything but carrier pigeon, Trey. All I'm getting is radio silence," Marty said. "I've got a PI looking into it."

"A private investigator? That seems a little dramatic."

He steered the car out of the parking lot. Marty was overreacting, as usual. Still, Trey was suddenly anxious to get back to his mother's place and check in with Pops. Surely Jay had left word with someone about his whereabouts.

"I'm sure it's something having to do with the yacht," he insisted. "You know how Jay likes to keep everything about his toys top secret. If there's anything that needs to be fixed, he won't want to give his competitors an advantage in the next race. It's likely he is hiding out somewhere, throwing people off the scent while the repairs are being made quietly elsewhere."

It's exactly what Trey would do.

"Or, like I said, there's a woman involved," Marty argued. "Either way, he owes his sponsors an explanation. Let me know if you hear from him. And, please, don't agree to any more damn deals before running it by me first."

Trey called his grandfather from the car. As Marty mentioned, Pops had nothing to add about Jay's whereabouts. Unlike Marty, his grandfather wasn't all that concerned.

"You know your father, Trey," Pops said. "He always lands on his feet. That man has more lives than a cat. He'll be in touch with one of us soon. No need for anyone to worry."

Pops' reassurance only marginally settled Trey's nerves. What he needed was a long, hot shower and an evening in his mom's home theatre studying film. It was well past time he began focusing on the upcoming season. As for his father, Pops was right. Jay was a big boy and could take care of himself.

He parked the car in the garage and cut through the pool area toward his suite. With luck, his mother would already be headed out for a cocktail party or something. The last thing he wanted tonight was to have to make small talk with another socialite who simply wanted to hang on his arm in front of the paparazzi.

"There you are," his mother drawled from one of the chaise lounges strategically placed beneath a large Banyan tree. "We've been waiting for you."

Her use of the word "we" had Trey's gut clenching until he spied the gorgeous blonde reclining on one of the chaises next to his mother.

"Hello, Bree."

It had been a few years since he'd seen the realtor-turned-reality-star. He smiled fondly remembering the two weeks several years ago they'd spent ensconced in a bungalow on Key West exploring each other's bodies. Despite her mild-mannered demeanor onscreen, Bree was enterprising between the sheets. Best of all, she kissed and did not tell. There was no revealing article detailing every aspect of their fling for all the world to read when Trey walked away.

The corners of Bree's artistically full lips turned up slightly and her cheeks grew pink as though she were recalling their affair with the same appreciation.

"Oh my gosh, Trey. I'm so glad you're here." Bree's husky voice was normally a Bat Signal to his crotch. Not today, however. Which pissed him off because she would be the perfect diversion from his daily fantasies of London.

Bree slowly rose from the chaise, allowing her flimsy cover-up to float to the ground. Trey was treated to quite the show when she sauntered toward him wearing a skimpy leopard print bikini that likely set off her brown eyes were he looking up that high. The smell of coconut oil reached him seconds before she threw her arms around his neck and pressed her body against his. Her skin was warm from the sun beneath his hands, but her contact didn't arouse any corresponding heat within him.

Well, damn.

"I need your help," she murmured against his chest. "Your mom is standing me up tonight so she can have a spa night with her cousin." She lifted her face and fluttered her lashes at him.

Trey was the one who needed help. He had a sure thing in his arms and his libido had hightailed it to Siberia. Swearing beneath his breath, he untangled himself from her embrace and put a few inches between their bodies. "I'm sure if you ask her nicely, she'll take you with her."

Behind her, his mother shook her head.

Bree swatted his chest. "I don't want a spa night. I'm expected at the Polo Club. I've already got a gown to wear. I just need someone to escort me."

She trailed her palms up his chest to rest on his shoulders before executing a perfect pout. Trey's brain tried to remind his body what those lips once did to him, but nada. Bree rocked up onto her toes and pressed her mouth to his.

"Pretty please," she murmured against his lips. "I promise to make it worth it."

His mother shot him a pleading look over Bree's shoulder.

Ahh, what the hell. He was a male, after all. And a professional athlete to boot. His body couldn't withstand cold storage forever. Once he used the willing woman in front of him to jettison his erotic dreams of London from his system, he could get back to concentrating on football.

"Okay, okay. I'll take you to dinner."

"Yay!" Bree was already bouncing back to her chaise where

she retrieved her things. She blew a kiss to his mother before calling over her shoulder. "Pick me up at seven!"

His mom clapped her hands. "Wonderful. Now you don't have an excuse to hole up in my theatre again tonight and watch football. You're a young man in your prime. You should be out having a good time at night. You've only been out twice since you've arrived. And dinners with me don't count."

"Watching film is part of preparing for my job, Mom. Training camp opens next week. I don't have time to be out partying every night."

She kissed his cheek. "You always were that kid who studied more than anyone else. But if you don't want the reputation of being a stick-in-the-mud robot everyone believes you to be, you need to let loose more often. It will do your image good to show up in photos with a beautiful woman on your arm." She actually winked at him. "I'm sure Bree will be very *grateful.*"

For fuck's sake.

And just like that, his mother killed any hope of getting his libido in the game tonight.

"I'm headed back to Milwaukee tomorrow," he announced.

"So soon?"

His mom's pout was nearly identical to the one Bree had just treated him to. It was probably something women practiced in socialite school.

"You promised you'd take me to the Breakers before you left."

"Next time. I added a last-minute endorsement that's going to take up time during the pre-season. I've got to rearrange a few things in my schedule to make room for it."

She wandered back to her chaise to retrieve her drink. "Oh. Well, of course. You don't want to let the fans down."

He sighed. "I get paid a lot of money not to."

"You already have millions in your trust fund. I cannot believe I'm saying this but maybe you should take a lesson from your father and not be so uptight about things. You put too much pressure on yourself. I worry about you."

It was familiar refrain from his mom. Although the reference to his father was a new tactic.

"You don't have to worry about me, Mom. I'm perfectly happy. But speaking of Jay, have you heard from him?"

She appeared momentarily perplexed. "Why would I?"

Trey debated whether to tell her about Jay's abrupt withdrawal from his latest yacht race and seeming disappearance. But on the off chance one of her friends might have heard something, he decided to mention it.

"He seems to have dropped out of his race and then out of sight. Do you know if anyone here in Palm Beach might have heard from him? Or is there someone here he might reach out to?"

If he hadn't been already staring at his mom, he might have missed the sudden pallor in her cheeks. She recovered almost immediately.

"Why would it matter?" She scoffed and sliced her hand through the air. "I'm sure he's fine. You know him. He's probably chasing some woman he couldn't resist."

"Yeah. That's Marty's theory, too. Still, if you hear anything, will you let me know?"

Trey looked more closely at his mom. She blinked several times. He wasn't sure but he thought her eyes might be damp. *Dammit.* He cursed himself for bringing up the man who still seemed to have the power to hurt her.

She reached her sunglasses on top of her head and dragged them down to obscure her eyes. "Of course, darling," she said before disappearing into the nearby cabana.

CHAPTER TWELVE

As it turned out, Alek—and the rest of the world—did find out about London's ER visit in the arms of Trey Van Horn, thanks to a patient sharing cellphone video to *TMZ*. She suspected the video was bought and leaked by Trey's management team. It was the perfect human interest clip to counteract the *Vanity Fair* article. London would have done the same had she been handling Trey's PR.

There was also the annoying coincidence that the two athletes shared the same agent. A man who, if she had to guess, couldn't wait to share the details of London's hospital adventure with the goalie. She'd been dealing with Collin Slater for a little over a week now, and it was already abundantly clear to her that the guy was an egomaniac. Not to mention, a colossal thorn in her barely healed side.

"I'll need you to run any and all social media posts by me beforehand," he announced.

London was grateful they were having this conversation by phone and not video. She'd lost count of how many times she'd either rolled her eyes or flipped the guy off.

"I'm not in the habit of posting anything offensive, if that's what you're concerned about. My job is to promote Gunther Cheese. If that means making their spokesperson look good on social media, that's what I'm going to do," she told him, working hard to keep her tone neutral.

After a week at home, she'd been looking forward to returning to the office and her clients.

All except for one.

And his obnoxious agent.

Collin laughed. "Van Horn has over six million followers on his accounts, and he's posted roughly twenty times in the past seven years. Not only that, but his reputation is unimpeachable."

London bit back a snort. Had this guy not read the *Vanity Fair* article?

"Our concern," he continued, "is that nothing too ridiculous gets posted."

Trey's agent was correct about him posting rarely on his accounts. London should know. She'd been stalking him for years. But that didn't mean others hadn't tagged him. Namely women.

She picked up her cellphone and scrolled through his Instagram account just to torture herself. A photo popped up of Trey with a leggy blonde wearing a dress the size of a dinner napkin. The blonde looked at the quarterback like a lioness stalking her quarry.

For his part, Trey wore his patented bemused smile. A look he'd cultivated over the past decade. London often referred back to the photos she'd taken of him that summer just to reassure herself that the smile she remembered wasn't a figment of her overactive imagination. Of course, doing so never failed to make the ache she thought she'd alleviated begin to bite at her chest again. Had it all been real? As usual, swift anger followed.

"I have no intention of making my client's spokesperson look ridiculous, silly, inane, or any other description you care to use," she snapped. "In fact, I won't need to post on Mr. Van Horn's social media at all. I'll manage everything from the Gunther Cheese account. Problem solved. As soon as we finalize the arrangements for the commercial shoot, I'll be in touch. Have a nice day."

Trey's agent was still babbling when she abruptly ended the call.

"Nicely done."

London lifted her head toward the entrance of her office. Alek Bergeron stood with his shoulder propped up against the doorframe, a lazy smile on his full mouth. His hands were shoved into the pockets of his jeans. The navy Mayhem golf shirt he wore stretched neatly over his muscled shoulders and chest. Not for the first time, she was jealous of the long, sooty lashes framing his ice blue eyes.

"Alek! I thought you weren't getting back until later today?" She slipped on her shoes before coming out from behind her desk. "I didn't think I'd see you until dinner."

Since her surgery, Alek had been texting a couple of times a day to "check on her." He'd also called nearly every evening. He told her it was to report on Kyle's progress at camp, except that part of the conversation usually lasted only a few minutes.

The rest of the time, Alek had her laughing about the crazy antics of his teammates who joined him at the hockey clinic. Or he'd give her suggestions of what to binge watch while she was recuperating. He dished about his large family who he made sound overbearing in the most loving way. For a superstar athlete who was worth millions, Alek was surprisingly unassuming and easy to talk to. London found herself looking forward to his calls each night.

She wasn't looking forward to the dinner conversation she needed to have with him tonight, however. Now that Trey was on board with the Gunther account, her move to Chicago was inevitable. As much as she wanted those phone calls to continue, it wouldn't be fair to continue allowing Alek to believe she could offer him anything more than friendship.

"That was the plan." He stepped away from the door and into her office. "But I couldn't wait that long. I wanted to see with my own eyes that you're okay. You gave us all a scare."

The genuine concern in his eyes was hard to miss. London felt guilty her first thought was to wonder why Trey hadn't even bothered to check up on her once during these past two weeks. She shoved the emotion deep inside her, instead offering up a smile for the hot guy standing in front of her.

"That's very sweet of you," she said. Because it was. "Although you may not think too highly of me right now. I'm pretty sure I just pissed off your agent."

His eyes danced with admiration. "Good. He can be a total dick sometimes. And, technically, he's my agent's son." He waved a hand in the air. "Long story. But it doesn't matter. All that counts is that you look well. No. Check that. You look stunning." He took a step closer. "I wish we weren't in your office because I'd really like to kiss you."

Could he get any more perfect? If she were still looking for a Prince Charming, Alek would definitely be at the top of the list.

"We should probably save that for some place more private," she replied, not realizing how flirtatious her words sounded until they were out of her mouth.

His nostrils flared. *Great.* Now she was giving him mixed signals.

"But I don't think a hug would cause too much gossip." She draped her arms around his neck at the same time as he gingerly wrapped his fingers around her waist.

"Mm," he groaned, burying his face in her hair. "I may have to rethink our dinner plans."

London's body reacted subconsciously, sinking in closer to his before she could admonish it not to. She inhaled. He smelled crisp and clean. Not that there was anything wrong with that. It just wasn't the fresh, outdoorsy scent that had been haunting her dreams the past few weeks. She scolded herself for comparing his smell to the other hunky jock she knew.

As if she'd conjured him up, Trey's voice echoed throughout the room.

"Well, don't you make a cute couple."

London gasped with embarrassment as she tried to scramble from Alek's embrace. The goalie's arms were slow to disengage, however. He kept one linked tightly around her waist as he turned them both to face Trey.

"Nice to see you, Van Horn." Alek's tone sounded as if he didn't think it was nice at all.

"Bergeron." Trey jerked his chin up and down in what was likely supposed to be a nod but looked more like an obscene gesture.

For crying out loud!

London shook off Alek's arm and moved back behind her desk before the two men began wrestling like Neanderthals.

"What are you doing here?" she demanded. It seemed she was constantly asking the man the same question.

Trey arched an eyebrow at her. "I was told there was a meeting about the gala here today."

Seriously?

London had a hard time believing the man left his leggy blonde and the rest of the accommodating women of Palm Beach to return to Milwaukee for a meeting about the gala. Not when training camp was still four days away.

Alek looked between Trey and London. "For real? I'm representing the Mayhem this year. No one told me about any meeting today."

She crossed her arms in front of her. "That's because it's a logistics meeting with the representatives from the venue. The team figureheads chairing the event aren't expected to attend."

"When my name is associated with something, I'm all in.

Meaning, I like to be involved in every aspect." Trey's eyes never left London's.

She choked out a humorless laugh. "Control freak much?"

Alek chuckled at her comment just as his phone buzzed. He frowned when he looked at the screen before his face paled.

"Alek? Is everything okay?" She moved back around her desk toward the goalie, placing her palm on his upper arm. She was sure she imagined the low rumble coming from Trey's direction. Fortunately, Alek was too absorbed in whatever was in the text message to notice.

"My twin is having some issues with her pregnancy." He swallowed roughly. "I'm sorry. I need to cancel for tonight. I have to head back to Ottawa."

"Of course." She gave his biceps a gentle squeeze. "You should be with your family."

Alek quickly typed out a response to the text before giving London a grateful smile. "Thanks for understanding. And I'll definitely make the rain check worth it."

Before she could react, Alek's fingers were on the back of her neck, guiding her lips forward to meet his. It was a kiss filled with promise, not to mention a hint of machismo. London would have enjoyed it a lot more had Trey not been watching. Of course, she suspected the enthusiasm of Alek's kiss had a lot to do with their audience.

"I'll call you tonight," Alek announced rather loudly when he pulled away.

London couldn't decide which male was aggravating her more at the moment. Alek deserved her empathy, however. He'd been a good friend this past week. She knew how close he was to his family—his twin in particular.

"Please do," she replied. "I'll be anxious to know how she is doing."

"I'll be sure to take good notes at the meeting," Trey remarked when Alek passed him on his way out the door.

In return, Alek mumbled something that sounded dark and dangerous. Trey snorted. London fumed.

"The meeting is over in the conference room," she snapped as she returned to her desk and shuffled some papers pretending to look busy. Her hope was that he'd leave her in peace.

He didn't.

Instead, he closed the door before venturing farther into the room, only to stand quietly in front of her desk until she finally lost her patience and looked up at him.

"How are you?"

His softly uttered question had her breath hitching slightly. Or maybe it was the sincerity in those golden eyes studying her critically. Either way, her pique at his arrogance slowly ebbed away.

"I'm well," she replied. "Fit as a fiddle, in fact."

The corners of his lips kicked up and he nodded. "I'm really glad to hear that."

"Thank you, by the way." London cleared her throat.

Why was it so difficult to find the words to thank him? Who knows what would have happened if she had passed out on her floor? Were he any other person, she'd be offering to name her first child after him.

Except that at one time, she'd dreamed of naming *their* child after him. She tamped down on the sudden surge of bitterness and pushed out the words. Her mother had raised her better, after all. "Thanks for, you know, helping me the other night."

"Don't mention it."

He rocked back on his heels and a ghost of a smile she'd seen that long ago summer flittered over his mouth. Her stomach began to flutter wildly.

He does still exist.

"I didn't do anything any other guy wouldn't have done. I'm sure even Bergeron would have managed to carry you a few steps."

Annnd, just like that he ruined the moment. *Asshole.* Her annoyance was back threefold. The sooner she kicked him out of her office, the better. Still, her curiosity got the better of her. She had to ask the question that had been nagging her for a week now.

"Why did you do it?" she demanded.

He blinked in confusion. "Why did I take you to the hospital? How about because you were sick for a thousand, Alex?"

"No!" She snatched up the contract from her desk. "This! Why did you agree to represent Gunther Cheese?"

Something that looked a lot like remorse flashed in his eyes before he managed to extinguish it.

He shrugged. "Because it sounded like a kick."

London's throat grew tight. She hated the realization that deep down she hoped he'd say he agreed to the campaign because he wanted to be around *her.* That he wanted to make amends for how he'd left things. How could she still be so naïve? So foolish? In twenty-eight years had she not learned her lesson? She wasn't anyone's forever girl. Especially not Trey Van Horn's.

The regret she had detected in his expression was likely because he'd accepted the sponsorship as a lark. Hadn't he just referred to the sponsorship as a "kick"?

This was all a joke to him. With her luck, he'd come here today to worm his way out of the deal.

Well, too damn bad.

He'd signed on the dotted line. Bennie's livelihood depended on it. Her professional future depended on it. No way was she letting him back out now.

She squared her shoulders. "Well, aren't you lucky to be blessed with a bottomless trust fund and superior athletic ability that you can make decisions just for. . .*kicks.* But hear me loud and clear. I take my clients' livelihoods very seriously. And this campaign *will* be successful."

The air in the room nearly crackled as the two stared each

other down. Trey was still for a long beat as if he expected her to say more. When she didn't, he nodded once.

"At the risk of repeating myself, when my name is associated with something, I'm all in."

London scoffed. "Pardon me if I'm skeptical. Your track record where I'm concerned is questionable."

He rocked back on his heels again as if she'd struck him. London doubted he was wounded. Nor did she care. She grabbed her phone and purse from her desk.

"Your meeting starts in five minutes." She pulled out her sunglasses and plopped them on her head. "Don't forget to take good notes."

"You aren't going?"

"Nope." Score one for her for beating him at his own game. "I've got more important clients to deal with this afternoon."

She moved to slip past him, but his fingers quickly brushed against her hand, making all the nerve endings in her arm dance. *Damn him.* He slid his palm against hers before lacing their fingers together.

"I'm all in," he repeated softly, his breath teasing the skin near her ear. "You can count on me, London."

Could she?

It wasn't like she had a choice. Besides, Bennie said Trey's reputation with advertisers was nothing but professional.

"I'd like it if we could get through this without every moment in each other's presence being a battle," he added.

Well damn if he wasn't being the mature one.

She was the one being ridiculous by reading too much into everything he said and did, that's all. If he could approach the situation like a grown up, then so could she. After all, she wasn't that naïve eighteen-year-old any longer. No way was she falling for Trey Van Horn again. If he could keep things light and busi-nesslike, she would put on her big girl panties and do the same.

But not if he kept touching her. It was impossible for her to think with his body so close to hers. She hurriedly untangled her fingers from his and put some distance between them.

"I'd like that as well." Too bad her voice didn't sound as steady and committed to the new plan as she'd like. She managed a smile that she hoped looked more assured than she felt. "I'm looking forward to making this campaign a success."

He returned her smile with one of his own. Only his bordered on sly, as if he knew what the words were costing her.

"Me, too." He opened her office door and gestured for her to exit first.

"Am I seeing things? Or is that Trey Van Horn holding our daughter?" Andi Fletcher demanded of her husband.

Her tone was more bewildered than panicked, however. Not that Trey could blame her. Hell, *he* wasn't even sure why he was toting her baby around. Except that Lily's blue eyes had crinkled with pure delight when her father opened the door of his penthouse moments earlier. The little charmer had thrust out her arms in invitation and the next thing Trey knew, she was being passed from Dex's arms into his. He carried her out onto the balcony overlooking Lake Michigan and settled into one of the sofas with Lily's back resting on his thighs as though they'd assumed the pose dozens of times before.

From his seat on the opposite sofa, Luke Kessler draped an arm over his fiancée Summer's shoulders. "The better question is what is QB One doing out of the film room? Training camp opens in two days and he still has a tan instead of that vampire pallor he gets from sitting in the dark breaking down plays. Could it be he's slacking off from his pre-season preparations?"

"Maybe he's pissed off the football gods and now he needs to sacrifice a small child to get his superpowers back," Summer teased, her artist's imagination working overtime, as usual.

Andi jerked forward in her seat.

"Relax," Dex reassured his wife as he set a bottled water down on the table next to Trey. "My reflexes are much quicker than his."

Trey snorted. "Like hell they are."

As if he didn't trust his own boast, Dex leaned his hip against the balustrade, creating a human barrier between Trey and the lake below. "Something is off with him though."

"Yeah. Rumor has it he's deviating from his iron-clad routine of no endorsement work during the season," Kessler added. "Not only is he chairing the gala, but he's promoting *cheese*."

"No?" Summer pressed a hand to her chest. "That's definitely a red flag. Everyone knows he doesn't eat anything that tastes good. Maybe we should pinch him to make sure he's the real Trey Van Horn."

"Except the real Trey Van Horn is actually a robot," Andi said with a smirk. "At least according to well-informed female sources. Pinching him wouldn't prove anything."

Trey made a noise deep in his throat. "You know I can hear you people, right?"

His so-called friends laughed. Lily kicked her chubby legs with abandon, adding her giggles to the mix.

"What happened? Did the heat and humidity in Palm Beach give you some sort of brain fart? You had to agree to any deal just to get out of there?" Kessler demanded.

"Nah." Dex studied Trey. "It's just a guess, but I believe our boy might be having an existential crisis."

Screw this.

He didn't come here so his brainiac kicker could spend the evening psychoanalyzing him. Luke was correct. His time would be better spent breaking down film. Trey stood so quickly, he had to rely on those quick reflexes of his to grab Lily and settle her on his shoulder. The baby chortled with glee.

Her mom, not so much.

"Give her to me," Andi commanded, reaching for her daughter.

Trey was suddenly reluctant to part with the snuggly infant. He'd been feeling untethered for days now. Something about the adoration in Lily's blue eyes grounded him. Andi was two seconds away from going Mama Bear, however, and, judging by her husband's snarl, Trey didn't have a choice.

The baby scrunched up her face in protest at being handed off. Fortunately, the pacifier her mother stuffed in Lily's mouth immediately soothed her.

"Bath time," Andi announced.

"I think I'll tag along." Summer stood, grabbing both women's wine glasses and followed them into the penthouse. "I sense some team bonding is about to happen and I'd rather avoid the chest thumping."

He moved to follow the ladies inside, but the stocky kicker blocked his path.

"Hit a nerve, did I?" The asshole had the balls to grin.

Trey's only response was a glare.

Kessler chuckled. "I'm beginning to think QB One is a red-blooded human after all. And his altered state has been caused by a woman. This doesn't have anything to do with your rescue of a pretty publicist, does it?"

Trey snapped his chin around, redirecting his scowl at the receiver.

"Huh," Fletcher murmured. "Interesting."

"Fuck you both," Trey grumbled.

He turned and placed his palms on the balustrade. The cool stone beneath his skin did nothing to quiet the maelstrom of emotions churning within him. The sound of gulls dive-bombing the beach looking for their dinner filled his ears while his teammates remained blessedly silent. He could feel their eyes boring into his back, though.

Trey would never live it down if he admitted that part of their theory was true. He had taken the endorsement gig because of London. But not for the reasons they thought.

The two men behind him believed in the happy ever after hype. Hell, they were living and breathing it every day. If he revealed he'd taken the endorsement deal to help London, they'd wrongfully assume it was because he was in love with her.

He cared for her, yes. But if what he'd felt for her all those years ago had been love, he would have never left her sitting alone at that boathouse. He would have never believed the malicious gossip of a stranger. The truth was, he didn't have the guts to really put his heart on the line. When the going got tough in romantic relationships, the Van Horns simply got going. End of story. Trey was incapable of the kind of loving commitments his two teammates enjoyed.

Not that they'd ever be able to understand that. But he'd have to give them something. His sudden departure from the structured way he lived his life was obviously causing talk. With training camp opening this week, Trey didn't need anything interfering with the team's preparation.

"London is a family friend." He kept his gaze focused on the darkening shore so his astute friends wouldn't see too much. "I'm doing her a favor."

There was no possible way either man could unravel Trey's explanation. Every word was true. The lie he didn't want them to ferret out? He'd never devoted so much of his time fantasizing about any of his other "family friends."

Hell, Bree was technically a family friend. And he hadn't even given her a passing thought despite spending two weeks in bed with her at one time. Not only that but coming face-to-face with her again hadn't registered any movement of his body—and she'd made it a point to display a lot of skin every time she was in his company last week.

His libido had been on to something, though. Bree had been using him to get the attention of some oil rich polo player from Qatar. She claimed to have some beachfront property she wanted to show him. More likely it was a private tour of her naked body she wanted to take the guy on, considering the way the two of them circled one another half the night at the Polo Club.

The only woman who continued to fascinate his libido every night was London. So he'd made up some lame excuse to drop by her office today. Only to find her in the arms of Bergeron. And if that wasn't bad enough, she looked like she belonged there. Trey rubbed at a spot on his abruptly tight chest.

Even worse, Trey was such a tool, he couldn't seem to keep his hands off her. He had no right to her body. Not then and certainly not now. Yet he couldn't help himself. Even if it was simply holding her hand. And he'd swear on his left testicle that she felt the same sizzle every time they came in contact. Only she was better at controlling her baser urges, apparently.

This was why he didn't let his emotions get involved in his relationships. He didn't have time for this shit. He'd dropped by Dex's place tonight to refocus. To get his head back into football where it belonged. He needed to get smart and leave London to Bergeron.

Alek was a decent guy. From a normal, tight-knit family by the sounds of it. The hockey player had been given a rock-solid example of what commitment looked like. He could give London the fairy tale that Trey could not.

"London is good people." Kessler's words were unexpected.

Trey turned around to find both men staring at him defensively. He didn't like it. Not one bit.

"You know her?" he asked.

"Sure," the wide receiver replied. "She's been handling the PR for my dog adoption foundation for a few years now."

"She promotes Andi's shop, as well," Fletcher added.

"Funny how she never mentioned knowing you." Kessler was just as bad as Fletcher when he thought there was a puzzle to be solved.

"She never mentioned working with you either," Trey replied, doing his best to throw his teammate off the scent. "But here we are."

"Just friends, aye?" Fletcher had that dogged look in his eyes he normally aimed at his teenage Mathletes when they got out of line.

Trey sighed. "Yep. If you're trying to get the deets on her love life, look in Alek Bergeron's direction."

"Bergeron?" Kessler cocked his head to the side. "Actually, that kind of works. They'd make a cute couple."

It took some doing, but Trey managed not to flinch at the receiver's comment.

Fletcher continued to stare down Trey. "Bergeron is a decent bloke."

Trey was sure he was grinding his teeth into stumps. Lucky for him, the sound of his cellphone buzzing in his pocket put an end to the conversation. His pulse shot up when he saw his father's name on the screen.

"Is there some place I can grab this call in private?"

Fletcher gestured to the glass door leading into his study.

"Dad. Where the hell have you been?" Trey demanded once he was alone.

"Wow. Good to hear from you, too, *son.*"

Trey swore violently. The guy was apparently fine. Especially if he was getting in a dig about Trey not using Jay's first name.

"Excuse me if I was worried about you," he said. "You've done some crazy shit in your life, but you've never skipped out in the middle of a major race."

Jay sighed. "One of the crew had a health issue he needs to deal with. The sponsors have nothing to complain about. The yacht is still on track to win the Cup."

"Would it have killed you to let someone know that? Marty probably set back his recovery by a month."

"Marty is turning into an old lady. I had it handled. Besides, I know how you get when you're headed into the football season. No distractions, remember?"

"Sure. Whatever." Trey was pissed at having his words thrown back at him.

"Pops mentioned you're throwing Kessler's bachelor party at the lake. Maybe I'll head back to the States and come hang out with you guys that weekend. Show you boys how it's done."

"Don't you have another race to get ready for in September?"

"We're finishing the prep work up as we speak. I'll have plenty of time. I'm sure your planning will be well thought out, but everyone knows you're not the party animal I am. I'll bring the fun," Jay announced.

Trey bit back a groan. That's exactly what he was afraid of. The Growlers' season opener was the Sunday following the bachelor weekend. The last thing anyone needed was Jay Van Horn enticing one of the guys to do something reckless and get injured. Everything was a party to Jay. Even his yacht races.

Trey would never do something as irresponsible as fly halfway around the world for a party while leaving his crew to get the boat ready to race. There was no way he would ever take the field without being totally prepared mentally and physically.

Not for the first time, he wondered how he and his dad could share the same genes. Hell, their physical appearance didn't even match up. Where Trey was six foot three with broad shoulders and a square head, his father was four inches shorter, with a round face and a wiry body. Even their coloring was opposite. Trey had inherited his mother's olive skin and dark hazel eyes. Jay, however, was blond and blue-eyed like Pops.

He shook his head at the mystery of genetics.

"Pops also mentioned you just got back from visiting your mother. How is Reese?"

Not this again.

"For crying out loud, why don't you ask her yourself! I know you're on speaking terms with at least one of your exes."

Jay had the nerve to laugh. "Yeah, I read about you rescuing Kim's daughter from death's door. Kim is a good friend. Probably because she's the only one of my exes who never took a dime from me. Hard for a man not to respect a woman like that."

Say what?

He was letting that stunning revelation sink in when Jay continued.

"Glad you got to show off your human side after that ridiculous article that woman wrote. Although, it's like I've been telling you for years, you're too closed-off. You need to open up more. Women want to think they can fix you or they'll move on. Stop giving the ladies material to roast you with when you walk away."

Trey clenched his teeth. The last thing he needed right now was relationship advice from his old man.

"You'd be happier if instead of having a routine for everything, maybe go where life takes you once in a while," Jay continued.

Like me, Trey inferred. *Like Hell.*

"I'll keep that in mind," he lied.

Jay sighed. "Send me the details on the bachelor party. It's always good to have an excuse to catch up with you and Pops. Besides, I need to meet this new wife of his. I'll talk to you before then."

It was just like Jay to drop a guilt bomb two seconds before he hung up.

Kessler stuck his head in. "Everything okay?"

Hell, no.

"Just Jay calling to say he'd be thrilled to come to the bachelor party."

"Awesome! The weekend is going to be something."

Trey bit back a snort. "Yep."

He just hoped it wasn't going to be something he would regret.

CHAPTER FOURTEEN

"You've never been interested in the bike parade when I've invited you before, Kyle. Why the sudden change of heart?" London juggled a poster board sign and her brother's water bottle as she guided him toward the stadium parking lot where several hundred fans were already lined up, waiting for the Growlers. Of course, it had to be a chamber of commerce July day in Wisconsin with bright blue skies and a soft refreshing breeze. The size of the crowd always doubled in good weather.

"That's 'cause I was a baby back then." Kyle wobbled on his bicycle slightly as he tried to maneuver around the other kids who'd already staked out a place on the front lines.

Lucy walked on Kyle's other side. "Yeah, London, he's going into third grade next month. He's practically a *man,*" she teased.

Kyle stuck out his tongue playfully. "Don't mess with me. I learned how to square up at hockey camp."

"See what I mean?" Lucy shot London a look over Kyle's head. "Our boy is growing up too fast." *Square up?* she mouthed.

London shrugged. Her little brother had come back from Canada with some never-before-seen swagger, that was for sure. Still, she really wished he'd given her a heads-up about his plans for today. Her mom and Chuck were taking the couples' vacation London interrupted when she was in the hospital, leaving Kyle in Milwaukee with her. She should have suspected something when he showed up with his bike.

Kyle wormed his way toward the front of the pack. He leaned his bike on its kickstand and grabbed the poster he'd spent the previous evening coloring. London took in the crowd and did some quick mental math. There were only ninety players on the Growlers' training camp roster. From the looks of it, two-thirds of the kids were going to be disappointed.

"Maybe you can text one of the Growlers you work with and point them toward Kyle?" Lucy suggested quietly.

London shook her head. "I already had to call in those favors to accommodate Seth's two grandsons."

Damn Seth. London had worked with Bridezillas who were less trouble than that man was turning out to be.

Lucy winked at London. "Sit back and watch a big sister of four work her magic," she murmured before raising her voice. "You know, Kyle, part of the fun of today is simply being in the middle of the action. Even if one of the Growlers doesn't choose your bike this time, you live close by. You can come back next year and try again. You know that, right?"

"Yeah, sure," Kyle said absently, keeping his eyes peeled on the tunnel the players were set to exit from. "But I'm not worried. Trey is going to pick me."

Lucy and London exchanged *oh, shit* looks.

"Kyle." London crouched down so she was eye level with her brother. "Trey doesn't participate in the bike parade, honey. He only comes out for a few minutes and signs autographs."

Her brother waved her off, his gaze still trained on the stadium. "Pops told me that. It's because Trey doesn't want to hurt any of the kids' feelings."

Bennie had explained the same thing to London last week when she floated the idea of getting some B-roll for social media of Trey riding a kid's bike. All these years she thought he was being a prick for not joining in the popular tradition. Instead, he was simply taking into account the feelings of his youngest fans.

She hadn't thought this version of Trey was capable of that type of empathy. The more layers she peeled back from his mechanistic personality, the more she realized the man she once knew still existed somewhere within him. Her head and her heart both ached to know why he'd buried that aspect of his character so deeply.

A deep dive into the man's personality quirks was going to have to sit on the back burner, however. The bodies were closing in next to her, nearly knocking her to the ground when several of the Growlers' community relations team emerged from the tunnel. The excited chatter among the fans climbed to a fevered pitch.

"Then you understand he's not going to pick you, right?" It was a crapshoot trying to reason with an eight-year-old, but she had to try.

Kyle looked at her then. There was an agonized glint in his eyes she'd never seen before, and it shook her to her core.

"No one will get their feelings hurt if he picks me. We're family," he argued.

Double shit.

"He has to ride my bike." His voice broke, nearly breaking her along with it. "If I have Alek and Trey as friends, the kids at school won't be able to tease me about my size anymore." He puffed up his chest. "They'll have to answer to Alek and Trey if they do."

London's heart was suddenly in her mouth. Was he saying what she thought he was? Were the other kids bullying Kyle at school? *Holy hell.* Did her mom and Chuck know about this? Her head was suddenly swimming with questions. She needed to get him out of here so she could get some specifics.

"Oh, honey." She tried to wrap her arms around him, but Kyle pulled away.

His mulish expression stunned her. He'd never refused a hug.

The Growlers' staff began herding the kids and their bikes into the roped off area where the players would come out and meet them. Kyle side-stepped past London so he could jockey his bike toward the front of the crowd. A cheer went up when members of the team began to make their way into the parking lot.

A chorus of "awes" followed when a player the size of a small tank chose a tiny scooter to ride. The scooter's owner was a young girl dressed in a Growlers' cheerleading outfit. She hefted the player's helmet into her arms as if she were carrying a pumpkin, only to make it a few steps before her father had to relieve her of it. The ribbons in her hair bobbed up and down as she skipped along ahead of the parade with a huge smile on her face.

London groaned. "This is a disaster."

"It may not be as bad as we think," Lucy said.

"Really? Because from where I'm standing, I'm looking at five more days with a heartbroken kid who has obviously been holding onto a lot of ugly shit."

"Okay, when you put it that way, the situation looks pretty touchy, yes." Lucy sighed. "Look, I'd never, ever condone bullying. And you know I love that kid as much as you do. But it's an unfortunate fact that kids get teased about something at least once in their lives. It's survival of the fittest on the playground. We've all been there. But kids are fickle. And Kyle's almost nine. Who says he's not going to grow three inches this year?"

"That's not going to help the situation today," London all but snapped.

"Nooo," Lucy replied. "But he'll get over it if he has at least one super star athlete in his corner." She wiggled her eyebrows. "You could let things between you and Alek heat up. Instead of Trey being pseudo family, Alek can be his big brother."

"Are you kidding me right now?"

Lucy shrugged. "Can I help it if I have this dream about you settling down with a guy who adores you? We'll both live in the same neighborhood. Our kids will grow up together." She linked her arm through London's while she covered her belly with her other hand. "Kyle won't need to stretch the boundaries of the family tree. He'll have all of us. Alek will probably arrange for him to drive the Zamboni. The kids who are teasing him will be so jealous. It will be epic."

London wanted to scream. As if Kyle's revelation wasn't enough, now she was wracked with guilt about the secret she was keeping from her best friend. She needed to come clean. She needed to tell Lucy that finding a guy who was going to put her first was a fantasy. There wasn't going to be a relationship with Alek or anyone else. From now on, she was putting her career first.

And she was doing it in Chicago.

Of course, Lucy would be devastated. Mike had been her fairy tale since high school. Her friend believed she could simply wish that into existence for London. But that wasn't in the cards.

"Luce, I need to tell—"

A roar swiftly went up among the crowd.

"Trey!" fans called out.

"Van Horn!" other fans chanted.

Trey emerged from the tunnel looking like a gladiator stepping into the coliseum. He was dressed for practice, the green of his jersey picking up the flecks of green hiding in his golden gaze. The breeze even had the nerve to toy with his hair. Still, he looked untouchable and damn near invincible.

London's breath hung up in her lungs every time she laid eyes on him. But today, she was getting a glimpse of the legend in his element. To say it did strange things to her was an understatement. He raised his helmet in salute to the crowd, before stopping to sign a few jerseys and posters the kids held up.

"Oh, my." Lucy fanned herself with her hand.

The sound of Kyle frantically shouting for Trey refocused London's attention to the problem at hand.

"We've got to put a stop to this before Kyle gets his feelings hurt," she said.

With Lucy on her heels, she snaked through the crowd toward her little brother.

"Pregnant woman coming through," Lucy announced at the top of her lungs.

Miraculously the crowd parted enough for them to reach an opening along the rope behind Kyle.

"Trey!" her brother continued to scream.

"Kyle, honey—" London tried to get his attention.

Trey was moving in their direction. Kyle yelled louder while frantically waving his sign.

"Please, Kyle." She leaned over the rope barrier in an effort to reach him.

As if he heard her voice among the hundreds calling his name, Trey's eyes instantly found hers in the crowd. The surprise in them quickly morphed into concern at whatever he saw on her face. He moved toward her.

"Trey!" Kyle cried. "Over here. It's me, Kyle."

A wave of relief washed over her when Trey stopped to smile warmly at her brother.

"The hockey player. How are you doing, sport?" He tousled Kyle's hair much the way Pops always did.

The gesture brought a lump to her throat.

Kyle grinned from ear to ear. "I'm great now that you found me. I brought my bike for you to ride to the practice field. See?"

Trey took a moment to admire Kyle's bike while London held her breath. Any moment now he was going to let her little brother down. She only hoped that the guy she once knew, the one buried deep inside Trey Van Horn, MVP quarterback, would be gentle.

"She's a beauty," he said to Kyle before returning his gaze to London. "I see you also brought your sister along. Although, she's looking a little overwhelmed. Just between us guys, I don't want to have to carry her to the ER again. Why don't we have her join us so we can keep an eye on her?"

It was all she could do not to roll her eyes at him. He nodded to a security guard before lifting the rope and motioning for London to duck under it. Lucy didn't wait to be asked, quickly dashing under the barrier after her.

"Hi." Lucy sounded a tad too breathless for only having taken three steps. She aimed a coy smile at Trey. "I'm with them."

"See, I told you he'd choose me," Kyle said contritely when London reached him. "They both said you wouldn't want to ride my bike, Trey."

Suddenly, London wasn't sure who she wanted to throttle first. "That's *not* what we said."

"Actually, everyone is right, Kyle," Trey interjected.

Kyle's face fell along with London's stomach.

Here it comes.

But instead of breaking her brother's heart, Trey went off script. He waved over the Growlers' head coach.

"Coach Gibson, I know you were looking for an extra ball boy for practice today. This is my buddy, Kyle Prince. He's more of a hockey guy, but he's a promising young athlete. I'm sure he'll be a big help to you on the sidelines."

Kyle was suddenly bouncing on his heels with excitement.

The coach, however, was looking slightly perplexed. "A ball boy for today's practice?"

"Yes." Trey nodded slowly. "You know, the special one you choose every season on the first day of practice."

The two men seemed to be locked into a silent exchange that lasted a long moment before the coach nodded.

"Oh, sure. The ball boy." Coach Gibson turned to Kyle. "What do you say, Kyle? You down for shagging a few footballs this afternoon?"

"Heck, yeah!" Kyle shouted.

"That's a sweet ride you got there," the coach continued. "You haven't promised her to anyone else yet, have you?"

Kyle looked at Trey for a heartbeat before shaking his head. "No, sir."

"Excellent." Coach Gibson straddled the bike. "Let's roll."

Trey handed Kyle his helmet. "Don't let this out of your sight. I'll meet you there."

Kyle took off without a backward glance. The crowd of players, kids, and media quickly swallowed them up.

Not that London noticed. She was too focused on the man in front of her.

"What just happened here?" she demanded. "There's no such thing as a 'special ball boy,' is there?"

Trey wore a cat-ate-the-canary grin. "There is now."

She should have been grateful for his assistance. Thankful his quick thinking had come up with a solution where Kyle was able to keep his pride intact. Except she was uncomfortable with his help. She didn't want to be beholden to Trey Van Horn for more than she already was. Especially when, given the way he'd looked at her the other day, she wasn't sure what his price for repayment would be.

Or maybe it was the conflicting feelings swirling around inside her that she was uncomfortable with. After all, she had despised the man for so long now. Yet every time they touched, her desire for him simmered beneath the surface of her skin. She was angry at herself for being so weak.

So she took it out on him.

"That wasn't necessary," she said sharply.

His face instantly sobered as he closed the distance between them. "Really? Because two minutes ago, you looked as if your heart was about to shatter. And I'd do anything, London—Any. Thing—to prevent you from suffering any pain. *Anything.*"

She stood there in stunned silence wrestling with the fact that the source of her greatest heartache had just uttered such a statement.

"Oh, wow," Lucy muttered, reminding her they had an audience.

London whirled toward her friend. "I need you to keep an eye on him."

Lucy nodded, treating Trey to a silky smile.

"On *Kyle,* Luce!" London pointed toward the departing bikers. "I need you to keep an eye on Kyle."

"Oh, yeah, right." Lucy began walking backwards in the direction of the parade route. "Kim will want pictures. I'll just go catch up with them."

"I think that's the woman he carried into the emergency room," someone exclaimed behind them.

London noticed people in the crowd pointing their cellphones at her and Trey. No way was she letting her personal life become the story again. She wrapped her fingers around Trey's forearm and tugged him back toward the tunnel. "You come with me."

Luckily, he allowed himself to be led inside without argument. As soon as they were away from the prying eyes of the Growlers' fans, however, she dropped his arm. Touching him was wreaking havoc on her nerve endings.

Trey didn't seem to be suffering from the same affliction, though. He immediately reached for her hand, lacing their fingers together as he silently guided them through the maze of hallways. They ended up in a deserted press holding area outside the team's locker room. The quiet felt louder and more agitating than the din of the horde outside. London tugged her hand free and began to pace, hoping the movement would calm the turbulence swirling inside of her.

It didn't.

"Something on your mind, London?"

She whipped around to find him leaning a shoulder against the wall, looking cool and collected, as if he didn't have a care in the world. *How dare he!* She charged across the room and jabbed a finger into his chest.

"You!" She poked him again, ignoring the thrill that she was connecting with his taut muscles and not some sort of padding. "You keep messing up everything."

He had the nerve to hike an eyebrow at her. "Messing up? Excuse me, but I thought I was helping out there. Kyle seemed pretty jazzed with the solution."

"That's just it," she argued. "You think you can ride back into my life without a word in *ten freaking years*, like you're some. . . some damn White Knight or something and whoosh—" she flailed her arms "—you make everything better. Well, it's not better. It's making me crazy." She slapped her palm against his chest. "I don't want you rescuing me. I don't want your help with my job or my brother. I—" Another slap to his pecs.

"Don't."

Slap.

"Want."

Slap.

"You!"

Without even realizing it, she'd somehow managed to close the gap between them so that their bodies were practically touching.

"I don't want you," she whispered.

Her argument might have carried a lot more weight had she not immediately begun kissing him.

CHAPTER FIFTEEN

TREY WAS unprepared for the onslaught of emotions bombarding him when London's lips met his. Ten years of pent-up desire masquerading as anger threatened to overwhelm him. For the first time in over a decade, he felt fully alive again. It was as if he'd simply been going through the motions since the last time he had kissed her. And now, with her mouth fused with his, he was finally whole again.

She scraped her teeth along his bottom lip, and he was all too happy to grant her access to his mouth. The sweet taste of her was even more intoxicating than he remembered. She had learned a few things in the intervening years, too. He forced himself to ignore the irrational jealousy roaring in his chest and just appreciate the erotic way she sucked on his tongue.

Reaching up, she fisted her fingers in his hair, angling his head to give her better access to his mouth. The feverish and demanding way she kissed him had him painfully hard and cursing the asshole who invented the damn cup he was wearing. He felt as well as heard her contented whimper when he wedged his hand between their bodies and palmed her breast. The sound detonated something within him, and with a few thrusts of his tongue, control of their kiss belonged to him.

He reversed their positions, pressing her back against the cinderblock wall. Trey crushed her mouth beneath his, desperate to slow things down so he could savor the moment. Too bad London was having none of it. She dug her fingernails into his scalp, urging him to take the kiss deeper. He was more than happy to oblige.

Tongues and teeth collided as they both grew more frantic with need. He cupped her ass and lifted her up. She followed his lead, wrapping her long, glorious legs around his waist. His legendary control nearly snapped when his hands slid beneath her knit T-shirt dress and came in contact with her toned smooth skin.

She rocked her hips against him when he threaded a finger below the part of her thong dissecting her firm ass. *Dammit.* He needed them both naked. *Now.* Except he was having a hell of a time trying to round up his scattered brain cells so he could figure out the logistics of how to make that happen in the next thirty seconds.

The sound of a muffled announcement crackling over the PA system had them both freezing mid-kiss. London found her senses first, jumping away from him as though she'd just bolted awake from a nightmare. Trey leaned against the wall once again, trying to regulate his choppy breath and his highly-aroused body.

She resumed her pacing, her little white tennis shoes squeaking against the concrete floor as she raked her fingers through her hair. "That should never have happened."

And just like that, Trey didn't have to worry about his aching hard-on any longer.

"Of course. Because of Bergeron," he bit out.

The air in the room seemed to go still. She slowly turned to face him, the rubber soles of her shoes letting out one last wail.

"Really?" Her voice was calm. Her eyes, not so much. "Bergeron?" She stomped toward him. "You're going to drag Alek into this? He doesn't care who I kiss."

Trey snorted. "Bullshit. He very much cares who you kiss, sweetheart. Any man lucky enough to be with you wouldn't want another man to come within fifty feet of your lips, much less manhandle you with his tongue and his hands until you can't remember your name."

Suddenly wide-eyed, she sucked in a startled breath. "If that hadn't come out so high handed, I might take it as a compliment. But I'm not with Alek. I'm not with anyone. I'm done with men."

"Says the woman who just had her tongue down my throat."

Her eyes went all squinty. "That was a serious lapse in judgment on my part."

He laughed as he jerked his chin toward her chest where her nipples were still pebbled with desire. "Your body says otherwise."

She glared at him as she hugged her arms to her chest. Trey pushed away from the wall and cautiously made his way over to her. She shivered slightly when he traced his finger along her jaw.

"Alek and I are just friends," she murmured, her kiss-swollen lips grazing his thumb, sending a jolt of lust straight to his damn crotch.

Trey ignored it. He was suddenly anxious to know whether or not she counted him as a friend. Given that a few weeks ago she professed to hate him, the friendzone would be a promotion. Still, he was surprised at how acutely he wanted to be more to her.

Except that really would be a lapse in judgment on her part.

It took everything he had to push the next statement out.

"Bergeron is a good man. You should give him a chance. He can make you happy."

She absently leaned into his palm when his thumb caressed her cheek. "I don't need someone else to make me happy. I'm taking a page out of your book and I'm going to focus all my time and energy on my career."

The disappointment he felt nearly took his breath away. He didn't want her to live the way he'd been living. He wanted her to have her fairy tale. Yet, he couldn't lie. Part of him—the part that wanted to secret her away and keep her all to himself—was thrilled she was closing herself off from the rest of his species.

He brushed a kiss over her forehead. "You're incredibly talented, London. I'm glad you've decided to put your dream first."

She curled her body into his.

"Just remember, I'm here for any other lapses in judgment you want to take." He meant it as a joke, but his body didn't get the message, his cup suddenly painful again.

Heaving an annoyed sigh, she shoved away from him. The sound of footsteps headed their way had her anxiously patting her hair and adjusting her dress.

"You look gorgeous," he said quietly. "As always."

Her eyes softened and she gulped in a breath just as one of the equipment staff arrived to burst their sensual bubble.

"Here you are," the guy said. "The golf cart is waiting for you."

"Come on." Trey reached his hand out to London. "I'll give you a ride to the stadium and you can check on Kyle."

She curled her lips in that cute way of hers before nodding twice and taking his hand. They retraced their path through the bowels of the stadium with the equipment guy leading the way.

"What was up with Kyle when I arrived today?" Trey asked. "You looked a little frantic."

"Mm. He knew you don't participate in the bike parade and why." She squeezed his hand. "Very gracious of you by the way."

He wanted to tell her he wasn't being gracious at all by not riding in the bike parade. Just preserving his ass. Except the pride in her smile and warmth of words felt too damn good.

They reached the players parking lot where a four-seater golf cart waited. Trey helped her in, immediately missing the warmth of her hand in his. Draping his arm along the back of the seat, he slid in beside her, initiating a little manspread so at least their thighs were in contact. The equipment guy jumped in the driver's seat and jerked the cart forward. Trey wrapped his arm around her shoulder, telling himself the move was necessary for her own safety.

"Anyway, Kyle seems to think you and Pops are family. He believed that would give you a good excuse for participating this year. By picking him."

Trey laughed. "I like the way he thinks."

"Except his motive was to recruit you and Alek as human shields when the kids pick on him at school."

Memories of his days at boarding school had every muscle tensing up in Trey's body. No child should ever have to endure what he had. He swore viciously beneath his breath.

"Kyle is being bullied?" The anger in his tone caused the driver to swerve the cart sharply before he regained control and steered them along the side streets leading to the practice field.

"He only told me today." London sighed. "He was born premature. The pediatrician insists that he'll catch up at some point. Try telling that to kids who just want to make themselves look good by making their classmates feel bad. Or it could be a phase Kyle is going through because every other kid in his grade *is* taller than he is right now. My mom and Chuck are pretty involved in Kyle's school. I'm sure they've got a handle on it. At least I hope so." She patted his thigh. "But thank you for coming to the rescue today."

He covered her hand with his, keeping it right where it was. "I told you earlier, there's nothing I wouldn't do for you."

A shy smile broke out on her face just as the driver pulled the cart up beside the practice field.

"London!" Her friend Lucy pushed Kyle's bike toward them. Trey's helmet hung from the handlebars.

London quickly slid her hand out from beneath his. Trey resisted the urge to grab it back. He wasn't ready for whatever this was to end yet. But today's practice was open to the public and the fans crowded into the bleachers were already cheering and shouting at him.

"Where's Kyle?" London climbed from the golf cart.

"Having the time of his life." Lucy pointed to the fifty-yard line where the kid was running routes with Kessler and the other receivers.

London groaned. "He's not going to want to leave."

Trey took his helmet from Lucy. "So let him stay."

Both women looked at him as though he'd suggested Kyle run off with the circus.

"I have clients I have to see this afternoon, Trey. I can't just leave my little brother here unsupervised."

"He'll be fine," he reassured her.

"He can be a lot," she insisted.

Christ, did she think he was incapable of looking after her brother? "For crying out loud, the kid is what—eight? I think I can handle him. Besides, today's workout is more for show. We'll run a few drills to appease the crowd and then we head inside for meetings. Nothing can happen to him there. If he gets bored, he can play games on my phone. You can grab him from my place after you've finished work."

My place. Unbidden images of London in his home flashed before his eyes. London in his kitchen. In his pool. In his bed.

Dammit. There went the damn cup again.

She sunk her teeth into her bottom lip. "I wouldn't advise giving him your phone."

"Fine. I'll give him Kessler's phone. Either way, think of the insta-fame he'll have the first day of school," Trey added. "You don't want to deny him that."

"Think of your pregnant friend who has to pee." Lucy shimmied her hips. "Decide already!"

A whistle sounded on the field and Trey made the decision for her.

"We'll be back at my place at five. I'll text you with the address." He pulled his helmet onto his head and trotted in the direction of the field, leaving no room for argument.

CHAPTER SIXTEEN

THE LATE AFTERNOON sun bathed Lake Michigan in a dazzling array of colors. London always enjoyed driving through this part of the city. Something about being near the water grounded her, not to mention how it always eased the tension that knotted her shoulders. She glanced out the passenger window toward the lake, glad to know she'd be able to look out over the same water to find her peace when she moved to Chicago.

A move that couldn't come soon enough.

Visiting with Westbrook's clients was normally the favorite part of her job. She liked chatting with small business owners to find that one golden nugget she could use to promote them. Whether it was filming Orlando's ridiculous dad jokes or organizing a ribbon cutting on stilts for the new gymnastics place, London was all about it. No two accounts were the same and neither were the campaigns she designed for them.

Today, however, everyone had a gripe about something. *Why aren't my social media stats improving? Why weren't there more customers at the grand opening?*

Dealing with a myriad of clients with different budgets—even some with no budget—never used to bother her. Until today.

Variety, it turned out, was not always the spice of life. She was surprised at the relief she felt knowing that in a few weeks, the accounts would be someone else's problem.

At Nolan and Hemphill, London would be able to work on the larger media projects she'd always dreamed of. Evan was already dangling two international clients her way. Both wanted short films for their shareholders' meetings. Even better, both had killer budgets.

All she had to do was survive the Gunther Cheese campaign. Of course, that would be easier said than done after her foolish "lapse in judgment" earlier today.

"Arghh!" She adjusted the AC vents in an effort to cool the flush that scorched her skin every time she relived that kiss. Not that she would label what transpired outside the locker room as a simple "kiss." *Nope*. It was more like an assault. For God's sake, she'd climbed the man like a tree, practically devouring him like he was her last meal.

But his response—*oh, my*.

He met her breath for breath with deep, drugging kisses of his own. The touch of his lips immediately robbed her of any coherent thought. Not to mention her inhibitions. His very skilled fingers left a trail of fire everywhere they touched. And when his skin made contact with her skin? Well, she was surprised she hadn't climaxed right there on the spot.

She groaned again. What had she been thinking throwing herself at him like that? All she could do was chock it up to an out-of-body experience. One that would have her tangled up in her sheets for weeks. And one that could never, ever be repeated. Never mind the protests from the parts of her body that disagreed.

London had been wrong in her belief that Trey Van Horn's kisses were memorable merely because they were her first. She'd had a little bit of experience under her belt now, and she could safely say his kisses were all that and more.

So. Much. More.

The realization made her sad, though. Sad for what might have been. Sad that she would never have that with anyone else. That was something she was absolutely sure of. Trey was her "one" as Lucy would say. The problem was, she didn't have it in her to trust the man ever again. She didn't dare. It had taken her too long to find the wherewithal to move on. To choose her dreams.

But now she was choosing them. It was a good thing Trey wasn't aware of how much power he had over her body—mainly her heart. Because she had no intention of ever giving him that much power again. She was taking her life by the reins and steering it the way she wanted it to go.

Even if his tender words earlier continued to worm their way under her skin. Or if his championing of Kyle made her heart sing. She couldn't let those things deter her from her course.

Which begged the question: Where did they go from here?

There was no denying her behavior earlier was highly unprofessional. They had two days of commercials to shoot together in a few weeks. She had no doubt Trey would be able to shake it off. He was probably used to women throwing themselves at him. The other day, he'd promised her he was fully committed to seeing this endorsement deal through. To making it a success. In order for that to happen, London simply had to keep her wits about her—and her hands to herself—and trust him enough to believe he meant what he said. After all, her future depended on it.

She slowed down to allow the car coming from the opposite direction to pass before making a left turn into Trey's driveway. Trey didn't need to text her the address. She already knew it by heart.

The stately Tudor home was partially hidden behind an iron gate, but she had no doubt the views of the lake were breathtaking from its top floors. She'd seen photos of the home's interior a few years ago when a local magazine featured it as its cover story. Not that she'd ever admit to stalking Trey or anything. Her dog-eared copy of the magazine was simply research for when she owned a home like that one day.

Or so she told herself.

A buzzer sounded as soon as she reached the gate before it slowly swung open. Trey must have been watching for her.

"Down girls," she told the parts of her quivering with excitement. Trey wasn't anxiously awaiting her arrival because he wanted a repeat of earlier. More likely, he was drained from Kyle bombarding him with endless questions over the past four hours. Chuckling to herself, she pulled her car next to a Lincoln Navigator parked in the drive. She had warned Trey.

London was trying to decide which door she should approach when a side door, partially hidden among the wisteria climbing the brick, opened. A Kendrick Lamar tune blared from inside. Trey stepped out looking tempting as hell in a T-shirt and joggers. She cursed her nipples for their instant reaction. Clearly, her little pep talk on the ride over had been tuned out by parts of her body.

Trey flashed her a predatory grin as if he could sense her internal struggle, damn him.

"Hi." His eyes took a lazy tour of her from head to toe and back up again.

She felt her cheeks go pink knowing that he was probably picturing the skimpy thong she was wearing beneath her dress. It was all she could do to keep her gaze on his face rather than checking for a reaction on other parts of him.

"Trey." She cursed herself for the breathless way she uttered his name. Clearing her throat, she began again. "Trey, what happened today can't happen again." Her girl parts whimpered. "I need to know that you understand that."

His smile faded, but he nodded. "It's not in my nature to force myself on a woman."

"Okay. Good. That's-that's good." She mimicked his nod. "Is Kyle ready to go?"

"He may need a little coaxing."

Trey stepped to the side to allow her to enter. When she was beside him, however, he put his arm up, blocking the door. He lowered his lips next to her ear.

"For the record," he murmured, his warm breath fanning her neck. "I have a different set of standards for women who force themselves on me."

She bit back a moan. "It was—"

"A lapse in judgment." He lifted his head so that their gazes collided. "So you keep saying."

They stood there for a fraught moment, his pupils captivating her when they darkened to burnt gold. She tried to force her eyes away, but it was no use.

"You promised," she whispered. "I told you this account is important to me. I can't allow any complications to mess it up."

He dropped his stare to her lips, tenderly stroking the bottom one with his thumb. "So I did. I also promised I'd do anything for you, London. All you have to do is ask."

Her body was drunk on his smoldering looks, his sensuous touch, and his words laced with double meanings. It was screaming at her to "ask" him to take her inside and let his talented hands and mouth finish what they started outside the locker room. Fortunately, her brain was still sober enough to be the designated driver.

"I'd like for us to keep this professional," she managed to get out.

Trey studied her for a few seconds longer before dropping both his hands to his sides. "Done."

London knew she should be relieved at his quick acquiescence, but the lick of disappointment winding through her chest was sharp. *Decide what you want, girly-pop,* she chastised herself, before offering him a wan smile and hurrying into the house.

"Are you kidding me?" she gushed as soon as she entered his kitchen.

The magazine spread did not do the room justice. In spite of the kitchen's massive size, it was warm and homey. The high ceilings boasted wood beams that had been stained to match the off-white cabinets, making the space appear even roomier. A stunning copper hood gleamed above the professional range. Next to it was a wall of ovens that would be a baker's delight.

Across the room, the extra-large farm sink was tucked into an archway featuring a triple box bay window behind it, giving whoever had dish duty the perfect view of the pool and lush gardens out back. The entire room was set off by wide-plank wood floors stained the perfect honey brown.

Trey picked up a remote control, lowering the volume on the music. The sound of a video game being played in another room filled the void.

London spread her hands out on the quartz covering the massive island. "This is exactly what I've been picturing."

"You were fantasizing about my kitchen?"

Little does he know.

"No." Except maybe she had been. Maybe when she pictured Trey doing the Gunther commercials, she'd been subconsciously imagining him in his own kitchen. It made sense given how many times she'd peeked at the magazine images over the years.

"No," she repeated. "The kitchen I've been picturing for the commercials. I've been searching for locations all over the state, but I still haven't found the one that's a right fit for the aesthetic I want." She circled the island so she could trace her fingers along the oversized stainless steel fridge. "Do you mind if I look inside?"

He shrugged. "Suit yourself."

She pulled open both doors, sighing when she saw the entire thing was backlit. They wouldn't have to rig it with extra lighting. Even better, the fridge was nearly empty. No surprise there given his ridiculous diet.

"You're welcome to use this place for the commercial."

London spun around. "Really?" She resisted the urge to do a happy dance.

"Why not? It would make everything authentic."

"But you'd have strangers traipsing in and out of your house for two days. They'd have to set up and take down each day. It can get pretty intrusive. We typically use model homes."

Shut up already, she told herself before she talked him out of it.

He waved his hand. "That's no problem. I won't be staying here."

"What do you mean?"

Trey opened a drawer and pulled out a set of keys. "I stay at the hotel during training camp. Having people in and out won't disturb me."

Was he for real?

"You stay in a hotel when training camp is only eight miles away?"

"Quite a few of the guys have families that live somewhere other than Milwaukee. They stay in a hotel during camp. Rookies, too. It's optional for everyone else. But I like the team comradery that being together twenty-four seven fosters."

Of course he did. She leaned back against the counter, crossing her arms in front of her. "Like a frat house? Hazing the rookies by short-sheeting their bed?"

He rolled his eyes. "Sure. Exactly like that."

She was having trouble picturing Trey letting loose and actually acting silly. At least not this version of Trey.

"Well, I'm not going to turn down your offer to use this fabulous kitchen, then."

He tossed the keys at her. "You can use it whenever you want, London."

The sultry way he made the offer had her hands shaking and she nearly dropped the keys.

"London!" Kyle raced into the kitchen and wrapped his arms around her waist. "I had the best day ever!"

The pure joy in his smile melted away some of the worry she'd been feeling since his revelation earlier. Between appointments today, she'd called a high school friend who now taught at Kyle's school. Her friend was unaware of her brother being bullied. In fact, she said, Kyle was a favorite among kids of all grades. But that didn't mean things hadn't been said outside of a teacher's hearing. She promised to scope out the situation with Kyle's former teacher and get back to London.

"The best? Really? Even better than when I took you to Disney?"

Kyle shot her a sheepish smile. "Okay, the best day this summer." His smile faded. "Don't tell Alek, though, okay. Because hockey camp was really cool. Except I had to skate on the pee-wee line."

She brushed his hair back from his forehead. "Your secret is safe with me. Just remember, you're not going to be a pee-wee forever, though. Okay?"

His face lit up again and he pulled out of her embrace. "Did you know that Luke Kessler was my size when he was nine? And now he's the greatest receiver ever!!"

Trey snorted. "That's what Luke thinks. He's going to have to earn that title again this season."

"Go get your stuff," she told her brother. "We are going to Pirelli's for pizza." The restaurant was a long-time client of the agency. "Mama P is making your favorite."

"Yes! Can Trey come?"

Of course Kyle would ask that. It would be rude not to invite him after all he'd done for her today. Except she wasn't sure she trusted herself around him. Not that Trey was any help with his murmured sultry comments and casual touches. They needed to keep things professional if she was going to pull this campaign off. And that meant keeping her distance from the sexy quarterback.

"I'm having dinner with the rookies tonight, partner," he saved her by saying. "Next time, though, for sure."

Kyle sprinted back down the hall.

London grinned with relief. "Thank you for your help with him today."

"He's a good kid. I can see why Pops likes him so much."

"That's because he can take out his hearing aids and tune Kyle out when he needs to."

Trey threw back his head and laughed. The sound did strange things to her belly. She didn't think this version of him had any joy in it.

Kyle returned, trying to juggle a pair of footballs, a baseball cap, and some jerseys.

"Do you have everything?" she asked, reaching for some of his swag before he dropped it.

"I think so." Kyle checked the path he'd run from the other room. "Oh, and guess what? Trey has a big picture just like the one you have at your place."

London paused from folding a jersey. "What?" The only "big" pictures London had in her condo were prints of photos she'd taken.

"Back there." Kyle pointed down the hall. "In the study."

She glanced up at Trey. His face was unreadable. Dumping the jerseys onto the counter, she hurried down the hall, peeking into a dining room, a hall bath, and a butler's pantry before she reached what must be the study. There, above the fireplace, was a photo she'd taken of a sunset over the lake, the pink and purple sky the perfect backdrop for the tangerine sun sliding into the onyx water. Her timing had been perfect, allowing her to capture the rings of fading sunshine as they spread out over the rippling lake.

Kyle was correct. It was the same one she had hanging over her fireplace.

London stared at it for several moments, bewildered. How? Why? He'd left her at that boathouse without a word. He hadn't bothered to reach out in ten years. Yet, one of her favorite photos hung inside his home. He knew it was hers, too. He'd been the one to hoist her to the roof of the boathouse to capture the image.

"You sent it to my phone right after you took it. You were so proud of how perfect it was."

Trey was directly behind her. The heat radiating from his body was making all of her pheromones break out in a dance. It was all she could do not to sink back into him, remembering that long ago shared moment when he'd been her world.

Except she remembered the night he'd left her alone, too. The memory was tattooed onto her heart where it served as a constant reminder never to trust him again. Yet, he'd kept the photo all this time. He'd not only kept it, he had it blown up and framed where he could see it every day.

"Why?" she whispered.

An uncomfortable silence settled over the room, and London was beginning to believe he wouldn't answer her. Then she wished he wouldn't have.

"Because if I had to give you up, I still wanted to keep a piece of you with me."

It didn't make sense. What did he mean he had to give her up?

"London! I thought we were getting pizza," Kyle called from the kitchen. "I'm *starrrrrving.*"

"You know what? It doesn't matter," she told herself, not caring if Trey heard her or not. "I don't have time for this." She turned on her heel and edged around him. "I'll make the arrangements with the crew. As soon as the scripts are ready, I'll email them to you."

CHAPTER SEVENTEEN

TREY TOOK A THREE-STEP DROP, cocked his arm, and launched the football through the uprights. His teammates lined up on the sidelines of the practice field whooped and hollered with delight. At least those who had the wisdom not to take Kessler's wager did. Every year, the wide receiver talked his teammates into betting him that Trey couldn't throw a football seventy-five yards over the goal post in three attempts or less. And every year, Trey accomplished it on the first try.

"On behalf of the homeless pets of Milwaukee, thank you, gentlemen," Kessler said as he collected his winnings in the locker room thirty minutes later.

Grunting, Fletcher took his seat in front of the locker next to Trey's. "One of these days you're gonna miss and what will Kessler's mutts do then, eh?" The kicker tugged off his cleats.

"He won't miss," Kessler sat on Trey's other side counting his money. "He's a machine, remember?"

"I can't believe that article is still making the rounds," Trey groused. "Surely someone else has done something newsworthy —or stupid—this summer?"

"If you'd let me sue the woman, it would already be out of the news cycle."

Trey swore beneath his breath. He slowly turned to find Collin strolling through the locker room as if he owned the place.

Fletcher's laugh lacked any humor. "If he'd let you sue her, the story would still be front page news now and for months to come. 'Least said, soonest mended' according to my ma."

Trey gestured at the kicker. "What he said. What are you doing here, Collin?"

Except Trey could guess the reason his agent's son had dragged his ass from the parties in the Hamptons on a late August evening. The Growlers were playing a nationally televised preseason game against the league champion Baltimore Blaze tonight. With some strategic positioning on the sidelines, Collin would likely make it onto everyone's screens, looking like he's schmoozing with pro football players. It was a surefire gimmick to give him more cred with the college boys Marty's firm was angling to sign this year.

"I'm here to watch our number one client play football," Collin replied.

"This really is your first rodeo," Fletcher quipped. "It's our final game of the pre-season. Van Horn isn't even dressing for the game."

Collin flashed a coy grin. "Well, isn't that a shame? I guess we'll have more time to catch up on the sideline, then."

Bingo.

"Is your little brother coming tonight?" Collin went to slap Kessler on the shoulder, but the receiver abruptly stood before his hand made contact.

"He'll be around," Kessler replied.

"Cool. I can't believe he isn't repped yet. I'd really appreciate it if you'd hook me up with an introduction. I'd love to tell him what the Slater Agency can do for him."

Collin was ballsy, Trey had to give him that. Luke and Brody's father was an NFL legend who was still represented by the agent he'd signed with before he'd been drafted. Luke, being the illegitimate son, had to make his way in the league without the support of his superstar dad. And he had, thanks to the guidance of his own agent. For Collin to think he had a shot at Brody with two big-time agents already in the family was laughable.

Or desperate.

Trey immediately wondered about Marty's recovery. He hadn't talked to the man since their conversation about Jay the month before. Shouldn't he be back at work by now?

"How's Marty feeling?" he asked, giving Kessler time to slip away to his locker without having to commit to anything.

"Good, good." Collin waved the question off. "He'll be back at it soon."

His answer wasn't very reassuring. Trey made a mental note to reach out to Marty in the morning. Maybe Collin's father had some news about Jay. Trey hadn't heard from his dad since they last spoke weeks earlier. If Jay was really coming to the bachelor party, Trey needed to be mentally prepared. He tugged his jersey off and tossed it in the basket the equipment manager set out for dirty laundry.

"I'm sure you've got lots of other clients to look after with your father recuperating," he told Collin. "You don't need to babysit me."

"Dude, I come bearing gifts. Bergeron's girlfriend sent the scripts for the commercial shoot next week."

Hearing him refer to London as "Bergeron's girlfriend" had Trey wanting to shove his fist through a wall. Or Collin Slater's face. *She isn't the goalie's girlfriend,* he wanted to shout. She wasn't anyone's girlfriend, dammit.

He thought he'd been good at compartmentalizing. Concentrating on preparing for the season. Working out the kinks with his offensive line and his receiving corps so they were all on the same page with the playbook when the season started.

At night, however, when he was alone with his thoughts, London was always there. And now that he'd touched her again, that he'd had another taste of her, he kept picturing her in that formfitting T-shirt dress, with her cute white tennis shoes, looking all innocent on the outside. Except he knew what she was hiding underneath.

Then he remembered the way she'd looked at him after discovering the photo she'd taken hanging above his fireplace. Her crestfallen expression shriveled up his balls every time he relived the moment. Parts of her may want him, but the parts in control still didn't trust him. And they never would.

"You could have emailed them to me." He shucked his uniform pants and quickly wrapped a towel around his waist. The last thing he needed was for Collin—or his Nosy Nelly teammates—to see how any mention of London affected him.

"I thought we should go over them. Suggest a few changes. They feel a little metro-sexual for your brand."

Fletcher made a choking noise.

Trey grabbed his bodywash and headed in the direction of the showers. "I'm reading the scripts verbatim."

"Seriously, man? WTF? What did this chick do that she owns your balls?"

Collin was even slower than he was in high school. Trey pinned him to the wall before the idiot knew what hit him. His eyes immediately bulged out of their sockets when Trey pressed his forearm to Collin's neck. For some reason, Kessler felt the need to intervene. The receiver wedged his arm between the two men and shoved Trey back.

"Whoa there, Slater." Kessler slid Collin out from Trey's grip. "If you want a minute with Brody, it's now or never. Let's go."

Trey was still breathing hard when Kessler managed to perp walk Collin's sorry ass out of harm's way and into the tunnel leading out to the field. He knew he was breathing hard because it was the only sound in the now silent locker room.

"Nothing to see here," he told his stone-faced teammates.

Fletcher picked up the bottle of bodywash from the floor and handed it to Trey. Antonio cued up the sound system and the speakers began to blast Drake's latest.

"You wanna talk about it?" Fletcher asked when they reached the showers.

"Nope."

The kicker had the nerve to laugh.

"What's so damn funny?" Trey demanded.

"Just imagining that I sounded a lot like you two years ago."

"Nah, you were a real dick. And don't go assuming my situation is anything like yours. It's not."

"Whatever you say."

Fletcher let it go—for all of thirty seconds.

Which was probably a record for the kicker who considered himself to be the team's sage.

"But if you're going to take on Bergeron, you're going to need some backup."

Trey ducked beneath the shower head in hopes of tuning out his teammate. Unfortunately, Fletcher was still wearing his trademark smug smile when Trey finished his shower.

"Brody is happy to string Marty's spawn along for a while," Kessler said when Trey and Fletcher made their way back to their lockers. "Are you going to tell us what that was all about?"

"QB One is not inclined to discuss the situation," Fletcher answered for Trey.

"There is no 'situation,'" Trey snapped as he dragged on his warmup gear.

"That's not what Randy said," Kessler murmured.

"Who the hell is Randy?"

Fletcher shook his head. "How many times have I suggested it would behoove you to learn the names of the staff?"

"Randy is one of the equipment guys," Kessler explained. "He's also your chauffeur for the golf cart."

Trey suddenly had a very bad feeling. "What. Did. He. Say?"

Kessler took a step back. "He might have incorrectly assumed you and London were an item. Mostly because her little brother hung around for practice opening day."

"And the hickey you put on the lass's neck."

"What? No way! My lips never left hers! There was no hickey!"

Fletcher's face lit up with a shit-eating grin just as Trey realized he'd been had.

"So it is true." Kessler put his hands on his hips. "You do realize Bergeron is a hockey player? Those guys fight dirty."

"She and Bergeron are not together," Trey managed to push out through clenched teeth.

"Because you and she are?" Fletcher asked, no doubt trying to trick Trey once again.

Trey placed his street clothes into his garment bag he would take over to the locker room in the stadium. "No." The disappointment brought on by that one word stunned him. "No," he repeated, trying to sound a lot more convincing.

He could feel the stares from the two men he considered to be his closest friends. Not that Trey did friendship very well. Letting his guard down with people, letting them see the real him, wasn't his strong suit. His ridiculous childhood taught him that putting yourself out there usually got you burned.

Sure, he'd go through hell and back with any guy in this locker room because they were his teammates. His brothers on the field. That's what a team did. They fought for one another. Yet, he suddenly wondered if any of them would do the same for him. Did they consider him a friend? More importantly, when had that started to matter?

Had the years of being aloof cost him more fulfilling relationships? The last time Trey had let down his guard, had let someone in, was those few weeks with London. He'd liked who he'd been with her. But look how that ended up.

He sank down on the bench and dragged his fingers through his hair. "It's complicated."

Fletcher snorted. "Aye. It always is with women."

Kessler sat beside him. "But they're worth it. And as my Gram always says, nothing worth having is ever easy."

"You two are fonts of old lady platitudes today," Trey mumbled.

"Do you want our help or not?" Kessler shot back.

"Give it up, Luke." Fletcher grabbed a new jersey and pulled it over his shoulder pads. "Van Horn is a one man show. Always has been. Always will be."

Except he didn't want to be anymore.

"I first met London ten years ago," Trey began quietly. "She jumped off a moving boat to deliver Pops' mail. I think I was in awe of her from that moment on." He grinned at the memory of her fearlessness. "Everything about her was guileless. It was relaxing to not have to be the big man on campus with her, you know?"

Kessler nodded in understanding.

"She was perfect. We were perfect together."

"So what happened?" Kessler asked.

"I misread the play." Trey blew out a heavy breath. "And I totally screwed it up."

Fletcher whistled as he took a seat on the other side of Trey. "Been there. Done that."

The kicker arched his eyebrows at Kessler.

"Hey, don't look at me! It was Summer who misread the play in our relationship," Kessler argued. His shoulders slumped. "Okay, I still effed it up by keeping secrets. But we're not talking about me right now. Focus your Obi Wan wisdom on Van Horn."

"Do you want what you had with her again?" Fletcher asked.

With everything he had.

But what if he wasn't enough? What if he was like every other male in his family and he couldn't give her the fairy tale? Was it worth the risk?

His shoulders slumped. "Even if I do, she'll never trust me again."

Fletcher stood, slapping him on the back before grabbing his helmet and shoving it into his bag. "Funny thing about trust. You can only earn it with genuine effort. Good thing you're one of the most driven individuals I know. If you want her, focus some of your single-minded pigheadedness on earning her trust again."

LONDON DOWNLOADED and scheduled the last of the reels featuring Mooz-R-Ella onto the various social media platforms.

"You should consider a career in advertising," Evan quipped when he sat down beside her in the Nolan and Hemphill conference room she'd been using as a temporary office for the past two weeks. "Oh, wait. You do work in advertising." He smiled warmly. "This is one hell of a campaign, London. You should be proud."

"Thank you."

She was proud. Her first shot at big time advertising was working out better than she imagined. Relaxing against the back of her plush chair—she was certain it was the most comfortable work chair she'd ever sat in—she took in the breathtaking view from the windows surrounding the room. From high atop the fiftieth floor, she could see the shores of Lake Michigan, not to mention all of Chicago spread out below.

A girl could get used to this.

London was in the city putting the finishing touches on the first part of the Gunther campaign. The part geared for parents of school-age kids. After a tedious week of focus group testing, the ads had been tweaked and re-tweaked and were now ready to launch online, in print, and on radio and television next week.

Evan picked up one of the Mooz-R-Ella puppets from the

conference table. "I need to steal a puppet for my kids. My son will be the hit of the first day of kindergarten if he has one of these before kids can win them."

"Nothing is more effective at creating demand than kids who have to have the latest toy." She handed Evan a second one. "Here, take two. Just don't tell Seth Gunther. He's pretty possessive of his stock." She winked at him.

Evan shook his head slightly at the mention of Seth's name. "I gotta hand it to the guy. He knows what he wants, and he goes after it. This deal is the talk of the industry. Everyone is going to be sniffing around trying to lure you away. We can't afford to let that happen."

He leaned back in his chair and steepled his fingers as he eyed London. Unsure of what was coming, she found herself tensing up.

"Your contract with Westbrook runs through the end of the calendar year. Obviously when we absorb the firm, that contract will be with Nolan and Westbrook. We'd like to get ahead of the game and renegotiate as soon as possible. Given your new celebrity, we'd be foolish not to lock up your services for another two years."

Was he serious?

Her pulse began to flutter wildly. "I haven't even delivered the second part of this campaign yet."

Evan waved her remark off. "I've seen enough to know you'll be a tremendous asset to our team. The rest of the agency's leadership agrees. We're putting together a lucrative package that will include a salary I think you're worthy of, as well as some benefits to sweeten the deal."

"Wow."

She worked with words every day, yet right now she was speechless. Was it really happening? Could her dream finally be coming true?

"I know you're racing back to Milwaukee tonight. I saw the

work order to begin filming Van Horn's spots tomorrow. We can talk more about this next week when you get back." He stood up. "Oh, and my wife wanted you to know that if you need help finding a place to live, she'd be happy to assist. She loves that kind of thing." He sighed. "And you'd be doing me a favor. She's on her 'let's move' kick again. Helping you will distract her from looking for a new place for us. I'm not up for the hassle of moving right now."

London laughed. "Thank you. That would be nice."

Evan pulled on one of the puppets and waved to her. "See you next week."

As soon as he was out of sight, London twirled the chair around a few times and let out a little shriek. She couldn't wait to get back to Milwaukee to share the good news with Bennie. He was going to be thrilled. London was going to be a big-time account exec in Chicago!

The *in Chicago* part had her deflating a little bit. Things were getting real. And that meant they had to break the news to the staff. It also meant she would have to break Lucy's heart.

The two women had enjoyed a girl's weekend a couple of days ago thanks to the hotel suite on Lakeshore where Nolan and Hemphill were putting London up. The goal was to show her friend all the exciting and unique things they could do together in Chicago. That way, when she broke the news about the move, Lucy wouldn't be too devastated. Except the weekend had been so enjoyable, making memories with her friend before her life was changed by motherhood, that London didn't have the guts to ruin it.

Now it loomed over her even heavier than before.

Sighing, she closed her computer and packed it in her bag. She gathered up the remaining puppets and dumped them back into their shipping box. They were destined for an event at the Boys and Girls Club in Milwaukee later in the week.

With a wave to the receptionist, she carried her stuff to the express elevator down to the parking garage. It was time to face the music and head back to Milwaukee. These couple of weeks away felt as though she'd been in her own perfect bubble, focused on doing what she loved. Building her future in a new place. But reality waited.

She hopped on I-94, headed north and turned on the traffic station for Milwaukee. Arriving at rush hour meant a possible route change. Traffic was apparently already a mess around the city. The Growlers' final preseason game was tonight.

How has she forgotten that?

Probably because she'd banned all thoughts of Trey Van Horn from ruining her trip. Sure, his name came up in production meetings and script writing sessions. But she'd been able to relegate him to a character in a campaign. Nothing more.

The technique worked brilliantly—until she was alone in bed at night. The kiss they shared in the stadium seemed to get hotter and hotter every time she relived it. Memories of the old Trey morphed into images of the current Trey until she couldn't tell them apart. Which was even more ridiculous because they were the same person. Trey Van Horn was still the guy she'd fallen in love with.

Except something had happened to change him.

"If I had to give you up…"

London had spent several sleepless nights—not to mention a few bottles of wine—wondering what Trey had meant by that statement. He'd given her up? Why? And for whom?

Maybe it was just wishful thinking on her part, but his words offered some explanation for the abrupt way he left her, without so much as a goodbye or a backward glance. All this time she thought she'd done something wrong. That she wasn't good enough.

But maybe not.

It was too late to salvage the blow to her confidence that had set her back a decade. Today's job offer went a long way to heal that, though. Yet, the anger she'd spent years stockpiling toward Trey had begun to crumble, little by little, since he'd come back into her life.

That didn't mean there would ever be anything between them, she reminded her girl parts. They'd both grown into the people they were meant to be, with careers that were taking them in different directions. She didn't have time for distractions like Trey, no matter how sexy the packaging. Nope. The sizzle between them was nothing without trust. She could—and would —ignore it, finish the campaign, and move on with her new career.

Provided he didn't have any more bombshell surprises lying in wait for her when she got to his home.

CHAPTER EIGHTEEN

A MAKEUP ARTIST lightly brushed some bronzer over Trey's forehead. From his perch on the stool, he watched in awe as London whirled around his kitchen, adjusting the cameras and lights for the commercial shoot. She shared a laugh with the food stylist who was arranging a platter of fruit and cheese with exacting precision. The rest of the crew joined in on whatever the joke was.

Her enthusiasm for this project made Trey smile. He was glad he could do this for her. Not just because this campaign would advance her career, but for the opportunity to witness her delight doing something she loved and was clearly very good at.

"I thought I was paying those big shots from Nolan and Hemphill to shoot these commercials," Seth Gunther grumbled from beside Trey. "Instead, I get Bennie's pet project. That girl might be good at promoting parties, but social media is not the same as network television."

Trey jerked his head around to scowl at the man who'd turned out to be a massive pain in the ass. If Trey found Gunther's micro-management of every aspect of his cheese campaign annoying, he could only imagine how stressful it must be for

London. He opened his mouth to chew the guy out, but his agent beat him to the punch.

"Actually, social media is where it's at these days," Collin chimed in, not even bothering to look up from his phone screen. "There are more eyes on ads online than commercials on the old-fashioned boob-tube you love so much, Gunther. And 'that girl' is killing it."

Mumbling something under his breath, Gunther stalked over to the counter to inspect the cheese.

"You're welcome," Collin said.

It was bad enough having Gunther in his house, but Collin insisted on tagging along to today's shoot, as well. Since arriving in Milwaukee ahead of yesterday's game, Collin had been Trey's shadow. And try as he might, there was no way of shaking the guy.

"Gunther is already taking advantage of you," Collin maintained this morning when he'd railroaded Trey at the training camp hotel. "You'll need backup to make sure he doesn't do it again. I should be there."

Trey disagreed that anyone was going to take advantage of him, least of all Seth Gunther, but he had to begrudgingly admit Collin had earned his keep with his remark.

"Thank you, Collin," Trey replied.

Collin shoved his phone into his pocket. "Don't mention it. It's not every day I can make two clients happy with one putdown.

"Come again?"

"I get Gunther off your back and protect the reputation of Bergeron's girl all in one move. I ought to bill you both."

Trey didn't bother laughing at Collin's attempt at a joke. Still, his lips turned up at the corners anyway. Probably due to the relief of knowing something Collin didn't.

London was *not* "Bergeron's girl."

At least she claimed not to be. And given the way she'd kissed

Trey at the stadium a few weeks ago, he believed her. He knew now she wasn't the duplicitous women he'd thought her to be all these years. Not only that, but according to Trey's sources, the hockey goalie hadn't been back in the country since the day he'd left London's office. His sister had eventually had her baby, allowing Bergeron to make the rounds at other hockey camps. He wasn't scheduled to return to the States until the Mayhem started camp next month.

And that left the playing field wide open for Trey. He was fairly sure he still didn't have a fairy tale to offer her. But he did know that if he didn't get whatever was between them out of his system before the season began, he'd never be able to concentrate on football. She still felt something for him, too. London might not admit to it, but her body spoke volumes every time they touched. The only problem was the sticky issue of her not trusting him.

"Is he camera ready?" she asked from across the kitchen.

"Always," Collin quipped.

Trey thanked the woman with the bronzer as he removed the cape that she had put on him to protect his jersey and white uniform pants from harm. He made his way behind the island, stopping to stand on the piece of red tape indicating his mark. One of the two cameras being used for the commercial was mounted on a tripod directly in front of him. The other was braced on the shoulder of one of the cameramen. The sound tech maneuvered the boom microphone hanging overhead into position.

London pulled on a pair of headphones and stepped behind her laptop. "Okay, let's go for a quick sound check. Trey, can you read that first line from the cue cards?"

He glanced at the young woman standing beside London who was holding the large white cards. She smiled coyly at Trey.

"I don't need cue cards," he said. "I memorized the scripts."

London's eyes twinkled. "I have no doubt you did. The cards

are there for backup, just in case. But could you humor me right now and read from the first card so we can check the microphone's sound levels?"

Please, she mouthed with a teasing grin.

He'd do anything to keep that smile on her face.

"You know, in football, we're always looking for the perfect play, and in my kitchen, it's all about the perfect cheese," he recited into the camera.

The sound tech gave a thumbs up.

London looked up from her computer. "Is there anything you're not good at?"

He met her amused eyes head on. "I told you before. I give everything one hundred percent of my effort."

Their gazes locked for a long moment before she dragged hers away.

"Uh, Cliff," she said. "Can we adjust the bounce on that light over there slightly? There's a shadow on his face I don't like."

The lighting guy did as she asked, but London still wasn't satisfied.

"I'm going to have to move his mark." She stepped around the island to stand beside Trey. "Come this way a smidge."

He moved an inch closer to her.

"More," she demanded, before placing her hands on his waist to position him where she wanted.

They both started at the contact. Even through his clothing, her touch ignited a firestorm along his nerve endings. Not only that, but his head began to spin as soon as she uttered the word "more." The unbidden image of her naked and writhing beneath him as she cried out "more" had him sucking in a ragged breath.

She dropped her hands and her chin instantly. But not before he caught a glance of her pink cheeks. *Good.* At least he knew she was just as affected as he was. He moved closer, glad for the high countertop hiding everything below the belt.

"How's this?" he asked softly.

"Mmm." She nodded and began to turn away.

"Is there anything *you're* not good at?" he whispered.

Her chin snapped back up as she shot him a questioning look.

He gestured with his hand at the scene in his kitchen. "You're a natural at this, London."

The flush was back on her cheeks. She sank her teeth into her bottom lip before nodding swiftly. "Thank you." The smile she gave him was effervescent. "Okay, team. Now that we've established that we're all good at our jobs, let's get on with it."

She settled back behind her laptop and pulled on her headphones.

"Mike, let me know when we are speeding," she said.

"At speed," one of the cameramen said.

London nodded to the woman who had done Trey's makeup. She held the clapper in front of the camera.

"Gunther Cheese spot one, take one." She clapped the board together.

"Action," London called out.

Trey responded as if the referee had blown the game whistle.

It took them less than two hours to film the five different commercials. Trey only had to rely on the cue cards twice. When London wasn't behind her laptop monitoring the footage, she was wandering around catching the action with the camera on her cellphone.

"For B-roll," she explained. "We'll use it for the social media posts."

"When can I see the finished products?" Gunther asked as soon as London called cut on the final ad.

"I can send you some rough cuts tonight," she replied. "The voiceover actor isn't available until next week, so we won't have the final package until then."

"Fine. I'll be expecting them this evening." Gunther turned to Trey. "And I'll look forward to seeing you on opening day. My grandsons are excited about being able to toss the football around with you."

Collin moved closer as if to interject, but Trey waved him off. He'd fulfilled his part of the contract, but London still had to deal with the asshole. He hadn't agreed to do any such thing with the man's grandsons. It didn't matter though. He'd do it anyway, if only to make her life easier.

"It'll be my pleasure." The fib rolled off his tongue easily.

Gunther slapped him on the back and without so much as a thank you to London and the crew, he exited the kitchen. If London noticed, she didn't react. Instead she joked with the sound guy as he packed up his equipment.

"You ready to head out, too?" Collin asked. "I know you're chomping at the bit to get back to the hotel meeting room and break down film from last night's game."

Trey was eager to get back into training camp mode. Even though he hadn't touched the ball, several of his best receivers had played the first half. Kessler held his own, but two passes had slipped through McGraff's fingers, and that was two too many as far as Trey was concerned. He needed to study the game film to figure out what was up with the young receiver's timing.

Unfortunately, the crazy pull he felt toward London was keeping his feet rooted to his kitchen floor.

"You're done with him, right?" Collin called over to where London was packing up her computer.

God, I hope not.

He still had a photo shoot left to do for the Gunther campaign. The shoot was scheduled to take place at an actual grocery store the following morning at five am to avoid attracting a throng of customers. After that, she would be "done with him" professionally. He only hoped she wouldn't want to be done with him personally.

"Actually—" There was a pensive look in her eyes. "I was

wondering if you have a few more minutes to shoot a couple of posts for social media?"

"He doesn—" Collin began before Trey interjected.

"I can spare a bit more time."

Collin shot him the side-eye, but Trey ignored it.

"What did you have in mind?"

"I was thinking a little ten second segment with a one liner. You'd have to take a bite of cheese at the end, though." She arched an eyebrow at him.

It was on the tip of his tongue to remind her he'd do anything for her. Only there were too many ears listening in on their conversation.

"Challenge accepted," he said instead.

There was that grin again. The one that made his chest feel tight and his head feel light.

"Okay." She spun on her heel looking around his kitchen. "Hm. The light is fading in here. Did I read somewhere that this place has a wine cellar?"

"It does."

"Please tell me you have wine in it?"

"My dad wouldn't have it any other way."

She clapped her hands together. "Perfect! Cliff, can I borrow the light?"

"I live to serve, my queen." Cliff winked at London.

Trey led them toward the stairs at the back of the kitchen.

"Do you need a camera?" Mike asked.

London shook her head. "I'll film on my phone. That way it will have the look I'm going for."

Collin followed them downstairs. "Wow, this is pretty bougie," he said when Trey pulled open the heavy iron door and ushered them inside.

The twelve-by-twelve-foot room had been carved into the home's stone cellar a century ago. Nearly two hundred bottles of wine were housed in the small area, all of it stored in simple floor-to-ceiling racks. A wooden tasting table took up the center of the space, with leather wing chairs sitting at two of its sides. Beneath it was a colorful Turkish area rug. Another smaller table sat in a corner, while an intricately carved chest Jay had brought back from China was nestled in the other corner.

"It's stunning." London scanned the room slowly. "Cliff, can you set that up here?" She indicated a spot in front of the larger tasting table. "That way we'll get those cobwebs reflected behind him."

Trey hadn't even noticed the spiderweb. Leave it to London to find the most unique aesthetic possible. The food stylist placed the tray of cheese and fruits on the larger table before exiting the crowded room.

"Striking," Cliff warned them before bright light flooded the space. "You want a scrim?"

"Yes." London nodded as Cliff placed a metal grated circle over the light, immediately softening its output. She motioned for Trey to sit in one of the leather armchairs closest to the cheese tray.

"This is going to be pretty simple." She pulled a piece of paper from the back pocket of her black pants and handed it to him.

It was still warm from being held so close to her body. Ignoring the shiver of lust coursing through him, he unfolded the sheet and read what was on it. He laughed.

"So this is how you want to handle it?"

She shrugged, still fiddling with the settings on her phone. "Seth didn't want to address the elephant in the room that is your strict diet. Bennie and I thought it would be better to meet it head on."

"Well played."

"Mm." She pointed her phone at him. "That works. Can we clear the room, please?"

Cliff stepped outside the wine cellar with Collin following reluctantly.

"Don't shut the door all the way," Trey cautioned him. "It can get a bit twitchy if it isn't closed properly."

Collin saluted him and left the door open an inch.

"We can do this in as many takes as you need," London said softly. "Just look right at my phone and say the lines as if you're talking only to me."

He let out a long breath and settled into the chair, telling his body to ignore her bedroom voice.

"Whenever you're ready," she coaxed.

Focusing on her lips, he recited the lines from memory. "You might have heard a rumor about me adhering to a strict diet during the season." He let the corners of his lips turn up slightly. "Well, it's true." He reached for a piece of cheese and brought it to his mouth. "So let's keep this just between you and me." Without taking his eyes from London's, he bit into the cheese, chewed, and swallowed, letting his eyes drift closed with a soft moan of pleasure. He had to admit, Gunther did make mean cheddar.

London was still filming, her lips parted in what looked like awe. Trey winked at her, and she seemed to come to her senses. Collin whooped it up from outside the door.

"Holy shit, that's brilliant," he shouted. "No wonder my dad wants to hire her."

The expression of horror on her face made Trey laugh. He was so distracted that he didn't notice Collin shoving the door the wrong way until it was too late.

"Collin, wait!" he yelled.

But his words were drowned out by the groan of the big iron door locking them in.

CHAPTER NINETEEN

LONDON JUMPED at the sound of the heavy door slamming shut. Trey bolted from his chair and raced toward it, swearing as he tried to pull it open. But it was no use.

"Are we locked in here?"

He shot her a look over his shoulder telling her everything she needed to know. She sank down into one of the chairs.

"But there's a key right?" she asked even though, judging by Trey's frantic efforts, she already knew what his answer would be.

Someone was pounding on the other side, but communication through the thick cellar walls was virtually impossible.

"Your phone," Trey suddenly demanded. "Let me have it."

She glanced at the screen, taking in the lack of any bars before handing it to him with a shrug. "I'm fairly certain we just stumbled on one thing you can't do."

He snatched it from her hand, obviously not appreciating a good joke when he heard one. Moving back toward the entrance, he typed something into her phone before holding it toward the top of the door.

"Cliff and Mike will figure something out," she said, trying to calm herself as much as him. "They at least have the technical skill your agent is no doubt lacking."

Trey dropped his head to his chest, releasing a long sigh that sounded almost as if it ended on a chuckle. Wearing a tight smile, he returned to the table and placed her phone in front of her.

"I guess we figured out something else you're good at," he said as he returned to his chair.

She arched an eyebrow at him in question.

"You don't fall to pieces when life throws you a curve ball."

If he only knew.

Maintaining her composure took a lot of work. And it was a slippery slope. She'd barely been able to hold herself together for months after he'd left her. Simply going through the motions of college life. While everyone else was gaining the freshman fifteen, London had lost nearly that much weight. She walled herself off from would-be friendships and experiences because they required too much effort. It took everything she had just to make it through each day.

Eventually, however, she'd put the pieces back together. And she'd come out the other side a much stronger woman. One who guarded her heart ruthlessly. A woman who was determined to never again feel that kind of pain. Of course, she hadn't planned on Trey popping into her life story again.

And now she was trapped in a wine cellar with the man. He'd practically been oozing testosterone all afternoon. Testing her hard-earned composure with the sultry way he delivered his lines and those sexy secret smiles he aimed at her.

God help me.

She wasn't giving him the satisfaction of letting him know she was on the verge of snapping, however. Exhibiting a calm she didn't really feel, she snagged a piece of cheese.

"Well, life isn't all bad when you have Gunther's cheese," she quipped. "It's the cheese that makes you cheer."

He picked up his own piece. "It's the ultimate tailgate cheese."

"Nothing says game day like Gunther's cheese."

"It's a touchdown of flavor," he countered.

London groaned when he popped his piece into his mouth.

"That was one Seth insisted on," she told him.

Trey feigned surprise. "You don't say?"

Feeling slightly more relaxed, she grabbed one of the grapes from the tray. "Well at least we won't go hungry."

"Only because we're not dependent on Collin," he joked.

"I don't suppose you have a bottle opener in here?"

Wearing an appreciative smile, he rose from his chair and headed toward a chest of drawers in the corner. He pulled out a corkscrew and held out his hand to her. London dragged in a breath. Touching Trey Van Horn was never a wise idea. *Neither is drinking wine with him while trapped in his wine cellar,* she cautioned herself.

Ignoring her inner voice and his outstretched palm, she stood and began to stroll among the racks of wine.

"I should have paid more attention when Lucy was having tastings at her shop," she said. "I'm not much of a connoisseur."

Trey reached over her shoulder to pluck a dusty bottle from the rack. "This is one of Jay's favorites."

His breath fanned the back of her neck, lingering a moment longer than necessary. In the name of self-preservation, she slipped out from under his arm and picked up her phone.

"Put the bottle next to the cheese tray," she told him, doing her best to keep the focus on work. "I'll capture some more B-roll of you opening it."

He did as she asked, expertly popping the cork, and pouring the wine into two glasses he retrieved from the cabinet.

She took the glass he offered, put it to her lips and gulped a large swallow. Lucy would be appalled. But she wasn't trapped in a wine cellar with the man who could make her hot and bothered with a single look. Desperate times and all that.

The wine went down smoothly. Perhaps too smoothly. She

took another healthy sip, feeling the liquid warm her as it made its way down her body.

Or maybe the warmth was from the fiery way Trey was eyeing her.

Ignoring him, she pulled up her Taylor Swift playlist on her phone and hit play. *We are never ever, ever getting back together* echoed off the stone walls. Trey chuckled before returning to the door and gently jiggling the handle. He grabbed the cheese knife from the tray and squatted down in front of the door.

London stifled a groan, tearing her gaze away from the mouthwatering view of the very fine ass his football pants were showing off. She poured herself another glass of wine. The only sounds in the room now were Taylor singing about Karma, and the relentless clink of the knife against the hinges of the iron door. London closed her eyes and let the wine work its magic on her slowly unraveling nerves.

A sound from outside the door had her eyes snapping open. The room was suddenly spinning. She tried to recall the last time she'd eaten anything today. Something more substantive than a grape and piece of cheese. *Dammit.* Was her wine glass empty again?

Trey pulled a piece of paper from beneath the door. He quickly scanned the note. "They've called a welder."

"A welder?!" It came out more as a hiccup than actual words.

He scrutinized her carefully before looking over at the wine bottle. It was nearly empty.

"Yeah. There's no telling how long that will take. I'll keep trying to get it from this end."

He turned back to the door. She poured the remaining wine into her glass.

"You know, I think I finally get why you left." She took a sip of liquid courage, determined to address the elephant in the room. *Why not,* the grapes were saying. "I mean you must have gotten the news about our parents while you were in Chicago."

His hand was still on the door. Taylor crooned "the more that you say, the less I know."

Apropos.

"What I don't understand," she continued, the wine making her bolder, "is why you didn't reach out. Why you didn't at least have the guts to tell me what was going on."

The only movement he made was to rest his forehead against the door. "I was young and stupid, London. And I made a bonehead decision."

She waited several heartbeats for the apology that should surely be coming. Except it didn't come. *Damn him.* She took another gulp from her glass.

"And you never regretted it?" She hated how rough her voice sounded. How vulnerable she'd now made herself.

Before she could take a breath, Trey leaped up from his crouch in front of the door and stalked over to her chair. His hands gripped the armrests, and he leaned over her, his golden eyes dark as they bored into hers. She licked her lips. His nostrils flared.

"Of course I regret it." He seemed to be struggling to find the right words while his chest sawed in and out. "I regret walking away from what might have been, all because I was too much of a hothead dumbass to know better. But what I regret most London Headley—" he swallowed roughly, "—is hurting you."

The last words came out as a whisper, but London felt them in her core as if he'd shouted them with a bullhorn.

"Oh," was all she could manage.

Trey lifted her as though she was a ragdoll, reversing their positions so she was now seated on his lap. He brushed his thumb along her cheek just as he always did before he kissed her. Her stomach seized with need, anticipating the feel of his lips on hers. Except the kiss never came. Instead, his lips traced a hot path along her neck.

"We said we wouldn't do this anymore." Her protest was weak

at best, especially since she was tilting her head back to give him better access.

"No, *you* said that," he argued, brushing an openmouthed kiss against the tender skin beneath her ear right before he took the lobe between his teeth.

London moaned.

"Tell me you didn't mean it," he demanded in between nips to her collarbone.

Her nails dug into his biceps. He pressed his fingers to her chin, gently turning it toward him so they were nearly nose to nose. Maybe it was the wine buzz, but she was pretty sure his eyes were pleading with her.

"Tell me, London."

The realization that she'd never be able to resist this man should have sobered her up. It didn't. Instead, she became even more reckless, threading her fingers through his soft hair before dragging his lips to meet hers.

The explosion of need was instantaneous. Trey shifted her so she was straddling his legs. London pushed him against the chair back while their tongues engaged in a wild dance. He tugged her blouse free from her pants, lifting it up to give his fingers better access to the bare skin of her midriff. Her body convulsed at the contact. A groan escaped the back of his throat, and he yanked his lips from hers.

"Let me taste you, London. Please," he begged as he tore at the buttons on the front of her blouse. He didn't wait for permission —or maybe she gave it to him. She didn't care as long as he didn't stop what he was doing.

His lips left a trail of heat everywhere they traveled on her body. He spread her blouse open, exposing her skin to the cool air, but it did nothing to quash the restlessness brewing inside of her.

"My God, you're still so perfect," Trey murmured. "I've

dreamed of this for so long." He spoke the words as if he were surprised by the thought.

Bending her back over his forearm, he slowly lowered his head and took a pebbled nipple into his mouth. The sensation of the fabric abrading her sensitive skin as he sucked her through her bra made her wild. She clawed at the hard muscles on his shoulders. He was so hard everywhere. She moaned when her core came in contact with the hardest part of him.

Trey shoved her bra down and continued to torture her other nipple. The pleasure and pain he doled out had London unabashedly grinding her hips against him. He growled against her skin, sucking even harder as he rocked his hard length against her.

"Oh, God!" She could feel the pressure building within her. "Trey. I need…I need—"

It was too late. The unexpected climax came over her in an intense wave, sending her over the edge into bliss. And as if that wasn't embarrassing enough, sparks began to fly along the hinges of the iron door.

CHAPTER TWENTY

Trey needed his head examined for agreeing to a photo shoot at five o'clock in the damn morning. He was tired and horny after a sleepless night breaking down the images of London coming apart in his arms. She was gorgeous in her ecstasy.

Except her pleasure rapidly evaporated when the door to the wine cellar began to budge yesterday. She'd scrambled from his lap and buttoned her blouse, hurriedly flipping up the collar to cover the marks he'd left on her neck. The welder and his team had pried open the door barely six inches when she slipped through and made her escape. He wasn't surprised to find his kitchen empty by the time he made his way upstairs a few moments later.

The only thing rousing him from his bed at zero dark thirty this morning was the knowledge that she'd be at the shoot. He knew he wasn't imagining the passionate way she responded to him. Yet, he didn't know if what they shared could become more than a few stolen kisses here and there. He did know he wanted her with a fervor he'd never felt for any other woman.

His increasing need for her was becoming a distraction. One he couldn't afford a week before the season kicked off. If it were any other woman, he'd take her to bed, slack his desire and get her out of his system so he could concentrate on the one thing that mattered most: football.

But London wasn't any other woman. She was the one in a million female who'd held his heart in her hands a decade ago. Until he'd failed her.

She'd stated unequivocally that she'd never trust him again. And that was on him. He knew her well enough to know she wasn't the type of woman who'd sleep with a guy she didn't trust. No matter how strong the attraction. That left him with two options: navigate the season with perpetual blue balls, or take Fletcher's advice and do whatever it took to earn back her trust.

Either way, he was screwed. Because the last thing he wanted was to hurt her ever again. Unfortunately, disappointing women was hardwired into his genetics. Ignoring what was simmering between them would be the wisest—and safest--choice. Turns out, though, Trey wasn't as wise as everyone gave him credit for. He'd decided to put everything on the line, going for the Hail Mary and hoping like hell it would end with a score.

His plan hit a snag right at the line of scrimmage, though, when London didn't show up for the photo shoot. Instead, she'd sent Bennie in her place. If her boss knew about the tonsil hockey she and Trey had been playing, he didn't let on. As an added bonus, Seth Gunther and Collin weren't early risers, making the hour-long session quick and painless. Except for the constant ache Trey felt knowing that he didn't have an excuse to see London again.

Five hours and one shitty morning practice later, he was roaming through the hallways of the Growlers' executive offices looking for the team's owner. It was a testament to how desperate he was to contrive an excuse to see London that he was willing to enlist the aid of his boss. He was hoping he could fabricate some sort of issue with the gala that necessitated Mrs. C calling a committee meeting. Or at the very least, something pressing enough that a visit to the Westbrook offices was warranted.

He hadn't counted on having an audience while he did so, however. Especially one that included Antonio McGraff, his least favorite wideout at the moment. Fumble Fingers had dropped seven passes in practice today. Sure, Trey had had some trouble getting the right spin on the ball. Given his current circumstances, it was understandable. But McGraff was getting paid millions to compensate.

"For someone who dropped more passes than he caught this morning, you've sure got a lot of time on your hands for flirting," Trey barked.

The young woman McGraff was chatting up squeaked softly before busying herself at her computer. For his part, McGraff barely flinched. The guy was a number one draft pick for a reason. What he lacked in ball control this morning, he more than made up for in cocky mental toughness.

The wideout lifted a brow and replied with a generous helping of snark. "Like my daddy always said, it's a poor mechanic who blames his tools."

Trey was about to give the little shit a set-down he'd never forget when a throat cleared behind him. He turned to see Mrs. C leveling a Mama Bear look at him. McGraff had endeared himself to the team's matriarch early in his rookie year and could do no wrong in her eyes. Trey blew out a frustrated breath.

Mrs. C edged past Trey to put something on the other woman's desk. "Thank you, Astrid. It looks like we're all set for the picnic this weekend."

Astrid smiled at her boss. With porcelain skin, doe-like eyes and an endearing grin, Trey could see why his teammate was so infatuated with the young Asian woman. Still, the guy needed to keep it in his pants and focus on the damn game he was paid so much to play.

Hello, pot. Meet kettle.

"Mr. Gunther called again asking if there was any chance he could secure an invite," Astrid said.

"Heavens, no," Mrs. C replied.

"Hell, no," Trey said at the same time.

The team owner studied him carefully while she directed her words to Astrid. "The picnic is strictly for players, staff, and their families. Advertisers get enough perks. And it will be my pleasure to remind him of that when I see him at the Boys and Girls Club event today."

Trey scoffed. "Good luck with that."

"I thought you two were pretty cozy given that you're promoting his cheese," she said.

"The man's an egomaniac."

"You have to admit his cheese is pretty good, though," McGraff chimed in.

"Well then, at least the girls and boys will enjoy their special treat this afternoon." She arched an eyebrow at Trey. "I take it you dodged a bullet and get to skip today's Gunther Cheese promotion at the Boy's and Girl's Club. London mentioned it would be centered around the cow puppet instead."

McGraff chuckled. "Dude, you've been replaced by a puppet already?"

Trey ignored his teammate's remark. He was too busy mentally patting himself on the back. He'd come up here looking to create an excuse to see London again and Mrs. C had just handed him one on a silver platter.

"Actually, I thought I'd drop by to see the kids. Without advance notice, the media won't be there to turn it into a circus."

Mrs. C eyed him shrewdly.

"What?" Trey demanded. "You're always saying I should put myself out there more. Show I'm human. What better way than to surprise a bunch of kids?"

This time McGraff's chuckle was more like a snort.

"And just for that, you're coming, too, Fumble Fingers," Trey told his teammate. "Hustle over to community relations and grab some swag. We leave in twenty." He turned to his boss. "Would you like a ride?"

She shook her head. "I'm planning to stay only long enough for the photo Gunther is insisting on."

Trey nodded, eager to get down to the locker room and change. "See you there."

"Oh, Trey," she called after him. "You didn't RSVP for a plus-one at the picnic. Are we to assume you're coming solo?"

Not if he could convince London to join him. The very idea had a grin teasing his lips. "Put me down for two."

***

LONDON HAD to be seeing things. Surely that was not Trey Van Horn strolling into the Vey Center with Antonio McGraff on his heels? The pair were instantly swallowed up by the kids in the room. Trey grinned at them as he slipped into the role of Santa, patting kids on the shoulder while doling out Growlers swag from a bag McGraff had draped over his shoulder. She was so mesmerized by the scene, London forgot all about the B-roll she should be shooting for social media.

"Well, isn't this a nice moment?" Bennie sounded as excited as the kids.

She was tempted to ask her boss to pinch her, but Trey continued to surprise her with his actions. Why should today be any different? She was relieved to see one of the interns filming the scene on his phone.

"He wasn't kidding when he said he gave everything one hundred percent of his effort," Bennie said.

Her nipples were suddenly hard just recalling the many ways his lips and tongue had given them 'one hundred percent effort' yesterday. Not that they had to work that hard. *Gah!* She could feel her cheeks flame at the memory of how fast she'd come. Trey must think she was some desperate virginal wallflower from one of Lucy's romance novels.

She wanted to blame the wine. But the truth was, Trey seemed to have a map to her body's erogenous zones and he wasn't afraid to use it. It made her angry that no other man bothered to take the time to perform their own due diligence. Life would be much easier if Trey wasn't the only one with this much power over her.

It wasn't lost on her that she had a similar power over him. She couldn't take it too seriously though. Because what man wouldn't respond to a woman who was constantly throwing herself at him? Or turning to putty the moment his lips met her skin? He was a male, after all. A guy who was suddenly aiming his panty melting smile her way.

London didn't have the patience for Trey Van Horn and his sexy wiles today. She'd purposely avoided the photo shoot this morning to rest her battle-weary senses from the havoc being in his orbit always caused. Besides, today's event wasn't about Trey and his football team. It was supposed to be Mooz-R-Ella the puppet promoting Gunther's string cheese.

She stormed over to where the kids were lined up waiting for their moment with Trey and his teammate. "Why are you hijacking my event?" she demanded. "I need them eating string cheese and playing with a cow puppet. Not footballs."

"Right. My bad." Trey grinned at the kids. "I'm pretty hungry for some cheese. Who else wants some?"

Twenty minutes later, the kids were all happily munching on Gunther's cheese. London was busy capturing as much video as she could only to find that her camera was constantly drawn to capturing Trey as he interacted with the youngsters. He was a natural, at one point even letting one of the girls paint his fingernails green and white for the Growlers. The video would make the perfect social media reel combatting his "robot" image. She ought to send it to his obnoxious agent.

"Remind me to leave McGraff home next time," he murmured when he wandered over to her side. "He's getting as bad as Kessler with the dares." A look of horror passed over his face when he glanced down at his hands. "This stuff comes off easily, right?"

She couldn't hold back her grin. It was amazing to see the playful, relaxed Trey she'd loved come back to life. "Nothing that a little nail polish remover won't cure."

"I don't suppose you have any?"

"Nope. I get my nails done at my friend's salon. You can pick some up at a drugstore."

His bottom lip curled into a sulk and London had to fight off the urge to kiss it away. She slammed her eyes shut.

"This was not part of your contract, Trey. Why are you here?"

London could feel his stare as it moved over her face, then lower. She flicked her lids open. His eyes were trained on her and the pout was gone. It had been replaced with a solemn expression.

"I wanted to see you. You left very abruptly yesterday." He stepped in front of her, blocking her with his body so that anyone watching wouldn't be able to make out what they were saying. "Things got a little out of hand."

That was an understatement.

A blush of embarrassment was heating her cheeks again. *Could this get any worse?* She aimed her gaze at his sculpted chest, not wanting him to see her humiliation.

"It was the wine," she lied, desperate to put an end to this conversation. "It makes me very…uninhibited, that's all. You didn't take advantage, if that's what you're worried about. I barely remember a thing."

A low growl rumbled from deep within his chest. His finger gently guided her chin up so their eyes met. She watched, mesmerized as his darkened with passion.

"Well, I remember every second. In fact, I haven't been able to stop thinking about it."

Oh my.

He stepped closer. "We need to talk about this, London. Because this—" he motioned between them "—is not going away. No matter how hard we try to ignore it."

"We'll just have to try harder," she whispered, hating how futile the words sounded. Hating that she couldn't seem to step away from him. Hating that he'd rekindled the desire she felt for him. Desire she'd believed to be long extinguished.

He slowly shook his head. "I don't want to try harder. And I don't think you do either, London. Have dinner with me. We need to hash this out."

Something that felt a lot like panic gripped her stomach. The last two times she'd been alone with Trey, they'd "hashed things out" via a lip-lock. She wasn't sure she could trust herself to be alone with him again.

She shook her head. "I can't. Besides, we decided we weren't going to go there anymore."

"No. As I keep pointing out, you decided that. Which begs the question, why not?"

Why not?

There were a million reasons "why not." Too bad she couldn't come up with a single one right now. Not while he was touching her. Not while his smoldering gaze was locked in on her. Not while she could still remember the feel of his lips pressed against her skin.

For the first time in the past two months, she was grateful for the sound of Seth Gunther's overbearing voice.

"Are you kidding me? Is that our favorite quarterback over there?"

Trey swore violently. London took a giant step back. Seth was already charging across the room, Bennie on his heels. She was grateful for the shelter of Trey's body when he turned to face

Seth. It protected her from preying eyes, allowing her to regain her composure. Seth and Bennie were so busy fawning over Trey, none of them noticed when she slipped from the room and out of the Vey Center.

WHY NOT?

Hours later, Trey's question continued to ricochet through London's head. He was right about the "thing" between them not going away. Lucky for her, she was moving to Chicago in a month. Distance would help the feelings to fade. After all, it had worked once before.

Except she wasn't as confident it would work again. Because now she knew for certain the man she'd fallen for all those years ago still existed beneath the polished image he'd created for the rest of the world. Her heart ached wondering why he continued to hide that guy from everyone but her. The rest of her body ached for very different reasons. She squirmed in her chair.

"Are you listening to a word I'm saying?" Lucy asked.

"Uh—"

London glanced around the busy nail salon. The place was filled with Lucy's family and friends, all drinking wine and gossiping at the monthly spa night. Beside her, Lucy was eyeing London curiously while her feet soaked in the whirlpool bath at the base of the chair. London was embarrassed she hadn't heard a word her friend had said.

"Sorry, Luce. I'm still in work mode." Technically not a lie. Trey was still considered a client.

"Mm. You're supposed to leave 'work mode' at the door, remember? That's the whole point of spa night."

"Or you can tell us what's troubling you," Lucy's mom suggested. "Perhaps we can help. Many hands make light work."

No way was she dishing about Trey. Lucy would kill her for

not confiding everything weeks ago. Not to mention there was something even bigger she'd been holding back from her best friend: her move to Chicago.

Guilt clogged her throat. The time never seemed right, though. Upsetting Lucy while she was pregnant didn't seem wise. At least that's the excuse London kept leaning on.

But her friend was going to find out eventually. London was going apartment hunting while she was in Chicago editing the commercials next week. Perhaps Mrs. An was right. With all her friends and family here to comfort Lucy, maybe the news wouldn't be too painful.

"Actually," she began. "There is something I've been meaning to share with you all."

A hush fell over the salon as everyone turned expectant looks her way. London sucked in a breath trying to summon up some courage when she was quite literally saved by the bell when the chimes above the door rang.

Heads swiveled at the sound.

"Holy snot," Lucy murmured.

London could think of several other choice words she wanted to utter, none of them as tame as Lucy's, because, of course, Trey would be the person interrupting spa night. He quickly scanned the salon, a relieved smile forming on his lips when his gaze landed on London.

"Can I help you?" Mrs. An inquired politely, as if a sex-on-a-stick athlete wandered through her doors every day.

Trey pulled his eyes from London to beam at Lucy's mom. He held up his fingers. "I'm looking for some nail polish remover."

"Oh, for crying out loud!" London yanked her feet from the warm foot bath and shoved them into her flip flops. She could feel everyone's eyes following her as the rubber soles slapped against the tile floor. "I told you to get some at the drugstore," she hissed.

"You didn't tell me there were so many options. Was I

supposed to choose the Acetone free? Or one with lanolin? Or MEK? Which, I'm pretty sure is unhealthy, just because they have to use an acronym for whatever odious chemicals are in the bottle."

She slammed her eyes shut and counted to ten. Unfortunately, he was still standing there when she forced her lids back open. She didn't appreciate the teasing gleam in his eyes one bit.

"Sit here. I'll help you." Angie, Lucy's aunt, indicated one of the empty manicure tables.

Not happening.

London wrapped her fingers around his wrist and tugged him toward the table. "I've got it," she told Angie.

Lucy's aunt winked at her before stepping away. The older woman said something in Vietnamese that had everyone in the room laughing.

Great. Just great.

"Sit," London commanded.

Trey smirked in triumph as he relaxed into the high-back chair. London rifled through the drawers, pulling out cotton balls and a squirt bottle of nail polish remover. She saturated the piece of cotton and reached for his hand.

Bad idea.

The sizzle at the contact raced up her arm. Angry at her unwanted response, she swiped at his fingernail roughly. Thankfully, the salon was bustling with conversation again.

"Why are you really here, Trey?" she murmured, keeping her head tilted down to focus on her task. And to avoid his knowing expression.

"Because we didn't finish our conversation earlier," he replied quietly.

She gritted her teeth. "There's nothing to finish. Your commitment to Gunther Cheese has been met."

"That's not what I meant, and you know it."

His frustrated tone compelled her to risk looking up at him.

The hungry expression she saw in his eyes made her breath catch. It took everything in her arsenal to remind her body that she couldn't trust him. Would he still want her had their paths not crossed? London doubted it. After all, he'd never given her a compelling reason for why he'd left her without a word in the first place.

"Been there. Done that. And we didn't work," she told him as much as herself. "At the risk of repeating myself, my career comes first now. There's no room for anything else."

She wiped his hands with a wet towel, rinsing away the remaining nail polish remover.

"Then we're on the same page," he said. "My career is always number one with me. But know this, London, you're the one person I'll always make time for."

Her heart stuttered at the sincerity in his words.

"Hear this, too. What's between us is like nothing I've felt before. The fact that you're afraid to be alone with me tells me it's making you just as crazy." He leaned forward. "If you want to explore whatever this is and where it might lead, I'm all in."

The seductive way he spoke the words had her skin tingling. Not to mention a few other places, too.

He held his hands up, palms out. "No more stalking you. The ball is in your court, now." He stood up. "The team picnic is on Sunday. I'll leave your name at the reception tent. No pressure. But if you want to see where this leads, that's where you'll find me."

Dropping a twenty-dollar bill on the table, he waved to Mrs. An and sauntered out of the salon.

CHAPTER TWENTY-ONE

"I KNEW IT!" Lucy squealed.

After Trey's impromptu visit to the nail salon, London had no choice but to loop her friend in on the situation. For the next two days, Lucy vacillated between sulking over being kept in the dark and bubbling with euphoria as she thumbed through bridal magazines, searching for the perfect maid of honor dress.

"You know second chance romances are my all-time favorites," Lucy gushed on Sunday morning. "But your second chance romance is so much better than the ones in my books!"

"For the hundredth time, there is no romance story here, second chance or otherwise," London insisted.

"Mmm-hmm," Lucy replied.

Despite the fact they were having this conversation by phone, London had no doubt her friend was wearing a self-satisfied smile. Lucy was a dyed-in-the-wool romantic. London, on the other hand, was pragmatic enough to know that a romance with Trey was not in the cards. He just wanted her for sex.

She flounced down on the sofa in her living room, letting her eyes drift to the framed photograph above her fireplace. The same photo Trey had hanging above his fireplace. Every time she glanced at it, she wondered if he was looking at it, too. The thought unnerved her.

"Why do you think he has one of my lake photographs in his house?" she asked Lucy.

Her friend sighed softly. "Did you ask him?"

"Yeah. He gave me some vague answer. Just like all his replies to any question I ask."

"Maybe you're not asking the right questions."

London sat up. "What's that supposed to mean?"

"It means that you've already made up your mind how a relationship with Trey will end before you even dip your toe in."

"Maybe because the man has a proven history in that department. It's in print, for crying out loud."

"Okay, yeah. But do we really believe everything an angry ex spouts off in a magazine?"

"Hello! He left me without a word."

"Yes, but let's not forget you were practically kids back then. People change."

"Oh, Trey changed, all right. Just not for the better."

Did she really believe that, though?

These past weeks, she'd gotten so many glimpses of the guy she once knew that she questioned if he actually was the arrogant robot who was lionized in the media. Or was he simply portraying himself as the man everyone wanted him to be? The old Trey would hate having to pretend to be something he's not.

At least the Trey she thought she knew.

Gah!

"Why did he have to insert himself back into my life? It was so much easier hating him from afar."

"Of course it was easier. You could control the spin on it."

"Meaning?"

Lucy sighed again. "Don't take this the wrong way, but you manage a lot of your life by compartmentalizing. You tend to steer clear of things that are chancy. Or anything that will open you up to even a smidge of pain. You've put your relationship with Trey in a neat little box, labeled it, and tucked it away. By keeping that box closed you're safe from any further heartache. That's not healthy, London."

"Wow."

"Hey! Look at how much you keep from me? And I'm your best friend, for freak's sake."

Guilty as charged.

With all the hullabaloo after Trey left the salon the other night, London hadn't had a chance to break the news about her impending move. She needed to come clean with Lucy. Except she couldn't very well rip off the Band-Aid over the phone. The announcement needed to be made face-to-face. She'd do it first thing tomorrow.

Unfortunately, Lucy wasn't done slinging arrows. "I'm sure you rationalize it by wanting to protect me. And I love you for that. I really do. But maybe deep down you keep yourself buttoned up so you won't have to deal with anything negative."

And that arrow hurt.

"I'm not saying all this to be cruel," Lucy continued. "The significant men in your life have let you down pretty hard. I get that. It's only natural to want to protect yourself from more heartache. But is closing yourself off entirely from potential love the answer?"

"Trey never said anything about love." She ignored the tightening in her chest brought on by that truth. "He just wants a booty call, Luce."

"So? When was the last time you had one of those?"

It's been too long to count, her girl parts screamed.

"Dude," Lucy said. "A person would have to be blind not to notice the sexual attraction between the two of you. It is *hawt.* Honestly, it was a wonder the smoke detectors didn't start screeching in the salon the other night given the vibes you guys were giving off. My mom had to turn on the AC just to cool everyone off."

London squirmed on the sofa recalling how quickly he'd made her come in the wine cellar. *With barely any effort*, her body reminded her.

Imagine what it would be like if you had all the time in the world and no fear of being interrupted?

Great, now her brain was weighing in.

Why not? he'd asked.

"Look, you do you. But at the very least, I think you should go to the picnic and make him explain himself. Get the answers you need. It's the only way to close the chapter of Trey Van Horn."

Lucy's suggestion made some sense. Once London moved to Chicago, she might not get the opportunity to confront Trey again. To get the truth she deserved.

"And if those answers involve the two of you getting naked? Even better," Lucy added with a giggle. "Who knows? He might be a total dud in bed. That's one way to jettison him from your fantasies."

"With my luck, I'd have to name my vibrator after him," she mumbled.

"Ohmigod, but wouldn't that be *sweeeet?*"

"Why not?" London heard herself saying.

Her girl parts were screaming along with Lucy. *Down girls.* She was going to the picnic to finally have the frank conversation that had been a long time coming. To get the answers she needed for closure. If getting answers meant getting naked, well, then at least she'd get him out of her system.

Her body let out another whoop.

Sex with Trey didn't have to mean anything, she rationalized. He'd made it very clear his career was his top priority. And so was hers. Besides, she'd be living in a different city in a few weeks. London didn't have to open up the box all the way. She was a mature, self-evolved woman. Her heart would be perfectly safe as long as she never trusted Trey Van Horn with it.

SHE WAS WEARING another one of those flowy sundresses. This one in lavender, setting off her flawless skin to mouth-watering perfection. Trey's junk was practically doing a touchdown dance at the thought of what London might be wearing beneath that dress.

Or not wearing.

From across the crowded tent covering the Growlers' practice field, he tracked her as she stopped at the opposite endzone to greet the caterer with a hug. The florist was next. She'd likely worked with both at some event here in town at one point. Hell, he wouldn't be surprised if they were clients. She and Bennie seemed to represent every mom-and-pop business in the city. Even the woman holding the reins to one of the ponies Mrs. C brought in for the kids leaned in for a hug when London passed.

Trey's chest swelled with unexpected pride. He may be the bigger celebrity in Milwaukee, but London Headley was a star in her own right. Her clients and contractors obviously trusted and adored her. While he would always carry the guilt from the part he unknowingly played in her abandoning film school, he found some solace watching how she'd reshaped her life and her career, successfully landing on her feet.

Mrs. C and her husband stopped London's forward progress at the fifty-yard line. The two women shared a laugh at something Mr. Ciaciura said. The Growlers' community relations director joined their circle and was bending London's ear when Trey felt the weight of someone's stare. He turned around to find Fletcher smirking at him.

"What?"

The kicker jutted his chin in London's direction. "Does her

being here mean you won't be such a dick to be around? Because you've been a bloody prickly bear the past few days."

It was true. Trey had been on pins and needles ever since leaving London at the nail salon. He'd been a jerk issuing that damn challenge to her. Acting like a cocky asshat wasn't exactly the best way to earn back her trust. He was going about this the wrong way. Thinking with the wrong head.

"Could go either way," he replied honestly.

Fletcher cocked a bushy eyebrow at him. "Meaning?"

Trey heaved a sigh. "Meaning I still don't know where I stand with her."

The bastard had the nerve to grin broadly. "It's about time a lass gave you a run for your money. You've wasted too much time on empty-headed socialites who agree to whatever you want as long as they get to parade along the red carpet by your side." He patted Trey on the shoulder. "You're a gamer, though, Van Horn. I've no doubt you'll win her over."

Buoyed by his friend's optimism, Trey headed in London's direction. As if she sensed him coming, she glanced his way. Her lips twitched with a shy smile. It was so sinful, Trey felt it all the way to his groin. He grinned back at her, surprised by the immense relief he felt that she'd shown up. She excused herself from the Ciaciuras and made her way toward him.

"There you are, Lover Boy!"

The sound of a familiar female voice had Trey freezing in his tracks, leaving him a sitting duck for Bree Moynihan. His former lover latched onto his arm tighter than a barnacle on his father's yacht. She curved into his body, her coconut scent overwhelming his nostrils. Of course she was dressed in a slinky dress that would have been more appropriate at a cocktail party than a picnic. Her hair and makeup were flawless, yet this close, Trey could see the red rims of her eyes and the tell-tale shadows beneath them.

"What the hell, Bree?"

"Surprise," she murmured. "Everyone is watching us, so I need you to play along."

Everyone is watching us? Trey's gaze darted around the tent. Sure enough, nearly every guest's eyes—not to mention several cell phone cameras—were aimed in their direction. Including a shocked blue pair.

Shit!

"I'm not playing along with anything, Bree," he growled, attempting to gracefully yank his arm free.

She untangled herself from his arm, but only so she could cradle his cheeks with both her hands. Her lips followed them in, taking his mouth by surprise. A few wolf whistles rang out among the crowd as Bree ate at his mouth. Trey cringed and jerked his head away before grabbing her by the wrist and marching her out of the tent.

Her ridiculous heels were tearing up the turf. Not that he cared. He just wanted the woman to go back to Palm Beach.

"What the actual hell, Bree?" he shouted when they reached the level ground of the parking lot.

"I know!" She pressed her hands to her face. "But I'm getting desperate. Idris only pays attention to me when he knows someone else wants me."

"Idris?"

She rolled her eyes. "My client from Qatar. You met him last month at the Polo Club."

Trey let a few choice words fly. "Client my ass. And you couldn't pick some other sucker to use to make this guy jealous?"

"I was in Chicago promoting the show. Your mother mentioned the picnic. Idris follows every athlete on social media. It was worth a shot." She shrugged.

Damn his mother to hell. No doubt she thought she was being coy trying to throw the two of them together.

"Well, there's a flaw in your plan, Bree. I don't want you!"

If his angry words hurt her, she didn't show it. "Of course,

CHAPTER TWENTY-TWO

"I CANNOT BELIEVE I fell for his bullshit a second time," London chastised herself as she pulled a quart of ice cream from her freezer. Not bothering with a bowl, she grabbed a spoon from the drawer and dug into the chocolate and peanut butter concoction.

"Nope. It's gonna take a lot more to dull this pain."

She took a can of whipped cream from the fridge and sprayed a shot directly into her mouth.

"That's a start," she mumbled around the food before heading over to the wine rack to explore her options. Memories of her embarrassing moment in the wine cellar flashed through her mind. She slapped a hand onto the quartz countertop. "Oh my God, the jerk has even ruined wine for me."

A loud pounding on her door made her jump.

"London. Open up. It's me."

Her anger ratcheted up a notch at the sound of Trey's voice.

"Are you even serious right now?!" she shouted.

How had he gotten through the building's front door? She gritted her teeth. He'd likely conned some star-struck resident the way he'd been conning her.

"London, please. We need to talk."

Damn right they needed to talk. Hadn't that been why she went to the stupid picnic in the first place? To get answers. To find closure. Instead, she'd fallen for his lines all over again. Lucy's romantic mumbo jumbo had somehow slipped beneath her defenses, falsely luring her to believe that maybe the Trey she'd fallen in love with all those years ago still wanted her. Hell, had he even wanted her back then?

"Come on, London. I'm not leaving."

Oh, he was leaving, all right. Just not before she got her pound of flesh. She doubted she'd believe a word that came out of his mouth. But after today, she could reseal the box she'd shoved Trey Van Horn into and kick the stupid thing to the curb.

She stormed to the door, threw back the deadbolts and yanked it open. Not bothering to even grace him with a look, much less a hello, she spun around and stomped back into the kitchen. The carton of Ben and Jerry's was still on the counter calling her name. Leaning a hip against the island, she scooped out a spoonful and shoveled it into her mouth.

Trey appeared at the other end of her kitchen, his movements hesitant and his expression guarded. She ignored him while she gulped down more ice cream.

"I can explain," he said after a painful moment passed.

London's laugh sounded more hysterical than she would have liked. "Really? Because that would be a first for you. You've danced around explaining yourself for over a decade now."

He actually looked chagrined.

Good.

"I was referring to earlier."

"Oh, well, then." She waved her spoon. "By all means, explain away."

He glanced up at the ceiling before exhaling heavily. "I didn't invite Bree to the picnic. She just showed up."

London scoffed at the ridiculous excuse.

"I'm supposed to believe that Bree Moynihan of "Oceanfront Dreams" just *showed up* in Milwaukee, Wisconsin, where there's not an oceanfront in sight? Not only that, but she wandered into an invitation-only picnic that you were coincidentally attending? Ha! Good to know you think I'm a fool."

"I know how it sounds. And I would never take you for a fool, London. She and my mom are friends." He pinched the bridge of his nose. "Bree and I were an item very briefly several years ago. My mom is still trying to throw us together."

That was *not* jealousy churning in her belly. *It's just the damn ice cream.*

"Well, I seriously doubt your mom has to push too hard. There were photos of you and Bree together earlier this summer. You didn't look like it was a trial to have her *draped all over you.*"

His eyes narrowed. *Dammit.* Now he knew she stalked him. She'd shown her hand too quickly.

"That's not how it was. She was using me to make her polo player boyfriend jealous. That's all. They both like to play mind games with each other for some reason. I was simply a handy prop."

The ice cream was giving her a headache. Or maybe it was this conversation. She found it ironic that a woman as wealthy, beautiful, and famous as Bree Moynihan needed to resort to "mind games" to keep a man. Or maybe it was just sad. She dropped her spoon onto the counter.

"I'm not buying it. Beside the fact there wasn't a single polo player in attendance, the woman is a stick figure. She wouldn't have been kissing you if you didn't want it."

The words hurt to even think, much less speak.

"Dammit! The only person I wanted to kiss today is you! You're the only woman I've dreamed about kissing for—" His voice trailed off and he dropped his chin.

Her breath hung up at the back of her throat. She hated how desperately she wanted him to finish his sentence.

"I'm not good at this, London. At relationships." The laugh he let out lacked any humor. "But you already know that. If you didn't know it firsthand, you could read about it. The fact is, I didn't really have the best role models. Another fact you've seen for yourself."

The ice cream began to churn deep in her belly. When had he moved across the room?

"The only time I've ever felt comfortable letting someone in was that summer with you," he said softly. "The feelings I had for you then haven't diminished one iota. If anything, they've gotten more intense. And I don't want to throw this away again. Not without exploring where it takes us."

He stepped in closer. His warm breath fanned her cheek. She tamped down on the shiver that threatened.

"I know you feel it, too," he whispered.

She swept her eyes away, too afraid of revealing her feelings beneath his hypnotic gaze. Because she did feel it.

Why not? It doesn't have to be about anything more than a booty call. A fun way to get him out of your system.

God help her, Lucy had taken over her subconscious.

He lifted his hand toward her face. She jerked away.

"You have whipped cream—" He gestured to her cheek.

Mother of God. All this time she'd been trying to appear cool and collected while she'd looked like a six-year-old who'd just snuck into the cookie jar. She hastily swiped at her face.

He shook his head. "Not there."

Her knees threatened to buckle when he wrapped his fingers around her wrist, guiding her fingertips to a glob of whipped cream stuck to her cheek. Their gazes locked. He didn't relinquish his hold, maneuvering her hand to scrape off the remnants of her comfort food binge. She watched, mesmerized, as he slowly steered her fingers toward his mouth where he took the whipped cream laden fingers between his lips and sucked.

She drew in a swift breath at the sensation. It was impossible to tear her gaze away from his, watching raptly as he tenderly sucked and kissed each of her fingers. Each slow flick of his tongue had his eyes darkening with arousal. It was the most erotic thing a man had ever done to her. So provocative, her body began to tremble with need. Heat coursed through her as her breathing grew more fractured.

Her eyes never leaving his, she tugged her hand away and grabbed the whipped cream. She reveled in the way his nostrils flared when she shook the can and proceeded to spray a healthy glob just above the V of her dress. She'd never done anything so spontaneous and sexy like that before. His low groan told her it hadn't been a dumb move. He spanned her waist with his large hands and lifted her up onto the island. The movement caused the whipped cream to dribble between her breasts.

Trey shot her a wicked smile before taking his sweet time sliding his palms up her legs. Her hips twitched with joy when he rolled her dress up to her waist and stepped between her thighs. He dropped his eyes to the lacy thong she wore.

"Mm," he said as he reverently skimmed his thumbs along the edges of the panty.

Her trembling was growing out of control. The whipped cream was sliding farther south, down toward her navel.

"Trey, I'm wet and sticky."

His chin shot up. The look in his eyes was positively diabolical now. She groaned at her word choice. Arching an eyebrow, she gestured in the vicinity of her chest. He leaned over, carefully positioning her so her back was pressed against the quartz.

"Allow me to take care of all the places you're wet and sticky," he teased.

And then his tongue was on her skin, setting her on fire as he lapped up what remained of the whipped cream. He tugged at the spaghetti straps of her dress. She helped, eagerly working her arms free. He pushed the material down around her waist while he continued to lick at the messy cream flowing toward her navel.

Every stroke of his tongue had her writhing with need. She clawed at his shoulders, wanting to feel his skin beneath her hands. He chuckled against her belly.

"When I'm done with you," he murmured along her skin.

He blew on her belly button and her insides contracted. His fingers found their way beneath her back where he made quick work of her bra. It was on the floor before she even knew what was happening. She watched as he stared down at her, an awestruck expression on his face.

Embarrassed at being laid out on her kitchen island like a buffet, London tried to sit up.

Except Trey was having none of that. He pinned her back down with his gaze. "Don't," he commanded. His perusal of her body was agonizingly slow. "You are even more beautiful than I remembered."

"You've seen it all before."

His eyes snapped back up to collide with hers. They were darker than she'd ever seen them. "Not all of you."

He slid his hands down her sides, easing her hips up so he could slip her dress off and toss it over his shoulder. It landed on her tea kettle. London barely noticed. She was too busy watching Trey licking his lips at the sight of her.

"Even more gorgeous than I dreamed."

She wanted to ponder his comment further, because, really, *he'd been dreaming about me?* Unfortunately, pondering anything was impossible once he bent at the waist and began dragging his thumbs along the inside of her thighs. Her stomach grew tight at his touch. She was so close to the edge, and she didn't want to embarrass herself again. Not when she wanted him inside her when she found her release.

"Trey," she begged, tugging at his hair to get his attention. "I need you. I don't want it this way."

He aimed another one of his take-no-prison-looks at her. "Hush, woman. You've never had it my way." The next second, he was shoving her thong aside and sliding his tongue inside her.

He was correct. She'd never had it his way. The man was just as talented with his tongue as he was with his million-dollar hands. Her hips arched of their own volition, pulsing against him as the pleasure built. Her head flailed from side to side on the countertop, the cool of the quartz doing nothing to calm the fire spreading over her skin. He stroked and sucked with more force than he had used with her fingers, pulling her to the brink once, then again before backing off with a satisfied growl.

"Don't you dare," she nearly screamed when he left her hanging a third time.

It sounded like he said "anything for you" before his mouth was on her again, this time taking her even higher, until her body was strung so tight, she thought she might snap into a million pieces. Instead, a climax washed over her, so fierce it brought with it a million shining stars. She wasn't sure but she thought she heard someone chanting his name as though he were a deity.

SOMETHING STIRRED within Trey's chest as he stared down at London's limp, sated body. She was stunning with her skin flushed from head to toe and a contented smile curving her lips. But she was also probably quite literally freezing her ass off lying on the slab of quartz.

He slipped his hands beneath her shoulders and lifted her to his chest. A murmur of appreciation escaped from her lips when he began rubbing her chilled back with his hands. He buried his face into her neck breathing her in, while she slowly began to return to the here and now.

She shifted forward, pressing her body more solidly against his. He winced, letting out a groan as he forced himself to step back. London brushed her hair back from her face, her eyes still glassy but quickly becoming alert. And annoyed.

"Yeah, um, about that." He winced. "My plan was to go back to my house. I didn't exactly come here prepared."

She rolled her eyes at him before sliding off the counter and strutting into the living room. Her movements had Trey struggling to breathe normally. Damn, the woman had a very fine ass. His body grew even tighter thinking of all the things it wanted to do to that heart-shaped natural wonder.

When she bent over to pull something out of a cabinet, black spots blurred his vision, and he was pretty sure he might expire where he was standing if he didn't have her in the next thirty seconds. She stood and tossed a box at him. He almost embarrassed himself by fumbling it, but thankfully his reflexes were still in the game. Gripping the economy box of magnum XL condoms—the ones labeled "ribbed for her pleasure"—an ugly thought popped into his head.

"Please tell me these are not Bergeron's."

Shit. He said it out loud.

London charged across the room, looking spectacular dressed in nothing but a lacy purple thong. Except for the squinty-eyed expression she was aiming his way. She stopped in front of him and yanked the box away in annoyance.

"I told you there is nothing going on between us."

He knew that. He was a first-class jerk for even mentioning it.

"Yeah." He dragged his fingers through his hair to keep from touching her. She looked angry enough to snap them in half. "I'm an ass. Mostly because I can't stand the idea of another man touching you. I know I have no right, though. But it is what it is. Please don't hold it against me."

Her face softened instantly. She dug her fingers into his shirt and pulled their bodies closer. "They were Lucy's idea of a birthday joke."

He pressed a kiss to the top of her head. "She's a keeper, your friend Lucy."

She nodded, then lifted her face to his. "Are we going to do this or what?"

Hell, yeah!

His body nearly wept with relief. He grabbed the box back and tore it open. Pulling out a sleeve of the condoms, he dangled them in front of her wide eyes. "We are going to do this until neither one of us can move."

The gorgeous blush was back on her body. She draped her arms around his neck. He dug his fingers into her sweet ass and lifted her against him. When she wrapped her legs around his waist it took every ounce of restraint he possessed not to take her against the nearest wall.

"Down the hall," she demanded against his neck, sounding as edgy as he felt.

Her bedroom was bathed in summer sunlight thanks to the wall of windows looking out over the city. A thin layer of sheer curtains provided the privacy they'd need for all the things he wanted to do with her. The room was decorated in muted shades of blues and greens, matching the stunning photograph of Lake Geneva in winter that was mounted above the queen-sized bed. The bedroom was exactly what he'd expect of London, cool and relaxing.

He gently laid her onto the center of the fluffy comforter, tossing the sleeve of condoms down beside her. She eased herself up onto her elbows and arched an eyebrow at him.

"Shirt. Off."

Her bossiness had his junk growing painfully tight. Without hesitating, he reached a hand behind his neck and tugged his polo over his head. Her pupils dilated when he dropped the shirt to the floor.

She purred. "Wow. Those magazine covers were definitely not photoshopped."

The pride he felt at her approval was ridiculous. "You've seen it before," he mocked her.

"Not all of you." London shot him a coy look, echoing his words from earlier.

She crawled up onto her knees and toddled to the edge of the bed. It was a struggle not to reach for her, but her assertiveness was really turning him on, and he didn't want to stifle it. He sucked in a tight breath when her fingers made contact with his zipper. A playful smile twitched at her lips as if she just realized the immense power she wielded over him.

Trey couldn't remember ever having a woman undress him before. Which wasn't saying much because he wasn't sure he could recall his phone number right about now. But he knew it was arousing as hell and he'd gladly ignore the parts of him screaming for release and let her undress him all day long if she wanted to. She sunk her teeth into her bottom lip while taking her sweet time lowering the zipper, her curious fingers stoking him all the way down. He groaned with pleasure at the contact.

The sound spurred her on. Her palms skimmed his ass right before she shoved his pants down over his hips. He stepped out of them and toed off his shoes in one furious motion before stripping off his socks. London rocked back onto her heels. Trey stepped forward against the mattress.

"Mm." London leaned forward and flicked her tongue against one of his nipples. At the same time, she reached down and cupped his balls.

Something inside him snapped. A sound escaped his chest that sounded more like a feral animal than civilized human, but he didn't care any longer. He had to have her. Now.

Before she could even react, he had her flipped on her back and pressed beneath him on the mattress. He ripped the flimsy thong from between her legs and tossed it away. Not that she seemed to mind. Her hands and mouth were all over him, her teeth sinking into his shoulder when he slipped a finger inside her.

"Jesus," he groaned.

She was so hot and wet his pulse began to pound with agonizing need. Her hips jumped when he slid another finger into her.

"Trey," she cried.

"I know."

He blindly patted the bed for the condoms just as London whacked him on the thigh with them. Using his teeth, he tore back the foil. She immediately snatched the condom from his hands.

"Roll over."

His cock jumped at her command. He did as she asked, but not before leaning down and sucking on a nipple until she cried out, just to let her know two could play at this game. Tucking an arm behind his head, he watched her straddle his thighs. *Damn,* she was a sexy hot mess. Red splotches were blossoming where his teeth had left a trail of love bites. Her skin was dewy with sweat from their foreplay. She pushed her hair from her face and grinned slyly with kiss-swollen lips. He let out another growl at the sensual torture she inflicted rolling the condom over him.

It was his turn to make demands. "Come here."

With annoying slowness, she crawled up his body, dragging her tongue over his navel and up to his chest. Jesus, she could be a porn star with what she was doing to him. Reaching between them, she wrapped her fingers around his rock hard erection and rose up on her knees. Her eyes drifted shut as she seductively lowered herself over him. Her teeth found her bottom lip right before she took him fully inside her. A puff of a sigh whispered from her throat when she sank home.

"Christ," Trey gasped.

She was so tight he was afraid things would be over before they even got started.

"Yeah," London whispered right before she bent forward and touched her nose to his. "You feel so unbelievably good."

Trey took her face between his palms and guided her lips down for a kiss. He meant for it to be tender, but the instant he tasted her, things got wild. Tongues and teeth rammed against one another. One of them moaned frantically. *Probably him.* His fingers slid from her face to tangle in her hair. She nipped at his lip while her fingers fanned out on his pecs. When she rocked her hips against him, he was a goner.

His pelvis rose up to meet hers, thrusting into her at a punishing pace. She was up to the challenge, however, easily meeting his rhythm. Her hair formed a curtain around their heads and Trey couldn't resist stealing another drugging kiss. Her breathing was growing more erratic at the same time as his body was becoming impossibly tighter. Gripping her ass, he flipped them over.

Once beneath him, she hitched her legs higher on his back. Her nails dug into his shoulders while he pumped into her again and again. He groaned with pleasure when her muscles began to contract around him. Her response to his body was so unbelievably perfect. It was as if she was built just for him.

"Come for me," he begged her.

She sank her teeth into his biceps. He coaxed her on with another hard thrust and she went flying, her velvety heat wrapping around him and pulling him over the edge right behind her.

CHAPTER TWENTY-THREE

London wasn't a post coitus cuddler. *Go figure.* Although Trey gave her extra points for that. He hated the clingy pillow talk most women seemed to need. The dull pain in his chest was *not* because, for the first time, he wanted to lay around tracing lazy circles on her body while they talked about . . . whatever it was couples were supposed to talk about after sex.

When he emerged from the bathroom after disposing of the condom, the bed was empty. The sound of running water came from the kitchen. He pulled on his boxer briefs and went to look for her.

Hard to believe, but the woman in the kitchen was even sexier than the one he'd left in the bed. She'd pulled her hair up into a messy bun and donned a peach-colored silk robe that brushed her bare feet. She appeared to be cleaning her kitchen. Definitely a first for him.

He stepped up behind her and wrapped his arms around her waist. "Having fun?"

She wiped a sponge over the counter. "I remembered that I left the ice cream out. It all melted."

The dejection in her voice had his heart nearly melting too.

He'd overheard enough locker room chatter to know to never get between a woman and her ice cream.

"I can go out and get you some more," he offered. Not that he was ready to leave her.

She leaned her back against his chest, dropping her head back to brush a kiss along his jaw. "You're sweet, but that's not necessary. I just wanted to clean it up before it got too gross."

The feel of her silk-covered ass was making him hard again. He pressed an open-mouthed kiss to her neck.

"Mm." She slipped from his embrace and padded over to the refrigerator. Grabbing two glasses from a cabinet, she filled one with water before handing it to him. He took it and pounded back its contents before she'd even finished filling hers. Propping her back against the stainless steel, she eyed him over the rim of the glass.

"What happens now?" she asked softly.

His body shouted ideas to his brain. None of them suitable to be repeated. His brain warned him to tread carefully.

"Whatever you want to happen," he replied. "I told you before, you're in charge here. I'll do whatever makes you happy."

She blinked a few times.

A lick of panic raced up his spine. Was that not the right answer? Trey never had to be careful with his words around a woman before. But he couldn't mess this up a second time. His breath began to flow again when a slow smile formed on her lips. She placed her glass onto the island and walked close enough that her body heat warmed his bare chest.

"By my count, you've made me happy twice already today."

"Twice is for amateurs." He tugged on the tie to her robe until her body was flush with his. "You're now in the hands of a professional, sweetheart. The sky's the limit."

He snaked a hand inside her robe to palm her breast, eliciting a lusty sigh. She pressed her lips to his sternum before licking her way to his jaw. Their mouths met in a kiss so feverish, it was as if they'd been apart for years and not minutes. The need Trey felt for London was too overwhelming to contemplate. He didn't want to consider that he may never have enough of her to be satisfied.

Pushing the thought aside, he used his hands and his mouth to work London into a writhing ball of lust. Somehow, they ended up in her living room where he bent her over the sofa. He plowed into her gorgeous ass while she screamed with encouragement. The skill and finesse he'd bragged about minutes earlier was long gone, stripped away by her wanton response to him.

With any other woman, he'd be able to hold on until she reached her climax first. But whatever this thing was with London it had short-circuited him. He was in high school the last time he'd left a woman behind. His climax lurking, he managed to tuck a finger between them, flicking wildly at the spot he knew now would set her free. She came in a frenzied rush, pulling him into ecstasy right along with her.

They stayed like that for several long moments, both of them trying to catch their breath, his bare chest pressed against her bare back. When she made a noise beneath him, he hurriedly stood to give her space. He headed to the kitchen to toss the condom and wash his hands. She was tying her robe again when she followed him in.

"I owe Lucy season tickets for her very useful birthday gift," he joked.

"I suppose the Growlers test you boys for all kinds of things that would be awkward if the media got wind of it."

"That and I don't want to have some woman show up with a surprise I want no part of nine months later."

She froze with her water glass at her lips. He didn't recognize the callousness of his words until they had left his mouth.

"Jesus, London. I'm sorry. I didn't mean—I. . ."

She held up a hand. "Don't apologize. At least you are thinking ahead." She hurried from the kitchen.

Shit.

He stood there for a long moment, feeling stupid in his nakedness and his thoughtlessness, cursing himself for hurting her. London's father hadn't bothered with preventing her creation. A mistake Trey for one was profoundly grateful for. That didn't mean he didn't want to kill the bastard. He scoured the floor for his underwear, yanking them on before he went groveling to London.

She was seated on the sofa, staring out the window at the partial view of Lake Michigan. He brushed his fingers over her shoulder, relieved when she didn't flinch or swat his hand away. Circling in front of the sofa, he cautiously sat down beside her. She lifted his arm and draped it over her shoulders.

"Please don't apologize or look at me with that pitying look."

His gut clenched with even more remorse.

"My life situation is what it is. It worked out the way it was supposed to."

He wrapped his other arm around her and pulled her back against his chest. "He doesn't know what he missed out on."

She scoffed. "Actually, he does."

Trey leaned in and brushed a kiss along her cheek. "You don't know that."

Sighing, she settled her body more comfortably against his. "Yeah, I do. That summer—"

He felt her swallow roughly.

"Um, the summer when we met, things were a bit crazy. First there was the whole situation of you ghosting me."

The guilt he was already feeling went from painful gnawing to a python squeezing his chest.

"Then there was the ridiculousness with my mom eloping with a man she barely knew. She and Jay were so hung up on each other, my mom barely paid attention to me."

Beneath his breath, Trey cursed his father.

"I was feeling really confused and lonely. I was so angry with my mom, I began to doubt all the things she ever told me, you know? I thought maybe my dad did want to know me. So, I stole her buddy pass and hopped on a plane to Connecticut."

He had a bad feeling about where this story was headed.

"I wasn't foolish enough to just show up on his doorstep. Before I left, I reached out by email. I was so excited when he sent a car to pick me up at the airport. We met at his country club." She tilted her head back to smile at him. "They do country clubbing a lot differently than we do in Lake Geneva. It was all I could do to keep my eyes from popping out of my head at the opulence of everything. You grew up with that. But for a girl from small town USA, it was pretty mind blowing."

"Mm." He brushed a loose strand of hair back from her cheek.

"My amazement quickly turned to anger when I realized what I'd missed out on all my life. And then he showed up at the table and . . . wow. I could easily see how my mom was duped by him. He's very handsome."

She patted his thigh.

"Not as sexy as you, though."

Her teasing made his chest ache even more.

"He was very formal and proper. No hugging his long-lost daughter when a handshake would do. He knew all about my life. Even that I was headed to LA. Can you imagine? I was crushed that my mom *hadn't* lied to me. Then he started in about child support. He assumed I was there to ask that he keep sending it even though I was eighteen."

The rat bastard. Trey wanted to demand the asshole's name and address.

"He gave me this eloquent lecture about how I needed to learn to forge my own way in life. Ha! As if my mom hadn't been doing that for years. He said I couldn't expect everything to be handed to me. The irony of it left me speechless. He rambled on about how teaching his kids to make their way in the world was the greatest gift he could give them."

She sucked in a shallow breath.

"I was shocked that he had other children. My mom had never mentioned that part before. He and his wife have a son and twin girls. At the time, the boy was ten and the girls were seven. He proudly pulled out his phone and showed me their pictures. The twins have hair my color. I asked if they knew about me." She chuckled. "You should have seen the look on his face. They were too young, he said. They wouldn't understand." Her voice seemed to grow smaller. "I'd never felt more like a mistake than I did at that moment. And unwanted. His three kids had each other. But I had no one."

Trey growled. How dare that pompous dipshit make London feel as though she wasn't good enough. Except, hadn't he done the same thing when he left her at the boathouse with no explanation? *Jesus.* No wonder she'd pivoted and stayed in Wisconsin. The men she thought wanted her not only broke her heart, but her spirit, too.

Now he was the one feeling small.

She patted his thigh again.

"Down boy. I got over it pretty quickly. Mom and I had a huge argument when I got home, but we worked it all out. I really did try to give Jay a chance. He and Pops have always treated me like family even after the divorce. Then my mom met Chuck. And Kyle came along and there went my desire to be a big sister." She laughed. "Just kidding. I wouldn't trade Kyle for anything. He's the best. My other half-siblings are probably spoiled rotten. Who needs them? Or my jerkoff sperm donor. I've got a really great family. And some amazing friends in Bennie and Lucy."

And me, he wanted to shout. *You've got me!*

He kept his mouth shut, though. Did he even deserve her? London certainly deserved the fairy tale. Not him. Yet, the idea of walking away from her again scared the shit out of him. Especially after the things they'd just done. Unbelievable as it was, his thirst for her wasn't close to being quenched.

"I need to shower," she announced.

"Mm." He tightened his hold around her. "I like that idea. I've got a very roomy walk-in shower at my house. We can head over there, enjoy the multiple shower heads and a few other perks I can provide. Afterward, I'll order some dinner. I'll even let you eat in bed if you want."

She spun around in his arms, pushing him down flat on the sofa. "That sounds ah-mazing. But as much as I don't want to leave this—" she trailed her fingers and her lips along his chest "—I have to head to Chicago shortly."

Wait, what?

"Chicago? What's in Chicago?"

"The editing bay for one. And the voiceover actor for another." She grazed her teeth along his jaw. "I have to package up your commercials, remember?"

"They don't have edit bays here?" The question sounded petulant even to his own ears.

London stacked her hands on his chest and laid her chin on top. "They do, but we'd have to rent one. One of the reasons we collaborated with Nolan and Hemphill is because they do everything in-house. They manage the crew, their brokers buy the media spots, and the production is all done under one roof. For one flat fee. This is Westbrook's first big national campaign. We didn't have the connections to pull it off on our own."

He tucked that pesky stray piece of hair behind her ear. "You would have figured it out. You're a genius where that's concerned."

"But you're not biased," she teased. "I could have done it all except brokering for the media spots. That's outside my field of expertise."

Trey sighed. "You have to leave before dinner?"

"Yep. If I wait too late, all the other out-of-town travelers get the good rooms, leaving me with one by the elevator or the dumpsters. I learned pretty quickly the early bird gets the best choice."

He had a better idea. "Or, you could stay at Pops' condo. It's right downtown."

"I know where it is. Olivia used to have a place in the same building. She invited Kyle and me to stay there a few times."

"Well, there you go. I happen to know it's empty right now. Pops and Olivia are extending their honeymoon at Lake Como another week."

She smiled wistfully. "They're so sweet together."

He snorted. "Give it time. Pops will mess it up. If there's one thing the Van Horns are good at, it's screwing up relationships."

Something shifted in her expression. "Good to know."

"Wanna know the best part about staying at Pops'?"

She arched an eyebrow in question.

"I can be there every night to keep you company."

Her brow crinkled. "It's a ninety-mile drive. Don't you have to practice your football moves every day?"

"Ah, but it's only forty minutes by private jet, door-to-door." He nuzzled her neck. "Besides, the season doesn't start for another two weeks. And I've got my football moves down pat. I'd rather work on my other moves. With you."

"I don't know. I think I'm going to need to see another demonstration of those moves before I agree."

She slipped off the sofa and held out her hand to him. Trey took it eagerly, ignoring the overwhelming feeling to never let go.

CHAPTER TWENTY-FOUR

"I CAN'T BELIEVE he's flying back and forth to Chicago every day. Ohmigosh, that is *sooo* romantic." Lucy gushed into the phone.

London weaved her way around a crowd of people taking photos in front of Chicago's famous bean sculpture. The upcoming Labor Day weekend brought with it an influx of tourists taking advantage of the final days to enjoy the city in all its summer splendor.

"There's nothing romantic about it," she reminded her friend for the umpteenth time. "It's just a long-distance booty call. That's all."

"For crying out loud! Will you stop selling yourself short, London," Lucy insisted. "Trey Van Horn is a sexy as sin, rich as crap professional athlete. He doesn't have to schlep ninety miles for a booty call."

"Gee, thanks. I think." She turned onto Columbus Drive, headed for her office. Trey was right, Pops' condo was very convenient to the Nolan and Hemphill offices. The nearly fifteen-minute walk would be brutal during wintertime, but London was enjoying it this week.

Not as much as she'd enjoyed the evenings, however. She

ducked her head to hide her blush from the strangers milling around her. True to his word, Trey had practiced *all his moves* on her, well into the wee hours last night—and the three nights before. The man's stamina knew no bounds. She could attest that he was going into the season in peak condition.

"Please don't make more of this than what it is, Luce."

Especially when I don't even know what it is.

Her friend sighed. "Okay, I hear you. But I'm not going to stop being happy for you. It's about time a man put you first. You deserve this."

London nearly lost her balance. "No one said anything about him putting me first, Lucy." She hated the punch to the gut brought on by the reminder that no man had ever done that. Certainly not her father or one single boyfriend. Especially not Trey.

Even now, when they were tearing up the sheets every moment they were together, he'd made it abundantly clear not to count on any commitment. In his own words, the Van Horn men sucked at relationships. Keeping that foremost in her mind, London locked her heart into one of those neat little boxes Lucy accused her of keeping. Meanwhile, she'd enjoy what he was offering.

"By the end of next week, he'll be so micro-focused on football he won't even remember my name."

"Oh, don't count on it. I'm pretty sure he still needs a way to blow off steam during the season," Lucy lowered her voice. "I read this sports romance book once where the dude couldn't pitch unless he had sex before the game. He was convinced it increased his testosterone levels. Given Trey's obsession with his performance, my money says he'll be interested in generating as much testosterone as he can get before hitting the field every week."

"See. You've made my point. I'm simply a booty call."

"Absolutely not. Booty call sounds too slutty. You guys are

more like friends with benefits. Two people bent on avoiding any kind of commitment who enjoy each other's company. Both in and out of the bedroom," she finished with a giggle.

London considered her friend's words. Lucy was right. Friends with benefits didn't sound as risqué. *Or limited.* And she and Trey were friends of a sort, weren't they? His admission the other day that she was the only person he could be "himself" with had touched her deeply. She felt freer with him, too. More relaxed, yet also more adventuresome. At least more daring than she'd been with any other man.

She wasn't ready to give that up. Friends with benefits would work. After all, they wouldn't be living in the same city in another month. London was putting a deposit on a cute place up by Lincoln Park at lunch today. Which reminded her…

"Luce, why don't we get breakfast this weekend?" She waved to the security guard monitoring the turnstile in the lobby of her new office building. "Trey is headed to Lake Geneva after practice tomorrow. He's got stuff to do for Luke Kessler's bachelor party Saturday night. Everyone at Nolan and Hemphill is working remotely to get a head start on the long weekend. I'm planning to head back to Milwaukee and check on a few clients, so I'll be around all weekend. We can go first thing Saturday, before the liquor store opens."

"Oh, I would love that, but I won't be in town. That's the reason I called. Mike surprised me with a babymoon! He rented a friend's place in Door County for the weekend."

"That's awesome, Luce. I told you Mike was perfect for you."

"He is, isn't he? We need some time alone. And my OB called Mike and told him he was being ridiculous with his hands-off policy. You won't be the only one enjoying some sexy times, girlfriend."

London couldn't help but laugh. It was worth putting off the conversation they needed to have so Lucy and Mike could enjoy some serious couple time before the baby arrived and made them a threesome. And who knew? Perhaps Lucy would return relaxed enough that she wouldn't have a meltdown when she heard the big news.

TREY WHISTLED a Harry Styles tune as he pulled on his street clothes after practice. He looked up to find the rest of his teammates' attention focused on him.

"What?"

The team's punter, Kane Palmer, shot him a foolish grin. "We've just never heard anything so sweet come from our QB One's lips. You usually use them for growling and ripping someone a new one. Who knew you had other talents."

His teammates laughed.

"Yeah," The team's big center chimed in. "You flying to Chicago every night for *music lessons*, Captain?" He turned and winked at the rest of the guys.

Guffaws and wolf whistles filled the room.

"Jesus," Trey murmured as he chucked his practice jersey at the laundry basket in the center of the aisle. "Is nothing private?"

Beside him, Fletcher chuckled. "Social media is having a field day with the rumors that you are hooking up with Bree Moynihan."

"Are you kidding me?" He glared at his friend.

Trey didn't bother with social media. He paid his agent to handle all of that. Collin should have put a stop to those rumors immediately. Unless it was Bree who was feeding fake news to the beast.

"Don't give me the stink eye. I'm not their source." The kicker gestured at Trey's shoulder. "But those love bites you keep arriving with every day only add fuel to the fire."

Trey swore beneath his breath as he tugged on a T-shirt to cover up the keepsakes from last night. Or maybe they were from the night before. He had no idea. What he did know was that every fantasy he'd ever had about London had been far exceeded by reality.

Just thinking about her passionate response to him stole his breath. Even better, she wasn't one of those needy or demanding women. There was no artifice with London, and it made their relationship so much more relaxed. Easy, even. She genuinely seemed content to take things day by day.

Like him, her career was important. He continued to be impressed by how hard she worked. How devoted she was to her clients. Even though he hadn't arrived until after seven every night this week, she'd still be on the phone chatting, smoothing ruffled feathers and making everyone feel as if they were the most important person in her life.

It was a chore to quiet the voice in his head demanding *he* be the most important person in London's life. Especially since that voice grew louder and more insistent whenever he was with her. Trey shook the feeling off. They needed to keep things status quo. Especially with the season kicking off next week.

But that didn't mean they couldn't enjoy their time together whenever they could. Tonight, he was going to surprise her by arriving early. He had big plans for them. Starting with dinner and a dessert that involved a can of whipped cream.

"Jay-sus," Fletcher said. "You might want to warn a guy before you break out that grin. No one here is used to seeing that, either."

Trey flipped him the bird.

Fletcher laughed. "I was going to extort some cash from you for my mathletes by promising not to let it leak who you're really spending your nights with, but it's nice to see you working your facial muscles for something more than a smirk."

"I know," Luke Kessler added, joining them. "I don't think I've seen you this loose, like, ever. I hope this means you're not going to be a party pooper this weekend."

"I'm hosting the damn thing. Isn't that enough?"

Kessler clapped him on the shoulder. "Thank you again, by the way. I didn't want one of those overly planned bachelor blowouts. Just some time with the guys who mean the most to me."

"Jay-sus, if you start getting all mushy, Kessler, I'm staying home with my wife and babe," Fletcher complained.

"Just for that remark, I'm adding circle time around the bonfire to the agenda," Kessler teased before turning to Trey. "Is your dad still planning to join us?"

"As far as I know." Which wasn't saying much, because Trey hadn't heard from Jay since their awkward phone call before training camp began. From what he could gather, no one else had, either. "But who knows with Jay? Something better could come along, and he'll forget all about Lake Geneva."

Kessler shrugged. "Either way, I really appreciate you letting us use your grandfather's place."

"Don't mention it," Trey said.

"Yeah, and no more mention of an agenda, either," Fletcher grumbled. "I'm using part of my time at the lake to catch up on some much-needed sleep. Lily is still teething, and Andi refuses to let me give the babe a nip of whisky before bed."

"Sleep is overrated," Kessler replied before ambling back to his locker.

"What are you still grinning like a fool about?" Fletcher demanded.

Trey hefted his duffel over his shoulder. "Just thinking about how much sleep I won't be getting tonight."

JOHN LEGEND'S *All of Me* was playing over the sound system when London arrived back at Pops' condo later that day. She dropped her messenger tote and her gym bag by the door and cautiously walked into the kitchen. A single glass of white wine was on the counter. It was barely five o'clock. Too early for Trey to arrive. Had Pops and Olivia returned from their honeymoon?

"Hello?" she called out.

No answer. She was pulling her cellphone from her belt bag when the front door swung open and a man carrying two shopping bags walked through.

"Trey," she said, her relief palpable. "You're early."

He hurried past her, depositing the delicious smelling shopping bags onto the counter. "You're the one who is early. I wanted to have dinner waiting for you when you got home. But you beat me." With a long-suffering groan, he pulled her into his arms. "Not that I'm complaining. It's been too long since I've kissed you."

She thought about rolling her eyes, but tilted her head back to give him better access to her neck instead. Trey was a master at neck kissing, and she didn't want to miss a moment of it. "It's barely been ten hours."

"Nine hours and fifty-five minutes too long," he murmured beneath her ear.

"Mm." She caressed his muscled shoulders and back. Judging by how quickly her body was responding to his, maybe he had a point. "Then I'm glad I was a good girl and got all my work done early."

He backed her against the Sub-Zero refrigerator. "I'm glad too. Right now, though, I really want you to be a bad girl."

Oh my.

"How bad?"

His erection jumped against her belly. "I bought some whipped cream."

"Gosh, I don't know. I just finished an hour barre class. I might not have the energy," she taunted. "And I'm awfully sweaty."

He teased the shell of her ear. "Have I told you how much I

like it when you're sweaty," he growled. "It means you're really enjoying my attention."

She didn't have the brain cells to tease him any longer. Besides, his dirty talk and his wandering hands had her legs nearly giving out.

"Shower."

The word came out of her mouth as a nearly unintelligible grunt, but Trey had no problem understanding her perfectly. He was cupping her butt with his hands, lifting her up against him before she even finished speaking. His lips were a breath away from hers when he whispered, "Anything you want."

And then they were kissing. Frantically. Madly. It was insane how badly she needed him. She clawed at his hair as if she could somehow bring their mouths closer than they already were.

Trey demonstrated his expert coordination skills when he effortlessly steered them to the large bathroom off the primary bedroom. He flicked on the lights with one hand while with the other one, he slowly guided her as she slithered down his body. A sigh escaped her throat, and he pulled her in closer. He gentled the kiss, but it did nothing to soothe her. Her entire body felt like it would implode if she didn't find her release soon.

She pulled away and, breathing hard, began wrestling with her clammy workout clothes. Trey stood and seemed to revel in her struggle. She stopped undressing—or trying to—and glared at him. He had the audacity to laugh at her.

"Damn, I love it when you act all feisty," he drawled.

He got the message though, toeing off his shoes at the same time as he pulled his T-shirt over his head. London swore as she tried to untangle her sports bra from her arms. His hands on her belly stilled her.

"Hush, woman," he whispered, using a voice she'd once heard on "Animal Planet" when a zookeeper was attempting to calm a hyena. "Let me help."

Her stomach quivered when his fingers stroked upwards. The

bra was sailing through the air seconds later, leaving them skin to skin. She sucked in a breath when he took a step back to roll off his joggers and briefs. One look at the work of art that was his fully-aroused body and she was glad for that breath because her lungs seemed to have shut down. Which was ridiculous because it wasn't the first time she'd taken in the delicious view. She'd had her hands and mouth all over that body multiple times over the past several days.

"You really are beautiful," she whispered.

He gripped her waist to move her closer. "And I'm all yours."

And I'm all yours.

Yet, he wasn't really. Just a friend with benefits, she reminded herself.

Really, really nice benefits.

Like, out of this world, benefits.

But nothing more.

And he never would be.

Her chest ached at the thought. It didn't matter that he was standing there eyeing her like she was the championship trophy he coveted. London Headley wasn't the type men stuck with. Trey had even told her so at the get-go. This was as good as it was going to get.

Not that she was going to complain about the benefits.

Friends with benefits. She was making that her new mantra.

Her attention was immediately refocused on the here and now when he slid his fingers beneath the waistband of her leggings and groaned.

"Do you have any idea what these things do for your ass?" He pushed them down to her thighs before leaning in to press a kiss to her belly. "I get so damn jealous just thinking about other guys looking at you." He shoved the leggings to her ankles, sinking his teeth into her hip as he did so. "Any part of you."

Snaring her fingers into his hair, she gently tilted his head up. "I'm all yours."

His nostrils flared and he was on his feet in an instant, his mouth eating at hers while he backed her into the wide shower. He turned her so his body shielded hers from the jets, then reached up to the panel that controlled the shower heads and the temperature, all the while, his mouth never leaving hers.

The water hissed and a blast of cold air filled the space. He flinched. She pulled him on top of her as her hips settled down onto the tile bench built into the back of the shower. His lips moved south to latch onto one of her breasts, the sensation making her cry out with pleasure.

The spray from the shower was warmer now and she wrapped one leg around his slick back in an effort to bring them closer. He had other ideas. Moving lower, he positioned her on the bench so she was opened wide to him. A guttural sound of pure male satisfaction filled the air before his tongue delved into her. Her release rocked through her fiercely. He let it happen without torturing her by stretching it out, seemingly just as desperate to be joined together as she was.

Warm water pelted her sated limbs when Trey stood to grab a condom. She forced her eyelids open to watch. Water cascaded off his powerful body when he came toward her.

"Mm." Her satisfied sigh floated through the steamy air.

He lifted her easily, supporting her legs with his forearm as he turned and pressed her palms down onto the slippery bench.

"God, you are so perfect," he murmured.

She gasped when he entered her with one swift movement. And then she was panting desperately while arching her back to meet him thrust for thrust. Her fingers struggled to grip the tile, but his hold on her never faltered. He growled words of encouragement against her ear. Sweet words. Dirty words. All of them driving her higher and higher until she was begging him for something more.

He eventually took pity on her, tweaking one nipple and then the other. She reached up and took hold of his wrist, guiding his fingers exactly where she wanted them. A savage sounding laugh echoed off the tile before his teeth sank into her shoulder. She screamed out when her climax came crashing over her, sending her soaring higher than she'd been before. Trey drove into her twice more until his body spasmed behind her as he groaned out her name.

CHAPTER TWENTY-FIVE

TREY ADJUSTED the towel London had wrapped around her damp hair. He pressed his bare chest to her silk-clad back before bringing his arms around her waist and meeting her gaze in the mirror.

"Have I told you how sexy that robe is on you?"

She rolled her eyes. "You're just saying that because you want to get it off me."

"Busted." He inched a hand beneath the silk only to feel her stomach growl. "Mm. I need to get some food in you first, though. You're going to need some more energy. I have plans for you later." He wiggled his eyebrows. "I'll go see what I can salvage from the dinner I ordered."

"I can help."

"You finish drying off. The microwave and I are good friends."

After allowing his lips a leisurely tour of her neck, he headed for the kitchen.

"I poured you a glass of wine. Do you want me to grab it for you?"

"I'll come get it," she called. "One sec."

Trey was humming that Harry Styles song when he rounded

the corner into the kitchen. The scene that greeted him had the tune dying on his lips.

"Well, that explains all this food," his father said with a laugh. "Guess that article about your clean eating must have been BS." Jay shook the can of whipped cream.

But it wasn't the sight of his father unexpectedly standing in the kitchen that had him stunned and suddenly furious. It was the woman who was caressing Jay's face.

"Mom?!"

For once, Trey's innate reflexes failed him. He should have intercepted London before she got an eyeful of Kim and Jay locked in an embrace.

"Whoa," Jay exclaimed. "That's not Bree Moynihan."

"London?" Kim went deathly pale.

"I—wha—I—" London's voice trembled along with her body.

Trey draped an arm around her shoulders, pulling her in close to him. "What the hell is going on here?"

The color had returned to Kim's face. Lots of it. Her eyes narrowed to slits as she aimed a glower in Trey's direction. "Certainly not what is going on *here*." She gestured to her daughter's robe and Trey's only clothing—low-riding joggers he was wearing commando.

He felt more than heard London's soft whimper of frustration when the front door opened.

"Pizza's here. And Kyle is happily enjoying a sleepover at my parent's. We've got all night, just the three of us."

Chuck Prince entered the kitchen to what had to be an assortment of perplexed gazes.

"Wow, this just gets more interesting by the moment," Trey said, his tone the steely one he used on confrontational reporters.

"London?" Chuck looked from his stepdaughter, to his wife, and back to his stepdaughter again. "What are you doing here?"

"I'd ask the same of you, but I don't think I want to know the answer anymore."

"Oh, for crissake," Jay shouted. "Can't a dying man have a piece of deep-dish pizza without it turning into something scandalous?"

The kitchen was suddenly quiet. Trey rubbed his chest with his palm, trying to jumpstart his heart. *Did Jay just say he was dying?*

"Dad?" he croaked.

Jay sighed heavily.

Kim made soothing sounds while she rubbed Jay's shoulder. Trey was amazed that he could feel it too, until he realized London was mimicking her mother's actions on his own shoulder.

"We should go and let you two. . . catch up," Kim said, softly. "Promise me you'll make that call, though, Jay. I mean it."

Jay gave her a half-hearted nod that seemed to appease her. She glanced over at her daughter. Some form of silent communication took place because London eventually nodded before stretching up on her toes and pressing a kiss to Trey's cheek.

"I'm going to grab my stuff and head out with them," she whispered. "Call me later."

He was this close to begging her not to leave him, when he caught sight of the far side of Jay's face. There was a bulky bandage covering his ear. "What the hell is going on with your face, Jay?"

His father headed for the fridge and pulled out a bottle of beer that hadn't been there earlier. He gestured to a second one. Trey shook his head.

"Suit yourself." Jay helped himself to a huge slice of the pizza Chuck left. "I'm not even going to bother asking if you want any of this."

Trey sucked in a breath, trying to keep his temper in check. "Can we get to the point here, Jay? What happened to your ear?"

"The sun happened to it," his father said around a mouthful of pizza. His eyes drifted shut. "Mm. They do not make pizza like this anywhere else in the world."

An annoyed sound rumbled from Trey's chest.

Jay chuckled. "You never did have a lot of patience. You get that from your mother."

"Dammit, dad!"

"There's no need to yell. I can still hear."

Trey suddenly felt like a first-class jerk. Bullying his father never accomplished anything. Not with Jay's chill demeanor. Case in point: The guy was downing a beer and slice of deep dish while discussing his own mortality as though they were talking about someone else.

Except they weren't.

"Did you really just say you're . . . dying?"

His father nodded as he finished chewing a mouthful of pizza. Trey waited in the charged silence while Jay drank from his beer.

"There's really no easy way to say this. I have Stage Four melanoma. The doctors thought removing my ear would take care of it. It didn't."

Trey would have reached for Jay's beer, but he was suddenly having trouble swallowing. None of this was making sense. His heart felt like it was hammering a hole through his chest. He couldn't imagine a world without Jay in it. The man was barely fifty years old, dammit. He was handsome, vital, wealthy and had everything to live for. There was no way cancer was taking his father from him.

"Well, that's just one doctor's opinion."

Jay chuckled. "That's what makes you a winner on the field son, you never give up."

"And you're not giving up either!" Trey shouted.

His father turned his head toward the living room where a wall of windows showcased the Chicago skyline. "Not everything in life goes according to a game plan, Trey." He sighed. "I've got appointments at MD Andersen next week. They're conducting some drug trial the doctors in New York recommended." His father shrugged. "Who knows? They've had good results so far."

A wave of relief washed over Trey. It was so profound he had to sink down onto the stool or else he'd be on the floor. "That sounds promising."

Jay's eyes were determined when he looked back at Trey. "I don't want you to get your hopes up. I'm only going because Kim will kick my ass if I don't."

And just like that, Trey was angry again. "Wow. Sure. By all means. Do it for Kim. A woman who's happily married to someone else." He shot up from his seat.

"Dammit, Trey!" His father slapped his palm on the stone countertop. "I'm trying to be a realist here. I've been living with this diagnosis for a few months now. I've done the research. And the math. There's only a one in one hundred thousand chance that I'm not too late for the treatment to work."

Trey slumped back onto the stool.

"And, I'm at peace with that," Jay said. "It's been a great ride. I was lucky to be born a good-looking dude with a silver spoon in his mouth, who literally sailed through life. Your grandfather was the one who made something of himself. Aside from a few yachting trophies, I have no real accomplishments to speak of." He placed his hand over Trey's. "Aside from you, of course."

The lump in Trey's throat threatened to choke him.

"I'm proud of the man you've become. No thanks to me." Jay shook his head. "You're so much like Pops, Trey. Driven to succeed at all costs. So much of life passed your grandfather by, thanks to his obsessive need to be the best. I'm really glad he's finally found someone to share the everyday things with. Someone to walk through the rest of life with."

"Does he know?"

His grandfather may be taciturn and gruff, but Trey and his dad were the only family Pops had. Trey worried his grandfather might take the news hard.

"He knows. I stopped in Italy to see the newlyweds before my surgery." His smile was melancholy. "Pops is a different man with Olivia in his life. It makes me wonder what he would have been like had my mother's death not broken his heart." He studied his beer bottle as if it held the answers to the universe. "Olivia is good for him. I'm happy he's got someone. You've made a good choice with London, too. She's good people. A man in your position needs a woman who is level-headed." He winked at Trey. "It doesn't hurt that she's easy on the eyes."

Trey waved his father off. "London and I are just—"

What?

He and London were just what?

"We're just having a good time." The words sounded a little hollow leaving his lips. "The season starts next weekend. She knows I don't want anything complicated."

The look of disappointment on his father's face had Trey's gut rolling.

"Does she, now?" Jay pulled his hand away. "That's too bad."

Trey snorted. "Says the man with four ex-wives."

Jay twirled his beer bottle between his hands. "Yeah. My biggest regret in life will be whatever pain I caused all those women. Especially your mother. She was the best thing that ever happened to me. And I screwed it up. Literally." His laugh lacked any real humor.

Jesus. Trey could have lived his entire life without having that rumor confirmed.

"All because I was a twenty-three-year-old horn dog who'd been overserved whisky." His eyes were shiny. "It's probably a good thing you avoid commitment. Because letting down your soulmate is more painful than any kind of cancer they could ever throw at me."

"You and I have always told each other everything." London's mom said as she poured herself a second glass of wine.

She and Chuck had followed London back to Milwaukee. There wasn't a hope in hell for London to avoid the conversation her mother insisted on having, so she invited them up to her place for late night sandwiches from one of her favorite clients, Between the Slices. Bennie had officiated at the wedding of the two women who owned the shop last summer. He and London enjoyed sandwiches on the house ever since.

"Except for anything about Trey," her mom continued. "Then or now. Why is that?"

London stared at her mom, wide-eyed.

Then?

Her mother arched an eyebrow and nodded as though London had asked the question out loud.

"How long have you known?"

Her mom shrugged. "Since that summer."

Of course, she had.

Would her freshman year in college not have sucked so badly had she confided in her mom? Shame clogged her throat. Except her mother had been a little distracted with Trey's dad at the time. And that hadn't helped London's woes.

She refilled her own glass. "The same could be said of you and Jay. Why is that, Mother?"

"Wow. It's 'Mother' tonight. Alright. My friendship with Jay has never been a secret. And for the past decade, it's been just that. A friendship." She quirked an eyebrow. "I wasn't exactly picking up those same vibes between you and Trey this evening."

Getting caught by one's mother moments after "doing the deed" in the shower was embarrassing at any age. Still, London powered through. "We're friends, too." She lifted her glass to her lips. "Friends with benefits," she murmured before taking a healthy sip.

Her mom worked hard to hide the disappointment in her eyes, but London glimpsed it anyway.

"It's not that big of a deal," she added, her tone a tad defensive. "Lots of people enjoy those kinds of relationships."

Her mother's expression softened. "Yes. They do. It's very progressive."

She waited for her mother to add more. When she didn't, London's hackles went up.

"But?" she demanded.

"No buts." Her mother shook her head.

London eyed her quizzically. Her mom glanced over at Chuck who was snoring quietly in his leather chair. The Timbers' baseball game droned on in hushed tones in the background. Turning back to London, she braced her elbows on the kitchen island and leaned in. Her eyes danced with a mischievous look.

"If he's anything like his father, those benefits are out of this world," she whispered.

"Mom!"

"Hey, every woman should be so lucky to experience those—" she made air quotes with her fingers "—benefits. But there's more to relationships than that." She glanced back over at her husband and smiled fondly. "And one day you'll find someone who satisfies your needs in more than one way. Someone you can count on not to let you down."

London had lost count of the number of "ways" Trey had satisfied her needs these past few days. Not that she was spilling that tea with her mom. Her flushed cheeks likely gave her away anyway.

"I'm not really looking for anything permanent right now, Mom."

Or ever.

"Of course not. You've got big things happening in your life. A move. A fascinating new career. You have no time for anything more than 'benefits.'"

Her mom's expression didn't match her words, however. "What?"

"Nothing." Her mom linked her fingers with London's. "I just want you to keep an open mind. Not every man is going to let you down. I promise. Would it hurt to give Trey a chance?"

London nearly choked on her wine. "Are you kidding me? I thought you'd be thrilled things between me and Trey aren't serious."

"I know. Even I think I sound crazy. But the way he looks at you. . ." She shrugged. "Besides, Trey is not his father."

"Wow. That's a ringing endorsement."

"They are both good men in their own way. Jay's issue is he wants a relationship desperately. Except he can't commit to anyone because he's still madly in love with his first wife."

This was news to London. "Seriously? That's kind of sad. Especially now."

Her mother and Chuck had filled her in on Jay's cancer diagnosis. She worried how the news would impact Trey. He and his father seemed as opposite as night and day. That didn't mean they didn't love each other, though. London grew up missing a father she'd never met—right up until she found out what a jerk he was. Losing someone after having them there for thirty years would certainly hurt.

"Mm," her mom continued. "Trey, on the other hand, seems to me to be a lot like you."

"What's that supposed to mean?" she asked before realizing she really didn't want to hear the answer.

"It means I don't think either one of you know what you really want."

London groaned at her mother and opened the freezer for some ice cream therapy, only to remember she'd sacrificed it for multiple orgasms the other day. She turned and rested her back against the fridge.

"You're way off base, Doctor Kim. Both of us know exactly

what we really want. Our careers come first," she announced as she crossed her arms over her chest. "And, before you ask, yes, we've both been very upfront with each other about it." An inexplicable lump formed in her throat. "Trey's one and only love is football. And I'm finally getting the chance at the job I've always dreamed about. The timing never seems to be right for us. I'm fairly certain the universe is trying to tell us friends with benefits is all we're ever going to be."

They stared each other down before her mom gave her a half-hearted nod and looked away.

"Well, I'm glad you're both being mature about this. It'll makes things easier to end when you move, I guess."

Her mother's cellphone vibrated against the countertop.

"It's Kyle." Her mom grinned. "He probably wants to know why his father stopped texting him about the game." She put the phone to her ear and strode into the living room. "Hi, sweetheart. Having fun?"

It'll make things easier to end when you move.

London corked the bottle of wine and put it back into the fridge. Did things have to end when she moved? She'd initially assumed they would, but the distance hadn't been an issue this past week. Why couldn't they continue to be "friends with benefits" while living in different cities? Parts of her did a high five just considering it. She ignored the fact that neither her brain nor her heart joined in.

<h1 style="text-align:center">CHAPTER TWENTY-SIX</h1>

TREY DEBATED CANCELLING the bachelor party, but Jay wouldn't hear of it.

"I've been looking forward to this all month," his dad insisted. "It will be a welcome distraction."

Too bad Trey was the one distracted. His friends greeted Jay with open arms, falling for the ridiculous yarn his father had spun about losing his ear in a yachting accident hook, line, and sinker. They were all a bunch of imbeciles.

Case in point, his idiot father was racing Pops' Chris-Craft across the lake at a speed well above the limit, towing an inner-tube carrying two geriatric thrill seekers. One who'd already lost his glasses to the lake when the tube hit a bump. The other guy—the grandfather of the bride—looked to be holding on for dear life. At this rate, the man would be paralyzed before he could walk Luke's fiancée down the aisle.

Trey stormed to the end of the dock, frantically waving at Jay when he sped past. Jay only grinned wider as he waved back.

"Oh, for fuck's sake."

Fletcher laughed. He and one of the other geezers were playing chess in the boathouse. Trey wasn't sure how they could concentrate, though. Brody and McGraff were tossing a football out on the floating dock. Their rap music was blaring so loudly, the ducks in Canada were probably ready to fly south.

"You sure you're not the dad and Jay the teenager?" Fletcher quipped.

His observation was apt.

"I just want everyone to leave here in the same condition they arrived," Trey said. "I should have had everyone sign a damn waiver."

Luke's future brother-in-law, Sterling, looked up from his computer. "Too late now. It will never hold up in court after the fact."

Trey glared at the attorney. "It's on you, then, if anything happens. You should have warned me ahead of time."

A football whizzed past Trey's ear and landed with a splash in the water just beyond him. He redirected his glare to the two morons on the floating dock.

"For crying out loud, Brody! Are you trying to ruin your shoulder before you even play a down of college ball?"

"How many yards was that?" Brody demanded. "At least fifty, right?"

"Nah, my guess is somewhere in the thirties," the geezer at the chessboard said.

Sterling got to his feet. "I don't know. I'd say it's closer to the forties." He turned to Trey. "You got a tape measure?"

The old man joined Sterling at the edge of the boathouse before looking at Trey expectantly.

"Yeah! Let's measure," McGraff hollered.

Trey shook his head before turning on his heel and heading up to the house. Let them all think he was coming back with a tape measure. They'd be waiting until hell froze over.

"What's with him?" he heard Sterling ask.

"That's what no sugar looks like on a man." The old guy

clicked his tongue. "My guess is he's not getting any sort of sugar, if you get what I'm saying."

Their laughter followed him up the wooden stairs leading to the terrace where Luke and several of the other receivers were playing a rousing game of bocce ball.

Hell, maybe the old guy was right. Trey should have made a pit stop at London's for some *ice cream* before he headed to the lake last night. God knows losing himself in her soft curves would have taken the edge off his ugly mood. She'd made plans with clients, though. And the last thing he wanted was to get too dependent on her body. *Or her.* Besides, he didn't feel comfortable leaving his dad. Which was ridiculous because his father had chosen a woman over him every opportunity he got.

He was into the great room before he realized Fletcher had followed him up.

"What? You don't trust me not to come back with a tape measure?" Trey asked.

The kicker groaned. "I came up here to ensure you don't. These guys have all been drinking since ten this morning. A tape measure will turn everything into a contest. Hell, they'll be measuring the length of their dicks by night's end."

Trey laughed as they entered the kitchen. Carter, Pops' cook, was supervising the caterers as they put the dinner together. Corn on the cob was soaking in a big pot, readying it for the grill where it would be cooked beside fresh salmon on seasoned wooden planks. Brody had talked two guys from Texas into hauling their trailer a thousand miles north to smoke some brisket. Based on the amazing scent wafting his way, Trey had to admit it was worth it.

"There's likely to be another potato famine somewhere based on the variety of spuds these people are preparing," Fletcher quipped.

He was right. The caterers were assembling a huge baked

potato bar along with pounds of French fries and several pans of scalloped potatoes.

"Kessler played his college ball in Idaho," Trey replied. "I decided to make that the food theme."

"Well, this ought to soak up the liquor in everyone's bellies right nicely."

The sound of Pops' boat roaring past had Trey grimacing toward the window.

"Everything okay with Jay?"

"Sure," Trey lied. "Why do you ask?"

"You're strung awfully tight for a guy who's getting regular sex, for one. And the giant bandage on the man's ear for another."

"He explained that. It was—"

"Jaysus, Mary, and Joseph, no one bought that shite he was shovelin', you dummy."

Trey glanced back out the window to watch the boat circle and head back out to the center of the lake again.

"Not to mention that troubled look you get whenever he's around. It speaks volumes," Fletcher added.

Not for the first time, he wondered if the Scotsman was part soothsayer.

"Jay has advanced melanoma. His odds aren't great."

Fletcher whispered something in Gaelic. "I'm sorry. Which always sounds wholly inadequate to say in this situation. How can I help?"

Trey sighed. "It is what it is. I'm good."

"I disagree, but I know better than to argue with your stubborn arse." Fletcher clapped him on the shoulder. "Just know I'm here for you, man. Whatever you need."

"Thanks, Dex. That means a lot." And it did. The weight on his shoulders felt a little lighter sharing the news with his teammate. His friend. "This won't affect my play this season, though. We're going all the way to the championship."

Fletcher let out a pacifying grunt and gave him another pat on the back. "Of course it won't. You're the MVP at compartmentalizing. I wouldn't expect anything less."

DINNER WAS A RAUCOUS AFFAIR. The food seemed to give everyone a second wind after a day of sunshine and beer. Kessler stood and tapped a knife against a glass to get everyone's attention.

"I'd like to propose a toast." He raised his glass. "To QB One for hosting today. Who is going to have to toast with water because he's already on his training diet of abstaining from anything fun."

"Someone has to be the designated driver for when one of you gets hurt," Trey teased.

The guys laughed before toasting.

"Is this the part where we get to give Kessler advice on marriage? Because I've got a few things to say," one of the offensive linemen asked.

"I've got a marriage tip," Jay called out. "Don't do it!"

A few uncomfortable chuckles followed.

"Take my word for it. Love is messy," Jay continued. "And painful. My son agrees with me. What was it that you said, Trey? Marriage is a trap."

Ah, hell. He had to go there, didn't he? Just when Trey was beginning to relax and enjoy the comradery of his teammates.

"For me and you, Jay. The rest of these guys aren't cursed in the matrimony area like us Van Horns." Trey raised his water glass. "How about a toast to the lucky groom-to-be?"

The guys saluted Kessler with their drinks. One of the old farts began the advice giving with the age-old remark about never going to bed angry. That was followed by numerous suggestions of how to placate a pissed-off woman. Several of them should have given the old men a heart attack. Except they were among the guys making the most scandalous suggestions.

Satisfied he'd diverted a crisis, Trey leaned back in his chair, only to find Fletcher staring at him.

"What?"

"The puzzle pieces are starting to fall into place," the kicker replied.

"What's that supposed to mean?"

"Why you date women who you'd never fall for in a million years. Women who are immature. Women who are vain. Women who aren't afraid to use you to get ahead. You gravitate to that type so you won't fall for them. Because you believe some shite about being cursed."

Trey shrugged. He could care less that his perceptive teammate thought he had him figured out.

"Surprised it took your MIT brain so long to solve the equation," he said.

"You're a fool."

And just like that, Trey *was* starting to care what his friend said. Fletcher was pissing him off, in fact.

"If you're going to give me some Highlander bullshit about how to live my life, save it. Just because it worked for you, doesn't mean you can paint me with the same brush," he bit out. "I'm perfectly happy with my life the way it is."

The Scotsman had the nerve to lift an eyebrow at him. "So you say."

He *was* happy, dammit. Trey was at the top of his game. The situation with Jay wasn't perfect, but he was going to get into that drug trial if Trey had to fund it himself. Everything would work out.

And then there was London. Reconnecting with her again was like finding a piece of him that had been missing. He'd never felt freer to be himself around anyone else. Ever. Not only that, but the sex was off the charts. His body began to hum just thinking about her.

Best of all, she was happy with the casual state of their relationship. It worked for both of them. She'd put her career in the top spot of her priorities and so had he.

"What are you two debating over there?" Kessler asked.

Trey looked up to see the expectant gazes from the men in the room zeroed-in on him and Fletcher.

"The Highlander was just recounting the finer things about marriage." Trey tossed the kicker under the bus. "Why don't you share your pearls of marriage wisdom with the boys, Fletcher."

Dex shot Trey a ruthless grin before speaking.

"Van Horn is almost right. Marriage isn't necessarily a trap. It is a gamble, however. And love is certainly messy."

Jay chuckled, but the rest of the guys eyed Fletcher intently.

"But nothing worth having is ever easy, right boys? A good marriage takes work. For starters, you're going to have to learn a new language. That's so you can decipher that most of the time she's not actually mad at you. It's just all her clothes are dumb. Or her hair didn't turn out the way she wanted. Maybe she's peeved you've left your socks on the floor. Or she's hangry but she has no clue what she wants to eat." He grinned at Kessler. "Here's a little pro tip. Chocolate always works."

"Yeah," one of the geezers chimed in. "And saying 'yes dear' will usually get you out of the dog house even if you have no idea why you're in there in the first place."

"Ain't that the truth," a teammate called out.

"Marrying the woman you love can be challenging, but it can also be rewarding, fulfilling, and healing," Fletcher rambled on. "In my opinion, it's worth every bit of effort, no matter how messy. Sharing my life with Andi has forced me to grow, learn, and connect with others. It has without a doubt made me happier, healthier, and more resilient. Best thing I ever did." He raised his glass at Kessler. "Good on you for gambling on it."

"Here, here," the guys cheered.

"It's navigating the love part that is the biggest gamble," Fletcher said just loud enough for Trey to hear him. "I was a fool to go so long thinking I didn't deserve it. And I've never taken you for a fool, Van Horn."

The rapid clicking of high heels on the wood floor saved Fletcher from the litany of choice words Trey would have regretted uttering later. He shot from his chair when he recognized who was storming in.

"Mom?"

"Where is he?" his mother demanded.

"Reese?" Jay stood so fast his chair tipped over backwards.

She jerked her head in the direction of Jay's voice, gasping when she laid eyes on him.

"Your ear! They really did cut it off," she nearly sobbed. "I always loved your ears."

What the ever-loving hell?

Trey tried to navigate the chairs around the room, filled with grown men entranced by the little tableau playing out before them. "Uh, Mom—"

"Ah, I'm sorry, Reesey," Jay said.

Trey had the profound sensation that his father was apologizing for a lot more than just losing his ear to cancer. His suspicions were confirmed when his mother threw herself into Jay's arms. He stood there in shock watching the two people who'd tortured each other for nearly three decades hug one another as if nothing had ever kept them apart. Behind him, the sounds of scraping chairs and clearing throats filled the air. He wanted to slink out of the dining room with his guests, but his feet refused to move.

"We're going to beat this. You and me, together," his mother said against Jay's chest. "My cousin is the director of the Miami Cancer Center. He pulled some strings to get you into the drug trial. You can stay at home while you are being treated."

Stay at home? You and me together?

Trey pinched the bridge of his nose. "Is someone punking me right now? Because this has to be some kind of a joke. You two haven't said a civil word to each other for practically my entire life. And suddenly you're back together? Just like that?"

His parents continued to stare into each other's eyes. Well, at least the part about them thinking of themselves first hadn't changed. His dinner rolled around in his stomach.

"Your father needs our help right now, Trey," his mom announced more to Jay than him. "He needs our love. I'm ready to put the past behind us and do that."

"Thank you," Jay whispered. "I don't deserve it, but you can't take it back. And you won't regret it. I promise."

They were kissing now. Trey checked behind him to make sure their audience had scattered because the way his parents were going at it, somebody was bound to shout "get a room!" In the end, it was Trey who said it.

"Maybe you two would like to take this somewhere private," he suggested. "I've got a house full of guys tuning up for a bachelor party tonight."

His mother pulled out of the kiss and laughed. "Are we embarrassing you, Trey?"

More like scaring the hell out of me.

He should be elated by this turn of events. At the very least, they'd both stop using him to mediate between them. It was just so out of the blue that none of it seemed real, though.

"He's right." Jay shot him an apologetic grin. "We need to go somewhere quiet where we can talk."

"Among other things," his mother cooed.

Argh! "Really, mother. I can't unhear that now."

She hurried over to Trey and wrapped her arms around him. At least the scent of her perfume was familiar. Maybe this wasn't a dream after all. He relaxed into her hold.

"Everything is going to be okay, sweetheart. Your dad is going to get better and we're finally going to behave like a real family. You'll see."

Behind her, Jay donned a sad smile. Trey knew his father wasn't optimistic about his chances. He also knew how much Jay loved his first wife. Maybe, just maybe, that love would be the thing that would ignite his father's will to fight harder.

God, he hoped so.

His throat was suddenly tight. He hugged his mother a little more firmly. It didn't matter how crazy and spontaneous his parents' reconciliation was. It only mattered that it happened.

"Thank you," Trey whispered to her.

"I love you," she replied.

Trey was pretty sure she loved his father more, but that was okay. He wasn't a child any longer. Jay needed all the love he could get right now.

Besides, she'd done him a favor. He'd been feigning confidence earlier when he told Fletcher his father's condition wouldn't impact his performance on the field. The truth was Jay's illness had rocked him. But with his mother taking the lead, he could direct his focus squarely where it needed to be—on the game.

CHAPTER TWENTY-SEVEN

IT WAS WELL after midnight when London made her way down to the boathouse. The lights from Pops' great room cast an eerie glow over the terrace. Music and male laughter floated through the air, but not loud enough to disturb the neighbors. It turned out the Growlers were pretty tame in their partying. Definitely not what she expected.

London was careful to stay in the shadows, not wanting to alert any of Trey's friends to her presence. She was sure there was some unwritten rule about women crashing bachelor parties. At least women like her. The last thing she wanted was to embarrass Trey.

So often over the past decade, she'd snuck down to the boathouse. Whether it was to torture herself with the painful memories or purge them, she never knew. Tonight, however, the feeling to be here felt urgent. She understood the meaning as soon as her tennis shoe hit the deck where she spied the shadow of a man leaning against one of the posts. A man she'd recognize even with her eyes closed.

She inhaled softly. Her pulse began to dance as she carefully approached him from behind.

"Dammit, Fletcher," he said. "I'm not in the mood for one of your heart-to-heart talks tonight. Go catch up on your beauty sleep before you have to return home to your teething baby tomorrow."

London pressed her body against his back, slowly sliding her hands around his waist. "Mm. Maybe you're in the mood for something else?"

Trey executed a move that probably stunned most opposing players, reversing their position so her back was to the pole and his lips were on her neck in less than a second.

"What are you doing here," he murmured against her skin.

She tucked her fingers into the back pockets of his jeans and squeezed. "No one saw me come down here, if that's what you're worried about."

He threaded his fingers through her hair as he nipped at her lips. "How did you know I needed you?"

Her heart squeezed at his admission. Fortunately, he'd already coaxed her lips open and was plundering her mouth with deep, drugging kisses. Because she wasn't sure how she'd answer him. How she'd explain that some instinct drove her to the lake tonight. Especially when she couldn't explain it herself. As much as she tried to keep things on a casual level with him, the universe kept finding ways to throw them together. Not that she minded right now, considering how good his body felt beneath her hands.

Trey groaned when her hips rocked into his. His fingers left her hair to slip beneath her hoodie, leaving a trail of warmth wherever they touched. A soft moan of need arose at the back of her throat when he fingered her hard nipples. Growling, he maneuvered her into the darkness of the boathouse. The back of her legs came into contact with one of the chaises right before he pressed her onto her back, covering her body with his.

Fumbling in the dark, he managed to unfasten her jeans and work them down around her knees.

"London, I'm not sure I have the patience for taking things slow tonight." His roughly voiced confession had her wet.

When he slid a finger inside her, she began kicking her legs free of her jeans. She worked her way out of her sweatshirt and bra while he stroked her.

"I want to see you." He reached up to one of the shades covering the screens and snapped it open.

"Trey," she warned.

"No one is looking down here. They're too wrapped up in their poker game."

The moonlight filtering through the screen illuminated her torso.

He sighed reverently. "Do you know how many times I fantasized about having you naked right here, beneath the moonlight?"

Her insides clenched when he leaned down to tongue one of her nipples.

"So many times," he murmured.

She dragged her fingers through his hair, gently tugging his gaze up to meet hers.

"Show me what you dreamed about."

Seconds later he was swearing as he agitatedly shucked his clothes. She might have laughed at his urgency were it not for the wild look in his eyes. The hunger she saw there incited her own. She reached for him and they were instantly a tangle of arms, legs, and tongues.

Trey wasn't kidding about not being able to keep things slow. It was only a matter of moments before the breeze carried her cries of release across the lake. He was right behind her, swearing with pleasure.

The quiet night surrounded them as their breathing returned to normal. He rolled onto his back, taking her with him. The body heat they were generating provided some warmth against the late-night chill. Laughter from the house broke into the silence. London shivered. He reached up to the shelf above their heads, pulled down a beach towel, and draped it over them.

"Better?" he asked.

She burrowed up against him. "Mm."

He cocked an arm behind his head.

"How are you doing?" she asked.

"Really? You have to ask after that?"

She could hear the smile in his voice.

"I meant with all the stuff about your dad."

She leisurely traced an L on his chest with her fingertip. They'd only exchanged a few texts since her speedy departure from Chicago. Knowing he had a lot on his plate with both his father's bombshell and the bachelor party, she'd given him space the past two days. Still, she'd worried about him. It wasn't unusual to worry about friends, she'd rationalized. She drew an O over his slick skin.

He sighed. "I'm still trying to wrap my head around all of it. Just when I worried Jay was prepared to throw in the towel without putting up any fight to try and beat his cancer, my mother shows up out of the blue. She acted as though they hadn't been bitter enemies for my whole life. Kissing and making up like they'd fought over who forgot to take out the trash. It all seems like a crazy dream really."

This time she traced an N. "I know. Your dad stopped by Mom and Chuck's earlier to share the good news. Apparently, *my* mom convinced him to reach out to *your* mom. She was very gracious in her thanks. My mom is very pleased with herself."

A chuckle rumbled through his chest beneath her cheek. She traced a D around his nipple.

"Well, she might want to hold off starting a matchmaking business. Give it time for the other shoe to drop."

An O went around his other nipple. "Why so pessimistic?"

"Because he's a Van Horn. Love never lasts for us."

Her finger froze in the middle of finishing an N. Her heart

froze along with it. He'd said the words so matter-of-factly. So prophetically. And it wasn't the first time. This time, though, she took his warning to heed.

Friends with benefits.

That's all they'd ever be. She laid her palm over his heart. It was beating out a steady rhythm. Proof, at least, that he had one. He simply refused to engage it, that's all.

At least not with me.

The back of her eyelids burned.

Stop it!

London reminded herself firmly that her heart wasn't available, either. She was putting her career first. Love wasn't on the agenda. Especially not with a man who didn't believe in it.

"I should go."

Trey sighed as she dug around on the floor for her clothes.

"I can't convince you to stick around and watch the sunrise with me?"

She dragged her hoodie over her head. "Too cold."

He sat up and pressed his lips to her back, halting the slide of her sweatshirt. "I'll keep you warm."

Parts of her were already growing warm—hot even—at the thought. Fortunately, her brain was fully in charge of the situation for once. She shook her head, not trusting that she might agree to if she tried to speak.

He gently righted her hoodie over her shoulders.

"Next time, then."

Her stomach sank. Would there be a next time? *Could there be?* Her head was swimming, wondering if suddenly the risk to her heart outweighed the "benefits." She tugged on her jeans and stood so she could step into her shoes.

He wrapped the beach towel around his bare shoulders. "We're all headed back in the morning. Why don't we have dinner at my place tomorrow night."

"Can't," she said as she bent down to tie her shoelaces.

"Chuck's family has a big barbeque. It's the only time I see most of them." *If you don't count the upcoming holidays.*

He rubbed his palm over her butt. "Monday then."

She straightened her body and stepped away. "Bennie is coming out for the day." They needed to strategize how they were going to break the news to the staff about Nolan and Hemphill absorbing the agency. "I won't be back in Milwaukee until late morning Tuesday. It's Kyle's first day of school. This may be the last time he wants me around to celebrate it with him."

Or the last time her soon-to-be busy schedule would allow.

"How's he doing?"

The genuine interest in his voice confused her. He was obviously capable of caring when he wanted to.

"Doing well. Ready to get back to school and show off the inch and a half he's grown this summer."

He laughed. "Good for him."

She took a step back. "Okay, well—"

The beach towel fell away when he sprung to his feet. Trey seemed unaffected by the cool air against his nude body. He cupped her cheeks, drawing her toward him. Her hands collided with the hard planes of his chest. A sigh got trapped in her throat at the contact. His mouth brushed against hers.

"Thank you for stopping by." He teased her bottom lip with his teeth.

"Uh, huh."

He kissed her then. It was both tender and demanding at the same time. And her brain cells began to scatter. She broke the kiss and stepped back before her sanity completely left the building.

"Yeah," he groaned. "If you don't leave now, we will be enjoying the sunrise."

Giving him a wave and a half smile, she darted toward the dock.

"London!" he called after her.

She looked back over her shoulder at him. *Big mistake.* Her mouth went dry watching the moonlight dance over his tousled hair and perfectly sculpted body. No woman in the world would be fool enough to walk away from those "benefits." She'd probably have to turn in her female card.

"Have a great rest of your weekend. If we don't catch up before, I guess I'll see you at the gala media shoot Tuesday."

Crap.

With everything going on, she'd forgotten all about next month's gala.

"Sounds like a plan." She nodded swiftly before hurrying away to find a safe place for her heart.

CHAPTER TWENTY-EIGHT

"How's Jay?" Fletcher asked when he and Trey crossed paths at the training facility Tuesday afternoon. Practice for Sunday's season opener wouldn't begin until the following day, but both men liked to take advantage of the quiet workout room whenever they could.

"In really good spirits," Trey replied. He'd FaceTimed with both his parents yesterday, and he couldn't remember ever seeing either one look so carefree. So happy. Even with the battle Jay still had to fight, his mom and dad acted like a couple on their honeymoon. "He got into the drug trial, thank goodness. There's still a long way to go, but the doctors seem optimistic."

"That's good to hear." The kicker adjusted his gym bag on his shoulder.

"Yeah. I still can't quite wrap my head around my parents facing down my dad's illness as a couple."

"That's because you let all that shite about your family being cursed influence your thinking."

Trey opened his mouth to object, but Fletcher held up a hand.

"I know you don't want to hear it," the kicker said. "And this is the last time I'll ever bring the subject up, mostly because you're not going to like what I have to say."

"When has that ever stopped you?"

"Just riddle yourself this. If the men in your family are so cursed, why would Jay and your Pops keep pairing up? I'm going to go out on a limb and guess they think the reward is worth the effort." Fletcher sighed. "There are no guarantees in this life, Van Horn. None. At the risk of repeating my advice, you'll never know if love is worth the risk unless you step off the sidelines and give it a shot."

He saluted Trey and strolled out of the gym. Trey sat down at the leg press and contemplated Fletcher's words. The kicker was just trying to manifest his own happiness on everyone else, that's all. Trey was happy. Things were going just fine the way they were. He had football and he had London. Admitting he loved London wouldn't change anything. His legs stilled on the machine.

Love?

Well, shit.

Of course he was in love with London. He always had been. Fletcher was right, dammit. Not that he'd ever admit that to his friend.

Trey had been a chickenshit all those years ago. The real reason he'd run back to Stanford was because he didn't know what to do with the feelings he had for her. He knew now, though.

If the game of football was suddenly taken away from him, he'd survive somehow. But if London was no longer in his life, he'd be lost. And the version of himself he was when she was around—the one he liked the best—would be lost, too. He needed her in his life. Long-term. All he had to do now was convince her of the same thing.

An hour later, he headed over to the stadium for the photo shoot. He chuckled to himself as he climbed the stairs to the conference room. He'd be a different Trey Van Horn in these pictures. People wouldn't be used to seeing him smiling ear-to-ear. But admitting his feelings about London made him feel lighter. Freer. Happier. He would have to resist the temptation to sweep her in his arms when he saw her in there.

"Here he is," the Community Relations Director for the Growlers called out when Trey stepped into the room.

"We've already finished with the Timbers' pitcher," she told Trey. "We'd like to get a few shots of the three of you so he can leave and we can finish with you and Alek."

"Sure," Trey agreed absently as he scanned the room, looking for the woman he couldn't live without.

"You're wasting your time," Bergeron murmured beside him. "London's not here."

Trey slowly shifted his gaze to the obnoxious hockey goalie.

Bergeron had the nerve to smirk. "I take it you haven't heard?"

LONDON ENTERED the crowded salon hoping her flagging courage wouldn't fail her when she finally dropped her truth bomb on Lucy. Breaking the news to the Westbrook staff had been more painful than she anticipated. They were a small office of twenty-one people, including her and Bennie. And up until today, they were tight-knit. The five younger staff—including interns—were all enthusiastic about the opportunity to work for a big-name firm like Nolan and Hemphill.

The rest of the staff, not so much.

Brenda openly sobbed at the idea of Bennie and London not being in the office any longer. The others grumbled about getting lost among the rank and file of an "advertising machine" while working in a "satellite" office in Milwaukee. One of the other account reps openly glared at London, obviously resenting the fact she'd be taking on larger accounts while he'd still be swimming with the small fish. The meeting left London feeling guilty and anxious.

"Shake it off, kiddo," Bennie told her. "This was my decision. I could have closed up shop and walked away and they'd all be scrambling for work. Everyone wins this way, whether they believe it or not."

She'd left early trying to ignore the incessant ringing of the phones, likely brought on by the email Bennie sent to clients an hour earlier announcing the merger.

"Out of the frying pan and into the fire," she mumbled to herself.

She caught sight of Lucy serving a small glass of wine to a woman getting a pedicure. Several months ago, London suggested her friend start hosting a "happy hour" a couple of afternoons a month where customers got a complimentary glass of wine from the liquor store with their pedicure. Lucy was pleasantly surprised at how many people purchased a bottle of wine on their way out the door. So surprised that now it was an everyday service.

Her friend smiled broadly when she spied London coming her way.

"Oh my gosh, you are glowing." London wrapped her arms around Lucy. "That must have been some babymoon."

"It was ahh-mazing. Just what Mike and I needed." She tilted her head and studied London. "You however, look a little ragged. I hope that means our favorite quarterback has been keeping you up with sexy times all weekend."

"I've had a few things keeping me up this weekend." *Not a total lie.* She gestured to the glass of wine one of the customers was holding. "Got any more of that?"

Lucy winked at her. "For you? Of course. Come on over to the shop."

They were headed to the back hallway that adjoined the two

spaces when the chimes on the door rang and a chorus of excited whispers filled the salon.

Lucy turned to investigate. "Speaking of our favorite quarterback."

Holy hell. Not now.

London's stomach seized up. He wasn't supposed to be here. She couldn't put this conversation with Lucy off any longer. Besides, Trey was supposed to be at the gala media day.

"Why aren't you at the gala meeting?" she demanded in lieu of a greeting.

Out of the corner of her eye, she saw Lucy's knowing smile fade into a confused expression.

Trey's expression wasn't any better. The flecks of gold in his eyes were hidden beneath the penetrating look he pinned her with. "Funny thing, that. I was under the impression that you'd be at that meeting as well."

Shit, shit, shit.

Trey stopped in the center of the salon, seeming to take up half the space in the room. He crossed his arms over his chest, showcasing his hard-earned muscles beneath his Henley. Muscles parts of her would likely never stop wanting to touch. Or taste.

"When were you going to tell me, London?" he demanded.

He must have seen the truth in her face because he swore violently.

Seriously?

They weren't in a real relationship. He wasn't supposed to care where she lived or worked.

"You know what, let's talk about this in the back," she managed to say around her suddenly tight throat.

"Why? There's nothing left to talk about. I already know Bennie sold his firm to Nolan and Hemphill in Chicago. And all his accounts along with it."

The salon went so still, the only sound was the staccato beat from the tango music playing in the ballroom dance studio two doors down.

Trey turned to Lucy's mom. "Don't worry Mrs. An. London will still be managing your account. Only she'll be doing it from Chicago."

That wasn't exactly true. London's Milwaukee accounts would be spread among the remaining staff. Not that she would be clarifying that right now. She was too concerned by the look of hurt on Lucy's face. Pain that she was responsible for.

"Is this true?" Lucy whispered.

Mrs. An rushed to place her arm over her daughter's shoulders. She shot London a well-deserved look of annoyance. But Trey deserved some of the blame, too.

This was not how this was supposed to go down.

She was furious at him for taking over the narrative. Grabbing his wrist, she marched him into one of the waxing rooms, slamming the door behind them. He was still wearing an inscrutable expression when he leaned a hip against the table. She fisted her hands on her hips.

"I was always very upfront that I was putting my career first."

"Yes, you have been. You just never bothered to mention that career would be in a different city. Imagine my surprise when I had to find out from *Alek fucking Bergeron!*"

His outburst had the thin walls of the room quaking. London pressed her fingers to her throbbing brow. Her stomach sank even further realizing that Trey wasn't angry about the move. His ego was bruised because Alek got the news from someone before he did.

"I'm sorry about that. I had plans to tell you in person."

His laugh rung hollow. "Good to know where I rate on your list of friends. Tell me something. How do you see *this*—" he gestured between them "—playing out? We'll just hook-up whenever we are in the same city?"

His affront was surprising to her because she was certain

that's how *he* pictured their relationship. And it was exactly how *she* saw their relationship, too. Until the other night at the boathouse. When she realized her heart was coming into play.

"There can't be a *this*, okay?" *Not without love.*

His head jerked back as though she'd punched him.

She blew out a breath. "I thought I could do this." She tried to clear the emotion from her voice. "But it turns out I can't."

"Only because you won't give it a chance."

It was her turn to recoil this time.

"Are you kidding me with that crap? And leave myself open for you to crush my heart when you walk away without a word again? Because you will. You said it more than once that you're not a good bet where relationships are concerned. That you don't *believe* in them." She sucked in a lungful of air in an attempt to steady her breath. "It's taken me ten years to get back the guts to go after what I really want. I can't afford the chance that you'll knock me off course a second time. I just can't, Trey."

Her lungs seized as she watched him seem to deflate before her eyes. The silence stretched for several long heartbeats. Eventually, he stepped away from the table with a heavy sigh.

"You're right," he said quietly. "I'm a bad bet long-term. Believe me when I say the last thing I'd ever want to do is hurt you, London."

Tears stung the back of her eyes at his admission. He stepped close to her, lightly brushing his knuckles along her cheek.

"Hold out for someone who'll put you first. He's out there. I promise you."

He moved for the door, pausing with his hand on the doorknob. "I believed in love once," he said, keeping his back to her. "That summer, you had me convinced it existed. But then I let someone convince me you were a mirage. A fake. My stupidity that day changed the direction of my life. And you're right. It's too late for a course-correction now."

His words confused her. She wanted to demand an explanation, but he was already gone. The tears came then. Tears of grief at the love she would never have. Tears of anger at the universe for making her want the one man on the planet who wasn't open to love. Tears of panic at the prospect of losing her best friend.

The door opened and closed. London hadn't realized she was sitting on the floor until someone slid down the wall and landed next to her.

"Of course you'd have to be on the floor," Lucy grumbled. "Well, you're going to have to help me up when the time comes."

Gulping sobs wracked London's body.

Lucy rubbed her back. "Shh. It's all going to be okay. I've got you."

"You're n-not mad at m-me?" London asked when she could finally get words out.

"Oh, girlfriend, I'm pissed as crap right now. Both at you and the fact that I can't share this bottle of expensive Prosecco with you." Lucy brushed a kiss over London's head. "But you're not getting rid of me that easily. I know the way to Chicago."

The tears now were from relief. *And love.* And happiness with the knowledge that she wasn't alone. She was going to be okay. Or at least better. She might actually survive this.

Someday.

CHAPTER TWENTY-NINE

THE WEATHER FOR THE GROWLERS' season opener matched Trey's mood perfectly: chilly and grey. His teammates knew enough to steer clear of him when he was in his pre-game mode. Too bad Collin hadn't gotten the memo. His agent was lying in wait outside the locker room when Trey emerged for his pre-game warm-ups.

"Another season to break some records." Collin fell into step beside him. "There are a couple of VIPs with field passes who'd like a photo-op with you."

"I don't care what they'd 'like.' I don't do photo-ops on game day. I'm sure your dad mentioned that to you," Trey told him curtly. "Photo-ops require random chit-chat and I don't have time for that bullshit. I've got a game to play."

They reached the edge of the tunnel leading to the field. Several players from the opposing team were headed in the direction of the visitor's locker room.

"Look guys, it's the big *cheese*," one of the linemen called out. "Good luck today, Van Horn."

Another player held up his cell phone. "Nothing says game

day like *cheese*," he teased. "Come on Van Horn, show me that *cheesy* smile of yours."

Collin snorted. "At least we know the campaign is resonating with viewers. Speaking of which, Gunther is out there with his two grandsons. He's expecting a photo-op and a little pass and catch action."

"Then he's going to be disappointed."

Trey had fulfilled his end of the contract with Gunther Cheese. He didn't owe the company's annoying owner another damn thing. He'd only agreed to meet with the kids to make life easier for London. She didn't need his protection any longer, however. Not when a big-name firm had her back.

In Chicago.

Part of him was so effing proud of her. The part that still felt guilty for not trusting his gut all those years ago. For causing her to lose faith in herself. London deserved this opportunity and she was going to do great things. Yet, there was a part of him that felt empty. Wounded that she hadn't trusted him with her dreams. Even though he knew deep down he didn't deserve her trust.

He gave a fist bump to one of the security guards, trying not to dwell too much on how things with London had ended. Going down that path had him wanting to punch someone. Himself, mainly, for thinking things would turn out differently. For hoping the Van Horn men weren't cursed in the love department. Sure, Jay and Pops were happy right now. Trey didn't need his Stanford degree to figure out it was only a matter of time before either man was crying in his beer again, though.

Beside him, Collin stopped short. "You sure you want to go that route? The kids will be disappointed, too."

Trey halted also, shooting his agent a *so-what* look.

Collin rubbed the back of his neck. "I get it. The guy's an ass. But those kids didn't choose Seth Gunther for their grandfather. Not to mention how bad it might look if Gunther opens his mouth."

As much as Trey hated to admit it, Collin was right. "Huh. Look at you being all responsible and agent-like." He sighed in exasperation. "Promise them each a signed jersey and ball at the end of the game. And *one*—as in a single—photo with the two of them at the locker room door."

"Got it. I'll take care of it right now."

Trey nodded and strode onto the field, headed for the fifty-yard line. A few cheers went up from the early bird fans who were already in the stadium. He glanced up toward the suites from where some of the cheers rained down. Likely from his mom and Jay who were watching from Trey's suite, along with Pops and Olivia. A week ago, he'd imagined London and her family up there with Pops. The idea that his mom and dad would be there wasn't even on his radar.

In the corner of the stadium, the Growlers' band was warming up. Kessler was waving his hands as if he was directing them. His fiancée, Summer, laughed as she tugged him back toward the tunnel where they'd likely be making out until someone dragged the receiver's ass into the locker room.

Fletcher was showing off his daughter to the other team's kicker and punter. In fact, several of the Growlers had their kids on the field running amok. Even Coach Gibson's daughter was practicing a cartwheel under the watchful eye of one of the cheerleaders.

Trey reached midfield, waiting for one of the trainers to show up to stretch him out. The guy was late. Probably lost in the pre-game frivolity that had settled over the whole damn team. Did anyone besides him care about preparing for today's game?

He slowly spun around, an island in the center of the gridiron teaming with media, players and hangers-on. The wave of loneliness that washed over him nearly took him out at the knees. His gut clenched.

The hell with all these people.

He'd just do what he always did and carry the team on his

back if he had to. He didn't need anyone to "complete" him. He had the game of football. A game where he was the best in the league. Football was his only love. The thing he put first above all else. The only thing he could count on for contentment. He'd prove it to them again this season. Starting today.

The Growlers went on to rout their opponents, scoring six touchdowns, three of those on passes perfectly executed by Trey. The locker room was jubilant after the game, as if McGraff hadn't dropped two passes. Or the offensive line had not allowed him to be forced from the pocket multiple times.

The team formed a ring three players deep around Coach Gibson who congratulated them on its victory before awarding the game ball to Trey. His teammates cheered.

Trey answered them with a scowl. "This is one game. We have twenty more to go before we can celebrate. Keep your eye on the prize, gentlemen. Today's win means bupkis if we don't win the whole damn thing."

The vibe in the room shifted to something less raucous but still upbeat. Trey wound his way through the crowd, headed to his locker and a shower. He'd take the photo with Seth's grandsons before spending the rest of the evening breaking down film and preparing for their next game. The familiarity of the routine soothed him. He understood football and the world within it. This was his life. And he was good with it.

LONDON STEPPED OFF THE ELEVATOR, juggling her coffee and the muffin she'd picked up at the Starbucks in the lobby. Since moving to Chicago five weeks earlier, she'd fallen into a routine of grabbing a quick breakfast to eat at her desk while she caught up on emails and other related tasks. Everyone else at Nolan and Hemphill did the same. She missed Swansons' freshly-made

Danish and the coffee the diner supplied to the Westbrook offices every day.

Mostly, though, she missed her morning chats with Bennie and the staff in the Westbrook conference room. She always enjoyed starting her day hearing about their families, their pets, or their weekend exploits. For some reason, she thought there would be lots of that type of camaraderie at Nolan and Hemphill given how many more people were employed at the firm. Instead, she'd found the opposite was true. People were friendly, they just kept to themselves.

"Give it time," her mother advised her. "You'll find your tribe within the agency."

She smiled at the receptionist who was already busy with the phones. He winked back at her, gesturing to the phone in his hand and rolling his eyes. Everyone here was so busy. That's probably why she hadn't "found her tribe" so to speak. As soon as she began working with a team on an account, she'd have a work family again.

London wove her way through the canyon of cubicles toward hers, with its obstructed view of the John Hancock building and the neighbor who insisted on burning popcorn in the staff microwave at least once a day. Evan was sitting in her extra chair, scrolling through his phone when she arrived.

"Good morning, Evan," she said as she hurried to put her things down and shed her coat. "I didn't realize we had anything scheduled this morning."

He waved a hand. "I just stopped by to compliment you on your meeting with the airline execs yesterday. They liked everything you pitched. Not that I'm surprised. Your ideas were spot on."

London bit back the enormous grin that threatened. She'd thrown her heart into creating that outline, working day and night for the last three weeks, not wanting her first attempt to be a flop.

Not wanting to regret any decisions.

She hadn't been a flop, though. And there were no reasons for regrets. She'd just landed a seven-million-dollar account with a major client on her first try. Even the music would be original to the campaign. It was all she could do not to pinch herself. Her wildest dreams were coming true.

"Thank you. I'm glad they liked them. So what happens next?"

"Contracts sends the paperwork over to their office, and as soon as all the 'I's are dotted and 'T's are crossed, we get to work. In the meantime, we'll start assembling a team for you to work with. They want the spots ready to air before the holidays, so your workload is going to be nonstop for a while."

"This is what I came here for. Bring it on."

"That's what I like to hear." He leaned forward in the chair, placing his elbows on his knees. "Once we kick this off, you won't have time to consult on any of the other Westbrook accounts any longer."

Something cold ran down her spine. "What do you mean?"

The expression in his eyes looked almost patronizing. "Darius in reception says you've been taking quite a few calls from the clients represented by Westbrook."

WTF, Darius? You wink at me while ratting me out behind my back?

Of course she had been fielding calls from Westbrook clients. Orlando had reached a hiccup in his social media campaign for the tire store and he needed someone to brainstorm with. The local pet store had received some bad press when a customer accused them of selling him a diseased hamster. Brenda was having problems with the printers for the auction booklets needed for the gala next week. Turns out the printers were having issues with the paper supplier they normally used. The gala wasn't going to happen without either matter being resolved today.

"I'm sorry. There have been a few bumps in the road with the transition of accounts. I didn't foresee a problem with pitching in since we are all under the same umbrella now. But I can see where it might present a clerical issue when accounting for hours charged. It won't happen again."

At least not here in the office. She'd tell Brenda to send clients to her cellphone or personal email.

"Technically, we are not under the same umbrella yet. We're still doing our due diligence deciding which accounts we'll keep."

Which accounts we'll keep? What is he talking about?

"I was under the impression you were buying the firm in its entirety, that all the accounts would be transferred over."

His mouth formed a thin line. "We can't absorb accounts that aren't paying on time, London. And from the looks of it, that's most of Westbrook's portfolio. The terms Bennie offered his clients were very generous. It's a wonder he kept the agency solvent for as long as he did."

She was aware Bennie was very lenient with clients who couldn't pay for services in a timely manner, but there was never a time when payroll wasn't met or the utility bill wasn't paid.

"The agency always operated in the black," she insisted.

"It did or we wouldn't have agreed to the deal. Don't get me wrong, Bennie is a shrewd businessman. His firm could have been three times the size if he hadn't tried to keep every small business in Milwaukee afloat. You can only be a nice guy and survive in business for so long, though."

Her mouth was suddenly dry. "How many accounts are you planning on keeping?"

"Gunther's, of course. It seems likely the paper companies will be onboarded, also." He shrugged.

"That's all?" she choked out.

"None of the others make sense from a profitability standpoint."

"And the staff?" She wasn't sure she could handle the answer to that question.

"We'll take on a few of them here in Chicago. The others will be given a decent severance package that they wouldn't have received if Westbrook was on its own."

London hoped he didn't expect a pat on the back for that last statement. She didn't trust her hand not to shake. The matter-of-fact way he'd discussed the people she loved had her reeling.

Her cellphone buzzed with a text. She glanced down at her watch and saw the text was from Mike.

Call me ASAP.

Lucy's husband rarely texted. Her stomach sank.

The baby!

"I'm sorry, Evan. I need to make a call. It's a family matter."

He eyed her curiously as he stood. "I'm sure I don't have to remind you that you signed an NDA with your contract."

She blinked twice. Did he really think she wasn't professional enough to keep her mouth shut? So much for making her feel like a valued employee.

"Don't worry. I'll leave the dismantling of Westbrook to your capable hands."

If he noticed her sarcasm, he ignored it. He nodded and walked away. She dug her phone out of her bag and dialed Mike's number. He picked up midway before the first ring.

"What's wrong?" she asked before he got a chance to even say hello.

"It's Lucy. Her blood pressure is through the roof. The doctor is admitting her to the hospital. They're saying she has preeclampsia."

"Oh, God."

"Look, Lon, I realize you've got this big account you're working on, but if you could maybe spare a couple of hours this weekend to come up and see her, I know it would do her a world of good. She'd never ask you because she likes to be tough. But, she's scared. Frankly, so am I."

London already had her coat on and was grabbing her bag. "I'll be there in two hours."

"Seriously? What about work?"

"The hell with work."

THE WAITING room was crowded with members of both Mike and Lucy's families. Mike's niece, Tina, raced over and wrapped her arms around London's hips.

"They won't let us all go back there," she moaned against London's stomach.

Given that there were twenty-nine people from three generations waiting to see Lucy, London could understand why.

"Isn't anyone working in the stores today?" she teased.

Lucy's mom quickly stood. London didn't think she'd ever seen the woman looking more anxious.

"It's going to be okay," London reassured her as they embraced. "Lucy wouldn't have it any other way."

Mrs. An nodded. "Down the hall. Third door on the left. She'll be glad to see you."

Even with her ever-growing belly, Lucy looked small in the hospital bed. So small that London had to stop and catch her breath.

"London? What are you doing here?" Lucy said when she spied London hovering in the doorway.

"I heard my godchild was giving you a hard time and I figured I'd better come and play peacemaker." She slipped off her coat and placed it on a nearby chair. "I figure I have years of this to look forward to. Especially if it's a girl."

Lucy laughed weakly. Mike pulled London into a bear hug before planting a kiss on her cheek.

"I'm going to grab a cup of coffee," he announced. "Can I get you ladies anything?"

They both shook their heads. Mike leaned down and pressed a tender kiss to Lucy's lips. "I'll be right back" He looked over at London. "I'd tell you both to behave, but since that never seems to deter either of you, I won't bother."

"I was only a little scared before, but seeing you here is making me really nervous," Lucy whispered. "What aren't they telling me?"

London adjusted some of the tubes and wires her friend was hooked up to. "Scooch over," she commanded.

Lucy moved to the far edge of the bed. London slid in beside her. She opened her arms and Lucy snuggled against her side.

"You and baby are going to be fine. You hear me. Perfect, in fact. It turns out Mike is a little skittish in hospitals. Who knew?" She stroked Lucy's hair.

She could tell her friend wasn't buying what London was selling, but she didn't protest. "I know you're really busy at the new firm. You don't have time to come take care of me."

"Actually, I had a free weekend. I landed the airline account, Luce. My first big deal. Can you believe it?"

"Of course, I can. You rock, girl." She hugged London. "I'm so proud of you."

Too bad London wasn't feeling as proud of herself. Not after everything Evan told her earlier. She'd gotten her dream job, sure, but she couldn't help feeling it was at the expense of her co-workers and the Westbrook clients. And that didn't sit well with her.

Did Bennie know about Nolan and Hemphill's plans? She brushed the thought aside. Now wasn't the time to be worrying about anything other than Lucy and the baby. To show her friend that even though she'd moved away, their friendship was still a priority.

"Now you're stuck with me for a few days while all this gets cleared up," she said. "Fortunately for you, I know a baker who is making your favorite red velvet cupcakes as we speak."

Lucy moaned. "I knew I kept you around as a best friend for a reason."

A contented silence fell over the room, punctuated only by the beep of the monitors and the pages over the intercom in the hallway.

"Isn't it ironic that my mother had five kids without incident. Yet here I am struggling every step of the way. Why do you think that is?"

London brushed a hand over her friend's belly. "If you are trying to blame yourself, stop it right now, Lucille. You've done nothing wrong. Absolutely nothing. Unfortunately, the universe is just being a fickle bitch right now."

Lucy covered London's hand with her own. "Why does it sound like you're speaking from experience?"

"Don't try to change the subject away from you."

The other woman laughed. "Uh, hello? I'm pretty sure that's why Mike called you. To distract me. Spill it, girlfriend. Get my mind off this mess."

She sighed. The words she'd refused to acknowledge for weeks now suddenly tumbled from her mouth. "What if what I thought I wanted at eighteen isn't what I want today?"

"I'm fairly certain the textbooks refer to that as maturity."

"Oh, Luce, I think I've made a big mess of my life."

Lucy squeezed her hand. "Are you regretting taking the job in Chicago?"

"I'm regretting everything."

"By 'everything,' do you also mean not allowing yourself to be loved?"

London turned to her friend with a shocked stare.

"God, I hope this child is not as pig-headed as the two of you are," Lucy huffed. "Yeah, yeah, Trey says he doesn't believe in love. Guys are idiots, Lon. It's up to you to convince him otherwise. But you can't do that if *you* don't believe a man could love you unconditionally. Because you weren't looking hard enough. Every time that man looked your way there was love shining in his eyes. So much love. He was just too dumb to know what it was. And you—" She poked London in the ribs. "You had blinders on too thick to see it. Or maybe it was just the lust blinding you both. Who knows?"

Lucy laid her head on London's shoulder.

"Not to worry, though. This mama has nothing but time on her hands right now, and she is going to manifest a way to fix this for you."

"I think it might be too late for that."

"Pfft. It's never too late. You just need a grand gesture. Every romance novel I've read has one. All we need to do is come up with yours." She patted London's thigh. "Leave it to me."

London was surprised at how light she suddenly felt. She wasn't so sure about Lucy's grand gesture nonsense. Yet, she was buoyed by her friend's insights about Trey. Could he love her and not realize it? More importantly, did she trust him with her heart?

"I'm so glad you can stay a few days," Lucy murmured sleepily.

"Mm." London smoothed Lucy's hair. A few days wasn't going to cut it. She felt lighter because she was where she belonged. *Home.* With her chosen family and found career. She'd tell her friend later that she was home to stay.

CHAPTER THIRTY

TREY TIMED his entrance to the gala perfectly, sauntering alone down the red carpet so there was video evidence of his presence. Once inside, he covertly dropped off a hefty check in the glass donation box in the museum's lobby. Now all he had to do was survive the director of the hospital board's remarks and acknowledgment of the gala chairmen. Then he'd be home free. Literally headed home. It was never too early to get ready for next week's game.

The Growlers were six and one through the first-third of the season. Trey was on track to break his own records from last year. Kessler and McGraff were proving to be the most reliable targets in the league. And the new tight end they'd picked up from waivers more than made up for his surly attitude with his strong blocking ability.

Football continued to be Trey's failsafe. The one area of his life he dominated better than anyone else. The game had kept him sane for the past seven weeks and for ten years before that. Stepping out of football mode for events like this was a necessary evil. But that didn't mean he wouldn't do it on his own terms.

Make an appearance. Leave a big gift. And get the hell out of here.

"Fletcher never wastes an opportunity to show off his hairy legs, does he?" Alek *fucking* Bergeron remarked when he came to stand along the perimeter of the crowded ballroom where Trey was currently lurking.

This was his fault for slowing down his movement around the exhibit hall. Small talk—especially with hockey players—was not in Trey's game plan tonight. Except the captivating view of the museum's glass roof brilliantly exposing the night stars had stopped him in his tracks. The image never failing to remind him of nights on the lake with London.

Focus, asshole.

London had moved on. At least physically. She continued to inhabit his dreams at night. And whenever he wanted to share something interesting or amusing with someone, hers was the first face that popped into his head. Football still dominated his life and his focus, but London Headley was always there, hovering on the periphery. He drew in a rough breath.

"You would think he's the only man ever to wear a kilt," Bergeron continued to gripe as he gestured to the Growlers' kicker. "He can't put on a pair of tuxedo pants like the rest of us?"

"You jealous, Bergeron? Or just peeved that you didn't wear your family's plaid?"

The goalie snorted. "Dude. I've spent most of my life on skates. These muscles would make Fletcher's look like chicken legs. I wouldn't want to embarrass the guy." He winked. "Or make the ladies swoon."

Trey shook his head. "Humble much?"

Bergeron was still crowing when one of the committee staff approached them.

"Mr. Bergeron. Mr. Van Horn," she said. "We will have the opening remarks shortly. Can you and your dates make your way toward the holding area behind the dais in five minutes? It's on the other side of the silent auction items." She pointed to the opposite end of the long room.

Nodding, Trey headed that way, skirting the crowd by sticking close to the curtained-off wall. Bergeron did the same.

For fuck's sake.

"Don't you need to collect your date?"

"I could ask you the same question. Where's London?"

Trey nearly stumbled over a cord bisecting the room. Why was the guy always asking him about London? Their affair had been brief and conducted in private. No way did the goalie know Trey's true feelings. "In Chicago, I assume."

"You assume?" Bergeron grabbed him by the arm, practically shoving him into a waiter carrying a tray of drinks.

"What the hell, man?"

"No! What the hell to you! Why don't you know where London is? Aren't you two together?"

The dull ache in his chest grew stronger.

Aren't you two together?

Trey suddenly wanted to scream. Or hurl something. *The goalie, perhaps.* Damn Bergeron for picking at a scab that had barely healed.

"Not that it's any of your business," he snapped. "No. We are not together. Never will be. She's all yours." The words tasted bitter in his mouth. He drew in a steadying breath so he could get the rest out. Because, above all else, he wanted London to be happy. And the arrogant swine standing in front of him could do that for her. "In fact, you two would make a great couple. She deserves someone who can make her happy. A decent guy who will put her first."

Bergeron swore savagely. "There's one problem with that, Van Horn."

"How can there be a 'problem?' You're moderately good-looking for a hockey puck. Some might even say you are success-ful. She seemed into you every time I saw you together."

The goalie gritted his fake teeth. "You're a dumbass, you know that? London was never 'in' to me the way she is with you. Hell, man, what I wouldn't give to have her look at me the way she looks at you."

The room seemed to spin as Trey absorbed his words. Luckily someone placed a strong arm around Trey's shoulders.

"How are my two favorite clients doing tonight?" Collin asked as he stepped between Trey and the goalie. He lowered his voice. "Tell me I'm seeing things, and you two are *not* about to throw down right here in the middle of a museum filled with everyone who's anyone in this town and beyond?"

Trey leveled a hard look at Bergeron before shrugging off Collin's arm. "Who let you in here?"

"I bought a ticket like everyone else." Collin straightened his tuxedo jacket. "You didn't think I'd miss a fundraiser chaired by two of our firm's biggest clients?"

"Then make sure you bid on several of these things." Bergeron swept his arm out to indicate the tables filled with items donated to the cause. "And bid high. It's for the kids."

A framed photo on an easel caught Trey's attention, drawing him closer. It was a stunning image of sunrise over Lake Geneva. He studied it carefully. It didn't take him but a minute to realize the picture could only have been taken from the vantage point of Pops' boathouse.

"Yo, Trey," Collin was saying. "Gunther is still furious at you for blowing off his grandkids on the field opening day. I've been holding him back at the games, but it's a lot harder in this environment."

Trey ignored him. He leaned in closer to inspect the inscription on the frame.

Every sunrise brings an opportunity for a new beginning.

London's initials were below it.

The room began to sway again. She was here. She had to be. But what did this painting mean? He needed to find her. To find out.

"Heads up. Gunther is at three o'clock. I think we should make a beeline in the other direction," Collin insisted.

The words registered with Trey a few seconds too late. Seth Gunther sneered as he jabbed a finger into Trey's shoulder. Trey didn't bother with subtlety as he shoved the offending hand away and pulled himself to his full height.

"Whoa. Hands off, man," Collin admonished Gunther.

"Will you call your pissy agent off, Van Horn. You and I have a beef to settle. No one breaks a promise to my grandkids. You're lucky I'm a forgiving man. I have a plan for how you can make it up to them. Starting with—"

Trey had heard enough. He stepped right into the overbearing asshole's face.

"Wrong. We are not 'starting' anywhere, Gunther. I never made a promise to your grandkids. That was all on you. I satisfied my end of our contract to the letter. And there was nothing in that deal about schmoozing with you or anyone else in your family." He kept his gaze focused on the man. "Am I right, Collin?"

"Yep. Not one word about it," his agent replied.

"We are done here. Enjoy the rest of your evening, preferably somewhere else in the museum."

Trey moved abruptly, attempting to step around the annoying man and begin hunting for London. Gunther flinched, knocking his elbow into the easel holding London's photo. The frame fell forward. Trey lunged, catching it before it hit the concrete floor. He released a long breath as he righted it back on the easel.

"She's still trying to get her claws in you, I see."

The female voice was vaguely familiar. Trey jerked his head around and nearly lost his lunch when he recognized the woman slithering up to Seth Gunther. Kellianne, Pops' caretaker who had set everything in motion all those years ago, in the flesh.

She made a tsking sound as she linked her arm through the older man's.

"Who's trying to get her claws in him, honey?" Gunther asked.

"London Headley." Kellianne scoffed. "Her mother was such a whore. Can you believe she has no idea who London's father is? She had to name her daughter after the city where she might have been conceived." Her shrill laughter made Trey's entire body vibrate with rage.

"Trey," he heard Collin mutter beside him.

Gunther was laughing now, too. "I always thought Bennie was a fool for that girl. So haughty, that one. I wonder who she slept with to get the job at Nolan and Hemphill." He smirked at Trey. "One thing's for sure, I don't want her associated with my account. I'll make sure everyone at the firm is well aware of her true character first thing Monday morning."

It turns out people really do see red when they are truly angry. Trey had no idea how he landed his punch through that flaming haze, but the sound of crunching bone resonating through the room told him he'd connected with his target. The pain shooting up his arm confirmed it.

The next minute was a blur of a woman shrieking—Kellianne —and a lot of panicked shouting. He tried to lift his hand to land another blow, but Bergeron had already pinned both Trey's arms behind his back. Good thing, because his knuckles were beginning to hurt like hell. Fletcher suddenly appeared in front of him, his big mitt shoving at Trey's chest.

"He nearly hit me," Gunther shouted, refocusing Trey's attention.

Wait, what?

If he didn't hit Gunther—

Kessler held a dinner napkin against Collin's obvious broken nose as he helped him to his feet.

Shit!

What had he done?

"I want to press charges," Gunther continued. "He tried to assault me!"

"If Van Horn wanted to assault you, you'd be the one bleeding right now," Collin said through the napkin.

"Because you stepped in the way!"

Was he kidding? Collin had taken the punch meant for Gunther? Or course he had. All in the name of protecting a client's reputation.

Trey was beginning to feel nauseous. The crowd around them grew larger. He caught sight of the Growlers' brass headed in their direction. Mrs. Ciaciura was leading the way, her dress billowing like the sails of the flagship in an armada as she weaved through the crowd. Her eyes were wide and her mouth grim when she stopped in front of them. The team's doctor reached for Trey's hand.

"No," Trey snatched it away and pointed at Collin. "Take care of him first."

"I didn't name you as a co-chair of this event so you could give us a little sideshow, Trey," his boss said through her tight smile.

Coach Gibson was already calling for ice as he led them to a small office off the main exhibit hall. Kessler stayed behind presumably to charm the crowd. The team's GM steered Gunther and Cruella De Ville in the other direction. Two paramedics descended on Collin, stuffing cotton up his nose.

The team's doctor returned to examine Trey's now throbbing hand. Trey hissed at his touch.

"This is why you should always leave the fisticuffs to us hockey players, Van Horn."

Mrs. C leveled her bulldog glare at Bergeron. The goalie shrugged.

Coach Gibson hovered anxiously behind the doctor. "What are we looking at, doc?"

"I won't know until we get some pictures. But it doesn't appear to be broken."

A chorus of exhales filled the room.

"That doesn't mean it won't still be swollen come Sunday," the doctor added.

"Send him over to the Mayhem facility. Our trainers are experts with swollen knuckles," Bergeron suggested.

"Lovely," Mrs. C said. "Do I even want to know what happened?"

Bergeron spoke up before Trey could. "The asshole deserved it."

Mrs. C hiked her eyebrows and pointed at Collin. "Him?"

"No. Gunther," Trey and Bergeron said in unison.

She scoffed. "Enough said." She turned to Collin. "And you deserve a medal for mitigating what would have been a public relations and legal disaster. I underestimated you, Collin. You do always have your client's best interests at heart. Nice work. Now let them take you to get some X-rays and get that handsome face of yours fixed up."

Collin tried to nod but he groaned instead. The female EMT brushed his hair back from his face as she helped him onto the gurney. Collin gave her a sloppy grin while they wheeled him out. Trey made a mental note to call Marty and let him know Collin would be handling all of his business from here on out.

"I'm going to head back in there to put a stop to any ridiculous rumors that might be going around. I'll speak to my brother about the Mayhem's trainer." She shook her head and sighed as she looked at Trey. "I hope whatever this was about was worth it. I'll see you in my office first thing Monday morning."

"Where the hell is that ice!" Coach Gibson yelled.

CHAPTER THIRTY-ONE

LONDON HURRIED through the museum's atrium. The gala crowd was already humming with excitement. Her body was humming with a different emotion, however: anxiety. She didn't hold out much hope that Trey would even recognize Lucy's cockamamie plan of a grand gesture.

"I should have just gone over to his house and laid my cards out on the table," she told her date.

"Too late for that now, kiddo," Bennie replied as he patted her hand on his arm. "Between Sunday's game in Seattle and last night's game in L.A., Trey hasn't been in town all week. Besides, you wouldn't want to deny him the opportunity of seeing you all dolled up. You look beautiful."

She squeezed Bennie's arm. "Thank you, sir."

Part of Lucy's plan involved a spa day and a figure-hugging beaded dress in deep indigo that practically lit up with every step she took beneath the subtle museum lights. Based on the double takes and polite nods, she figured mission accomplished on that front. She was surreptitiously looking around the large hall for Trey when a flurry of activity in the corner had everyone craning their necks to get a better view. A woman's cries rose above the din followed by a man shouting for the police.

A man who sounded an awful lot like Seth Gunther.

She and Bennie exchanged panicked looks before charging in that direction. It took them more than a minute to navigate through the guests. But when they did, it was to find an irritated Seth Gunther with a woman London never hoped to lay eyes on again hanging on his arm.

"You!" Seth practically spit the word out as he pointed a finger at London.

Bennie stepped in front of her, trying to reason with his friend. "Seth, are you okay?"

"Hell, no, I'm not okay! The product spokesman that *she* insisted I hire just tried to deck me."

Was he kidding right now?

Mrs. Ciaciura appeared at London's side. "It seems there was a bit of a scuffle over this gorgeous photo being auctioned off this evening," she announced loudly as she indicated the prop in Lucy's grand gesture scheme. Her laugh sounded forced. "It's wonderful to see such passion about this great cause. But I must insist you bid with your wallet and not your fists. Hurry though, the silent auction closes shortly."

A few weak laughs filled the air as the crowd began to disperse.

Seth made a choking sound before Bennie leaned in to whisper something in his ear.

London rocked back on her high heels.

This was not in the plan, Lucy.

Mrs. Ciaciura pressed a hand on her shoulder to steady her. "Trey is in the office. Astrid will take you there."

"Is he okay?"

The older woman smiled slyly. "Something tells me he will be soon." She gently shoved London in the direction of her assistant.

As she followed Astrid through a narrow hallway, they passed two EMTs wheeling Trey's agent on a gurney. His white tuxedo shirt was mired in blood.

London gasped. "Oh my gosh, Collin! What happened?"

"Trey's fist happened." He gave a thumbs up. "It's all good. He should be able to play next week."

Trey hit his agent? He should be able to play?

Lucy's grand gesture was turning into a grand nightmare.

"Where's that ice?" the Growlers' coach yelled from inside the office when they arrived.

London nearly collided with one of the catering staff who was rushing into the room carrying a pile of dishtowels and a bag of ice. She followed him in.

Trey was seated in a chair looking unusually dazed. The doctor took the ice and began filling a towel with some. Trey grunted when the doctor pressed it to his hand.

"You're hurt." She was stating the obvious, but she could sense that more than just his hand was aching.

"London," he said, the word coming out raspy.

Out of the corner of her eye, she saw Alek Bergeron moving toward her. How was he involved in this? She'd told him months ago they could be nothing more than friends. He'd accepted the news gracefully, still calling once in a while to check on Kyle and talk about their favorite shows.

"There you are, babe," Alek drawled. "I was wondering where you got off to."

He wrapped his arms around London's waist and leaned in to kiss her. London stiffened beneath his touch at the same time a loud roar coursed through the small room. Alek had the nerve to laugh.

"Yeah. That's what I thought." He dropped his hands. The grin he gave her held a touch of sadness. "I guess we found the one thing he'll always put above football."

Trey continued to struggle against the hold the team's kicker and doctor had on him.

"Sit down, Van Horn, before you do something else stupid," the coach ordered.

"She's all yours. Always has been."

Alek's words stunned her. How had everyone seen it but her?

The kicker pressed a hand to Trey's shoulder and guided him back down to his seat, chuckling as he did so.

"What do you say you and I go grab a glass of whisky, Canadian," he said.

"As long it's made with barley and not that rye crap you Scots insist on ruining it with." Alek winked at her as he followed Trey's teammate out of the room. "If he doesn't treat you right, let me know. I'll set him straight."

Trey snarled, making the two men laugh before they disappeared. The coach glanced between London and Trey. He tapped the doctor on the shoulder.

"A drink sounds good right about now. How about you, Doc?"

The doctor looked at the coach as if he'd asked him to rob a bank. "He needs to ice that hand. And I want to get him over to the training facility for X-rays."

"His hand is not going anywhere in the next couple of minutes. And he has more than enough help applying the ice." He hustled the doctor from the room and closed the door behind them.

London sat in the chair the doctor had just vacated, gently taking Trey's hand and placing it in her lap. She carefully rewrapped the towel around his hand. He groaned when her fingers brushed his wrist. She froze.

"Does that hurt?"

He shook his head. They were silent for several heartbeats while she readjusted the ice pack.

"I know your agent is a pain sometimes, but what did he do to deserve a broken nose?"

"It wasn't meant for him. I was aiming at Seth Gunther. Or rather, his date."

Well, then.

That wasn't the answer she was expecting.

"Kellianne?" She chuckled. "I think my mother would like first dibs at her. That woman has been spreading rumors about my mom since before I was born. They both worked together at the country club during the summers. Kellianne was jealous that my dad chose to have a fling with my mom. She wanted him for herself."

It was his turn to laugh. "Wow. That explains a lot."

She shrugged. "Come to think of it, he probably deserved Kellianne."

Trey reached over and cradled her chin with the fingertips of his good hand, angling her head so she could look into those beautiful golden eyes she'd missed terribly over the past seven weeks.

"Don't," he whispered. "If your mom and dad had not gotten together, there would be no you. And that would be a tremendous loss."

The sincerity in his words had her blinking several times. "Thank you."

He brushed his thumb over her bottom lip. It was all she could do not to kiss it. Except there were still some things unanswered.

She tilted her head. "Before, you told me that someone had sabotaged our relationship that summer. Kellianne was the caretaker for your grandfather's lake house. Did she--?"

Trey nodded. "It's not something I'm proud of. And it's my fault for believing her. I didn't even want to admit this to myself. But now I know I was afraid. Afraid of my overwhelming feelings for you. Scared to death I'd somehow screw it up. That you'd end up hating me." He swallowed. "She didn't have to do much of a sales job and I was out the door. That's on me. And you ended up hating me anyway."

"So you busted up your throwing hand because she said

something about me?" Her pulse began to pound. She could hear Lucy in her head squealing about a grand gesture.

"I told you, London," he said softly. "I'll do anything for you. *Anything.*"

His words and his gaze had her shivering. Maybe, just maybe, "anything" was his way of saying he loved her. Her face began to hurt at the smile taking over her lips. She stood, hiked up her skirt and straddled his legs so she was facing him.

"Anything?"

He groaned when she shimmied up his thighs. "Gunther is going to try to ruin you at your new firm," he blurted out.

She laughed as she draped her arms over his shoulders. "That's going to be hard for him to do because I no longer work there."

The parts of her that she thought had shriveled up and died when they broke up were making themselves known again when his good hand began to cradle the back of her neck, pulling her closer

"Why is that?" he murmured against her neck.

"I discovered I don't need the big city or bright lights. I don't need the big glamourous accounts to challenge me. I'm perfectly content to help the friends I've made here. I'm starting a new firm with Bennie's old clients."

He jerked up to stare at her in amazement. "Here in Milwaukee?"

She nodded. The look of delight on his face had her stomach doing somersaults.

"What brought this on?"

"It turns out the things I wanted when I was eighteen, I really don't want anymore." She pressed her forehead to his. "Except for one."

He stilled beneath her.

"You were always so concerned that I have the fairy tale. But here's the thing they don't tell little girls. Fairy tales aren't real. I want real, Trey. No matter how messy or how scary real is. And I want it with you. I know you don't believe in love—"

She didn't get the chance to finish because his mouth was suddenly covering hers. His lips met no resistance as they coaxed her mouth open. She nearly sang out when he deepened the kiss. It was equal parts demanding and reverent. As though he couldn't believe his good fortune. She responded in kind, trying to make up for lost time.

"I meant it when I said you taught me how to love. You give me a reason to believe in it," he said against her lips several minutes later. "I'm the best version of myself when I'm with you. Because of your love. I don't ever want to stop being that guy, London. And I will always put you first because you're first in my heart. I love you. And that idiot Bergeron is right. I always have."

She felt like her entire body was glowing.

"I think the universe is finally going to give us our new beginning."

He chuckled. "Ah. The photo. It's about *our* new beginning."

She pressed her forehead to his. "Mm. It was Lucy's idea. She read some romance novel where the character manifests a way to meet her hero. Lucy insisted the lake is what will always connect me to you. She said if I donated the photo, it would find a way to bring us back together." She shook her head with a laugh. "Honestly, I didn't think it would work." She adjusted the towel of ice resting between them. "And I hate that you hurt yourself because of me. I know how important football is to you."

He tilted her head back so he could meet her gaze. "Football is just a game. You, London, are my life."

And then, to prove his point, he kissed her again.

EPILOGUE

The water slapped up against the boat house with a steady, relaxing rhythm. There was a breeze blowing across Lake Geneva making the air cooler along the shoreline than it was higher up toward the house. Not that Trey minded as he sat on his favorite bench contemplating the lake, the bright sunlight dancing off its swells. Beside him, however, his mother was a little more bothered by the chill.

"You'd think it was the middle of January and not June," she groused, tugging her cashmere wrap up to her chin.

Trey wrapped his arm around her, pulling her closer to his body. "It's that thin Miami blood of yours," he teased. "This is a postcard day for this area. Brilliant blue skies. A nice breeze ruffling the water. And sixty-five-degree temps. You couldn't ask for anything more."

They both knew there was something more they could ask for.

More time with him.

Sighing, she rested her head on Trey's shoulder. "He loved the water. I'm so grateful to have had the last decade with him."

Trey fingered the urn on the bench beside him. He was still having trouble coming to terms with the loss of the man who meant so much to him. Despite knowing his death was imminent, Trey still felt blindsided by life without him. The pain of that reality would likely linger longer than the bruises after a game.

A cacophony of children's laughter floated down from the terrace, its sound making him feel lighter, relaxing the boulder that had been lodged in the back of his throat the past week.

"And I'm glad he had the opportunity to know your children," his mother said. "He loved them, you know."

No more than Trey did.

Love.

He'd gone most of his life not believing in it. Not trusting it. Not wanting the pain that came with it. Then along came the bright light that was his beautiful wife. Her smile had hit him like a thunderbolt right here on this dock twenty years ago. He cursed himself regularly for being a fool and running away from it.

Not that the past decade of making up for lost time hadn't been immensely pleasurable. He bit back a grin, recalling the enthusiastic way London and he had enjoyed each other last night. Except it wasn't just her body he loved. It was her very being. She made life softer around the edges and every day worth waking up to.

Life with London showed him that football didn't have to define him. In fact, the twilight years of his career hadn't been as difficult to accept as he'd imagined. Mainly because he had London and their two kids at home to temper the landing. He wasn't exactly sure what the future held, but he did know it would be filled with a lot of laughter and love.

"Uncle Bennie, my turn," his daughter Avery screeched at a decibel only five-year-old girls could achieve.

"Don't let them win, Grandpa Chuck," her brother, Jace,

shouted in reply.

Trey's mother chuckled. "The apple didn't fall far from the tree. You may not have saddled your son with the unfortunate name of Lars, but he's definitely got the genes. He might even be more competitive than you."

If Trey was skeptical of love at first sight when he met London, he'd certainly believed in it the first time he'd held his son in his arms seven years ago. The minute he stared into Jace's blue eyes, he was a goner. Sure, the kid was competitive—with Van Horn as his last name, it was to be expected. But he also had his mother's artistic eye and was fiercely protective of his little sister. Not that Trey could blame him. Avery had everyone in her orbit wrapped around her finger from her first breath. She was growing up fearless like her mother with the same impish smile.

"I should probably go up there before Bennie throws out his back," Jay said from the interior of the boathouse.

"Don't you go throwing out your back, mister. I have plans for you later." His mother winked at her husband.

Trey groaned. "Jesus, Mom. TMI."

London chuckled as she gathered up the paperwork she and Jay had been going over. It turned out their former agent, Marty, was right. Jay did have nine lives. To say that cancer changed Trey's father would be an understatement. It turned out, the man simply needed a purpose. Once he had one, he became as relentless as Pops or Trey about being the best.

Since his diagnosis, Jay had worked tirelessly with the medical community to help fund studies and drug trials like the one that had prolonged his life. He served on the board of directors for three different cancer research groups and was a frequent witness before Congress advocating for more funding.

Collin had even convinced him to write a children's book based on the cockamamie story he told his grandchildren about losing his ear to a pirate. It was an instant bestseller. He'd then teamed up with London to produce a documentary about the effects of global warming on skin cancer rates. The film premiered at the Sundance Film Festival last winter to rave reviews. There was even talk of an Oscar nomination.

Trey was so damn proud of his dad.

But he was even prouder of his wife. Not only had she given him the gift of two amazing kids, but she was realizing her dream every day. She was making the films that made a difference while still catering to the small mom and pop businesses in Milwaukee, treating them with the same respect and care as she would a global client. And she had several of those, too.

Her campaign for Gunther Cheese established her as one to watch in the industry. This summer, he and London were traveling to Italy so she could film an ad campaign for an Italian car company's new EVs. They'd rented a gorgeous villa on Lake Como. Spending two weeks ravaging his wife in Italy would definitely make missing his first training camp in eighteen seasons worth it.

Her lips lifted into a sly smile as if she could read his mind.

"You aren't going to dump that whole thing in the lake out there, are you?" Jay's question refocused Trey's salacious thoughts. "I thought you were going to save some of Pops' ashes for Lake Como. He was so happy there with Olivia."

His mother sighed again. "What a beautiful love story those two had. They spent the last ten years of their lives without being apart for a single night." Her eyes glistened with unshed tears. "And then to die within hours of one another. So romantic."

Jay tugged his wife to her feet and enveloped her into a tight hug. Even after all these years, it still blew Trey's mind seeing the way his parents looked at each other, how, after all the bitterness of his childhood, they had found their way back to one another.

"I'd say theirs is a pretty sweet love story, too," London whispered as she wrapped her arms around Trey's waist and pressed her cheek to his chest. "And you thought the Van Horns weren't capable of true love."

He pressed his lips to the top of her head. "I've never been so happy to have been wrong about something. And remind me to show you how happy I am tonight."

A boat horn sounded off in the distance. It was followed by screeches from the tribe of kids up on the terrace.

"It's coming!" Lucy's oldest daughter yelled.

Footsteps thundered down the wooden steps as everyone from the terrace made their way to the boat house.

"Calm down, Florence," Lucy called after her daughter. "Or you'll slip off the dock and miss Kyle's maiden mail run."

The *Walworth* came into view as it slowly cruised from around a blind bend in the lake. The captain sounded his horn again, making the kids cheer. Chuck stood at the railing of the dock with Avery on his shoulders. Kim beamed as she readied her cell-phone camera. Bennie hefted Lucy's youngest, Ivy, into his arms so the toddler would have a better view.

Jace stood arm and arm on the bench with Lucy and Mike's twin boys. Everyone referred to them as the Triplets because they were born the same day. Trey felt something in his chest shift every time he looked at the three of them together. They weren't related by blood, but by something just as powerful: love. It was the same fierce bond he felt for his teammates. Even after leaving the game. Fletcher. Kessler. They would always be part of his band of brothers. Hell, even Bergeron and his family were part of their social group.

"You need to keep the path clear, Florence, so the poor boy can have a spot to land," Lucy chastised her daughter before turning to London. "She told me this morning she's going to marry Kyle. Ten years old and she's crushing on a boy headed to college."

"Well, she is your daughter." London shared a sympathetic grin with Mike.

"Uncle Kyle!" Avery swayed on Chuck's shoulders as she waved at the incoming boat.

London gave Trey's hand a squeeze before he headed out toward the end of the dock. He pulled the plastic baggy from the pocket of his shorts. Kyle worshiped Pops as much as Trey did. It was only fitting that he be given the honor of leaving a little bit of Pops' memory at the center of the lake the old man had loved so much.

The kids were all clapping and chanting Kyle's name when the boat pulled up beside the dock. Kyle jumped off its bow, easily landing on his feet, much to the delight of the onlookers. Most of the tourists on the boat had their phones pointed at Trey, several of them calling out to him to look their way. Trey gave them a smile and a wave as he took the pile of junk mail from Kyle.

"You sure you're okay with this?" he asked his brother-in-law, now a healthy five foot eleven in height.

Kyle nodded. "Yeah. I know just the spot. We used to fish there."

The *Walworth* continued to crawl slowly forward. Kyle tucked the bag of ashes into his pocket and waved to his fan club on the dock.

"Gotta go. My sister is the only one who gets the honor of falling into the lake from this dock," he joked.

The kids and the passengers all cheered when he easily leaped back on board. London came to stand beside Trey as the boat pulled away. He placed his arm around her shoulders, grateful to have her by his side. She smiled up at him before stretching up on her toes and pressing a kiss to his cheek.

"You were worth taking a dunk in the lake for," she told him.

He took in her face, even more beautiful than it had been twenty years ago. Then he glanced around at the chaotic crowd on the dock, all of them dancing to some tune Jay was playing on his phone. Trey loved these people. And they loved him.

"It was the first best day of my life," he told her. "And every day with you keeps getting better and better. I love you, London."

And then he kissed her exactly the way he'd dreamed of kissing her that first best day of his life.

I hope you enjoyed Trey and London's story. If you are like me, I'm always sorry to say goodbye to the characters in books. How about a bonus chapter? It's yours for subscribing to my newsletter by scanning the QR Code:

If you want more day to day details about my books, my crazy writing life, and opportunities to name places and characters in my books, come hang out with my reader group, the X's and O's, on Facebook. Scan the QR Code for access:

Are you curious about Trey's teammates? You can read Declan Fletcher's marriage of convenience story in *Just for Kicks*. Then check out Luke Kessler's book, *Double Dog Dare.*

And please, don't forget to tell other readers how much you enjoyed *Catch and Release* by leaving a review on the site where you purchased it, as well as, Goodreads and BookBub. It's the best way to show an author some love and I ALWAYS appreciate it!

Want more football romance? Check out the Baltimore Blaze:
Game On – a grumpy hero sports romance
Foolish Games – a secret baby, marriage of convenience romance
Risky Game – a fake relationship sports romance
Sleeping with the Enemy – an enemies-to-lovers second chance sports romance

How about a little suspense with your romance?
Recipe for Disaster – a mistaken identity Secret Service romance
Shot in the Dark – a forced proximity Secret Service romance
Between Love and Honor – a second chance Secret Service romance

Do you enjoy books about small towns and big families—including some sports stars? Be sure to check out my Chances Inlet series:

Back to Before – a forced proximity romance
All they Ever Wanted – an enemies-to-lovers romance
Second Chance Christmas – age gap romance
It Had to Be You – a nanny romance

ABOUT THE AUTHOR

After years of writing reports and testimony for Congress, **Tracy Solheim** decided to put her creative talents to better use. The recipient of the 2020 Georgia Author of the Year Award, she's the *USA Today* best-selling author of contemporary sports romance, romantic suspense, and small-town second chance novels. Tracy lives in the heart of SEC country, also known as the suburbs of Atlanta, with her husband, two adult children who frequently show up at dinner time, and a neurotic Labrador retriever who keeps her company while she writes. See what she's up to by subscribing to her newsletter at Tracy Solheim (dot) com.

ACKNOWLEDGMENTS

My name may be on the cover, but this book would not have been possible without some amazing people propping me up behind the scenes. Thank you to Melanie, Shari, Gina, and Kim for the beta reads. Thank you to Jeannie Moon at Five Harbors Literary for the editorial feedback. Thanks also go to Mary Mullenbach for making sure all the i's were dotted and t's were crossed. And without a doubt this book wouldn't be possible without my assistant, Rachael, who keeps me on task and makes me look good, even when I mess up!

A huge thank you to my husband's Lake Geneva family, especially his cousin, Lisa Kenny, for telling me about the mailboat. I was so enthralled, I spent two days reading articles and watching videos on the boat line. It was a foregone conclusion that I would use it in a book. Now I have to visit during the summer months so I can experience the cruise for myself!

And for those keeping score, this isn't the first time I've hijacked an idea from our Lake Geneva crew. Lisa's sister in law, Patti Solheim, is the owner/operator of the original Patti Wagon ice cream truck featured in my Chances Inlet series. Thanks for the inspiration, ladies. I can't wait to see what else you come up with!

Finally, I'm humbled and grateful to all of you for taking the time to read my books, as well as, all the bloggers and booksellers who support my dream. I couldn't do it without you. You're the best!